To my husband R., who suggested that I write this, a departure from my usual genres.

And to the memory of R. D. Blackmore: an author who within Lorna Doone and his lesser-known works gave us some of the most lyrical descriptions ever created, and whose wit (and innuendo!) is sadly often not recognised.

Acknowledgments

My special thanks to the editors at Crimson Romance for the invitation to write for them in the first place and for their ongoing support and advice—such a friendly and knowledgeable group of people.

Lorna Doone

VOLUME 1

A Romance of Exmoor

M. J. Porteus *and* R.D. Blackmore

F+W Media, Inc.

This edition published by
Crimson Romance
an imprint of F+W Media, Inc.
10151 Carver Road, Suite 200
Blue Ash, Ohio 45242
www.crimsonromance.com

ISBN 10: 1-4405-7024-8
ISBN 13: 978-1-4405-7024-7
eISBN 10: 1-4405-7025-6
eISBN 13: 978-1-4405-7025-4

Cover art © 123rf.com.

CHAPTER I

ELEMENTS OF EDUCATION

If anybody cares to read a simple tale told simply, I, John Ridd, of the parish of Oare, in the county of Somerset, yeoman and church-warden, have seen and had a share in some doings of this neighborhood, which I will try to set down in order, God sparing my life and memory. And they who light upon this book should bear in mind not only that I write for the clearing of our parish from ill fame and calumny, but also a thing which will, I trow, appear too often in it, to wit—that I am nothing more than a plain unlettered man, not read in foreign languages, as a gentleman might be, nor gifted with long words (even in mine own tongue), save what I may have won from the Bible or Master William Shakespeare, whom, in the face of common opinion, I do value highly. In short, I am an ignoramus, but pretty well for a yeoman.

My father being of good substance, at least as we reckon in Exmoor, and seized in his own right, from many generations, of one, and that the best and largest, of the three farms into which our parish is divided (or rather the cultured part thereof), he John Ridd, the elder, churchwarden, and overseer, being a great admirer of learning, and well able to write his name, sent me his only son to be schooled at Tiverton, in the county of Devon. For the chief boast of that ancient town (next to its woollen staple) is a worthy grammar-school, the largest in the west of England, founded and handsomely endowed in the year 1604 by Master Peter Blundell, of that same place, clothier.

Here, I had risen into the upper school, and could make bold with Eutropius and Cæsar—by aid of an English version—and as much as six lines of Ovid. So it came to pass, by the grace of God, that I was called away from learning, whilst beginning the Greek verb.

My eldest grandson makes bold to say that I never could have learned ten pages further on, being all he himself could manage, with plenty of stripes to help him. I know that he hath more head than I—though never will he have such body; and am thankful to have stopped betimes, with a meek and wholesome head-piece.

But if you doubt of my having been there, because now I know so little, go and see my name, "John Ridd," graven on that very form. Forsooth, from the time I was strong enough to open a knife and to spell my name, I began to grave it in the oak, first of the block whereon I sate, and then of the desk in front of it, according as I was promoted from one to other of them: and there my grandson reads it now, at this present time of writing, and hath fought a boy for scoffing at it—"John Ridd his name"—and done again in "winkeys," a mischievous but cheerful device, in which we took great pleasure.

This is the manner of a "winkey," which I here set down, lest child of mine, or grandchild, dare to make one on my premises; if he does, I shall know the mark at once, and score it well upon him. The scholar obtains, by prayer or price, a handful of saltpetre, and then with the knife wherewith he should rather be trying to mend his pens, what does he do but scoop a hole where the desk is some three inches thick. This hole should be left with the middle exalted, and the circumference dug more deeply. Then let him fill it with saltpetre, all save a little space in the midst, where the boss of the wood is. Upon that boss (and it will be the better if a splinter of timber rise upward) he sticks the end of his candle of tallow, or "rat's tail," as we called it, kindled and burning smoothly. Anon, as he reads by that light his lesson, lifting his eyes now and then it may be, the fire of candle lays hold of the petre with a spluttering noise and a leaping. Then should the pupil seize his pen, and, regardless of the nib, stir bravely, and he will see a glow as of burning mountains, and a rich smoke, and sparks going merrily; nor will it cease, if he stir wisely, and there be a good store of petre, until the wood is devoured through, like the sinking of a well-shaft. Now well may it go with the head of a boy intent upon his primer, who betides to sit thereunder! But, above all things, have good care to exercise this art before the master strides up to his desk, in the early gray of the morning.

Other customs, no less worthy, abide in the school of Blundell, such as the singeing of nightcaps; but though they have a pleasant savour, and refreshing to think of, I may not stop to note them, unless it be that goodly one at the incoming of a flood. The schoolhouse stands beside a stream, not very large, called Lowman, which flows into the broad river of Exe, about a mile below. This Lowman stream, although it be not fond of brawl and violence (in the manner of our Lynn), yet is wont to flood into a mighty head of waters when the storms of rain provoke it; and most of all when its little co-mate, called the Taunton Brook—where I have plucked the very best cresses that ever man put salt on—comes foaming down like a great roan horse, and rears at the leap of the hedgerows. Then are the gray stone walls of Blundell on every side encompassed, the vale is spread over with looping waters, and it is a hard thing for the day-boys to get home to their suppers.

And in that time, old Cop, the porter (so called because he hath copper boots to keep the wet from his stomach, and a nose of copper also, in right of other waters), his place is to stand at the gate, attending to the flood-boards grooved into one another, and so to watch the torrents rise, and not be washed away, if it please God he may help it. But long ere the flood hath attained this height, and while it is only waxing, certain boys of deputy will watch at the stoop of the drain-holes, and be apt to look outside the walls when Cop is taking a cordial. And in the very front of the gate, just without the archway, where the ground is paved most handsomely, you may see in copy-letters done a great P.B. of white pebbles. Now, it is the custom and the law that when the invading waters, either fluxing along the wall from below the road-bridge, or pouring sharply across the meadows from a cut called Owen's Ditch—and I myself have seen it come both ways—upon the very instant when the waxing element lips though it be but a single pebble of the founder's letters, it is in the license of any boy, soever small and undoctrined, to rush into the great school-rooms, where a score of masters sit heavily, and scream at the top of his voice, "P.B."

Then, with a yell, the boys leap up, or break away from their standing; they toss their caps to the black-beamed roof, and haply the very books after them; and the great boys vex no more the small ones, and the small boys stick up to the great ones. One with another, hard they go, to see the gain of the waters, and the tribulation of Cop, and are prone to kick the day-boys out, with words of scanty compliment. Then the masters look at one another, having no class to look to, and (boys being no more left to watch) in a manner they put their mouths up. With a spirited bang they close their books, and make invitation the one to the other for pipes and foreign cordials, recommending the chance of the time, and the comfort away from cold water.

But, lo! I am dwelling on little things and the pigeons' eggs of the infancy, forgetting the bitter and heavy life gone over me since then. If I am neither a hard man nor a very close one, God knows I have had no lack of rubbing and pounding to make stone of me. Yet can I not somehow believe that we ought to hate one another, to live far asunder, and block the mouth each of his little den; as do the wild beasts of the wood, and the hairy outrangs now brought over, each with a chain upon him. Let that matter be as it will. It is beyond me to unfold, and mayhap of my grandson's grandson. All I know is that wheat is better than when I began to sow it.

CHAPTER II

AN IMPORTANT ITEM

Now the cause of my leaving Tiverton school, and the way of it, were as follows. I had spent all my substance in sweetmeats, with which I made treat to the little boys, and we came out of school at five o'clock, as the rule is upon Tuesdays. According to custom we drove the day-boys in brave rout down the causeway from the school-porch even to the gate where Cop has his dwelling and duty. Little it recked us and helped them less, that they were our founder's citizens, and haply his own grand-nephews (for he left no direct descendants), neither did we much inquire what their lineage was. For it had long been fixed among us, who were of the house and chambers, that these same day-boys were all "caddes," as we had discovered to call it, because they paid no groat for their schooling, and brought their own commons with them. In consumption of these we would help them, for our fare in hall fed appetite; and while we ate their victuals, we allowed them freely to talk to us. Nevertheless, we could not feel, when all the victuals were gone, but that these boys required kicking from the premises of Blundell. And some of them were shopkeepers' sons, young grocers, fellmongers, and poulterers, and these to their credit seemed to know how righteous it was to kick them. But others were of high family, as any need be, in Devon—Carews, and Bouchiers, and Bastards, and some of these would turn sometimes, and strike the boy that kicked them. But to do them justice, even these knew that they must be kicked for not paying.

After these "charity-boys" were gone, as in contumely we called them—"If you break my bag on my head," said one, "how will feed thence to-morrow?"—and after old Cop with clang of iron had jammed the double gates in under the scruff-stone archway, whereupon are Latin verses, done in brass of small quality, some of us who were not hungry, and cared not for the supper-bell, having sucked much parliament and dumps at my only charges— not that I ever bore much wealth, but because I had been thrifting it for this time of my birth—we were leaning quite at dusk against the iron bars of the gate some six, or it may be seven of us, and not conspicuous in the closing of the daylight and the fog that came at eventide, else Cop would have rated us up the green, for he was churly to us when his wife had taken our money. There was plenty of room for all of us, for the gate will hold nine close-packed, unless they be fed rankly, whereof is little danger; and now we were looking out on the road and wishing we could get there; hoping, moreover, to see a good string of pack-horses come by, with troopers to protect them. For the day-boys had brought us word that some intending their way to the town had lain that morning at Sampford Peveril, and must be in ere nightfall, because Mr. Faggus was after them. Now Mr. Faggus was my first cousin and an honour to the family, being a Northmolton man of great renown on the highway from Barum town even to London. Therefore of course, I hoped that he would catch the packmen, and the boys were asking my opinion as of an oracle, about it.

A certain young man leaning up against me would not allow my elbow room, and struck me very sadly in the stomach part, though his own was full of my parliament. And this I felt so unkindly, that I smote him straightway in the face without tarrying to consider it, or weighing the question duly. Upon this he put his head down, and presented it so vehemently at the middle of my waistcoat, that for a minute or more my breath seemed dropped, as it were, from my pockets, and my life seemed to stop from great want of ease. Before I came to myself again, it had been settled for us that we should move to the "Ironing-box," as the triangle of turf is called where the two causeways coming from the school-porch and the hall-porch meet, and our fights are mainly celebrated; only we must wait until the convoy of horses had passed, and then make a ring by candlelight. But suddenly there came round the post where the letters of our founder are, not from the way of Taunton but from the side of Lowman bridge, a very small string of horses, only two indeed (counting for one the pony), and a red-faced man on the bigger nag.

"Plaise ye, worshipful masters," he said, being feared of the gateway, "carn 'e tull whur our Jan Ridd be?"

"Hyur a be, ees fai, Jan Ridd," answered a sharp chap, making game of John Fry's language.

"Zhow un up, then," says John Fry poking his whip through the bars at us; "Zhow un up, and putt un aowt."

The other chaps pointed at me, and some began to hallo; but I knew what I was about.

"Oh, John, John," I cried, "what's the use of your coming now, and Peggy over the moors, too, and it so cruel cold for her? The holidays don't begin till Wednesday fortnight, John. To think of your not knowing that!"

John Fry leaned forward in the saddle, and turned his eyes away from me; and then there was a noise in his throat like a snail crawling on a window-pane.

"Oh, us knaws that wull enough, Maister Jan; reckon every Oare-man knaw that, without go to skoo-ull, like you doth. Your moother have kept arl the apples up, and old Betty toorned the black puddens, and none dare set trap for a blagbird. Arl for thee, lad; every bit of it now for thee!"

He checked himself suddenly, and frightened me. I knew that John Fry's way so well.

"And father, and father—oh, how is father?" I pushed the others right and left as I said it. "John, is father up in town! He always used to come for me, and leave nobody else to do it."

"Vayther'll be at the crooked post, tother zide o' telling-house. Her coodn't lave 'ouze by raison of the Chirstmas bakkon comin' on, and zome o' the cider welted."

He looked at the nag's ears as he said it; and, being up to John Fry's ways, I knew that it was a lie. And my heart fell like a lump of lead, and I leaned back on the stay of the gate, and longed no more to fight anybody. A sort of dull power hung over me, like the cloud of a brooding tempest, and I feared to be told anything. I did not even care to stroke the nose of my pony Peggy, although she pushed it in through the rails, where a square of broader lattice is, and sniffed at me, and began to crop gently after my fingers. But whatever lives or dies, business must be attended to; and the principal business of good Christians is, beyond all controversy, to fight with one another.

"Come up, Jack," said one, lifting me under the chin; "he hit you, and you hit him, you know."

"Pay your debts before you go," said a monitor, striding up to me, after hearing how the honour lay; "Ridd, you must go through with it."

"Fight," cried a fellow in my ear, the clever one, the head of our class, who had mocked John Fry, and knew all about the aorists, and tried to make me know it; but I never went more than three places up, and then it was an accident, and I came down after dinner. The others were urgent round me to fight, though my stomach was not up for it; and being very slow of wit (which is not chargeable on me), I looked from one to other of them, seeking any cure for it. Not that I was afraid of fighting, for at Blundell's I had fought a fight at least once every week. It is a very sad thing to dwell on; but even now, in my time of wisdom, I doubt it is a fond thing to imagine, and a motherly to insist upon, that young men can do without fighting.

"Nay," I said, with my back against the wrought-iron stay of the gate, which was socketed into Cop's house-front: "I will not fight thee now, Robin Snell, but wait till I come back again."

"Take coward's blow, Jack Ridd, then," cried half a dozen, shoving Bob Snell forward to do it; because they all knew well enough, having striven with me ere now, and proved me to be their master—they knew, I say, that without great change, I would never accept that contumely. But I took little heed of them, looking in dull wonderment at John Fry, and Smiler, and the blunderbuss, and Peggy. John Fry was scratching his head, I could see, and getting blue in the face, by the light from Cop's parlour-window, and going to and fro upon Smiler, as if he were hard set with it. And all the time he was looking briskly from my eyes to the fist I was clenching, and methought he tried to wink at me in a covert manner; and then Peggy whisked her tail.

"Shall I fight, John?" I said at last; "I would an you had not come, John."

"Chraist's will be done; I zim thee had better faight, Jan," he answered, in a whisper, through the gridiron of the gate; "there be a dale of faighting avore thee. Best wai to begin gude taime laike. Wull the geatman latt me in, to zee as thee hast vair plai, lad?"

He looked doubtfully down at the colour of his cowskin boots, and the mire upon the horses, for the sloughs were exceedingly mucky. Peggy, indeed, my sorrel pony, being lighter of weight, was not crusted much over the shoulders; but Smiler (our youngest sledder) had been well in over his withers, and none would have deemed him a piebald, save of red mire and black mire. The great blunderbuss, moreover, was choked with a dollop of slough-cake; and John Fry's sad-coloured Sunday hat was indued with a plume of marish-weed. All this I saw while he was dismounting, heavily and wearily, lifting his leg from the saddle-cloth as if with a sore crick in his back.

By this time the question of fighting was gone quite out of our discretion; for sundry of the grave and reverend signors, who had taken no small pleasure in teaching our hands to fight, to ward, to parry, to feign and counter, to lunge in the manner of sword-play—these great masters of the art, who would far liefer see others practise it than themselves engage, six or seven of them came running down the rounded causeway, having heard that there had arisen "a snug little mill" at the gate. Now whether that word hath origin in a Greek term meaning a conflict, as the best-read boys asseverated, or whether it is nothing more than a figure of similitude, from the beating arms of a mill, such as I have seen in counties where are no waterbrooks, but folk make bread with wind—it is not for a man devoid of scholarship to determine. Enough that they who made the ring intituled the scene a "mill," while we who must be thumped inside it tried to rejoice in their pleasantry, till it turned upon the stomach.

Moreover, I felt upon me now a certain responsibility, a dutiful need to maintain, in the presence of John Fry, the manliness of the Ridd family, and the honour of Exmoor. Hitherto none had worsted me, although I had fought more than threescore battles, and bedewed with blood every plant of grass towards the middle of the Ironing-box. And this success I owed at first to no skill of my own; until I came to know better; for up to twenty or thirty fights, I struck as nature guided me, no wiser than a father-long-legs in the heat of a lanthorn; but I had conquered, partly through my native strength, and the Exmoor toughness in me, and still more that I could not see when I had gotten my bellyful. But now I was like to have that and more; for my heart was down, to begin with; and then Robert Snell was bigger than any one I had ever encountered, and as thick in the skull and hard in the brain as even I could claim to be.

I had never told my mother a word about these frequent strivings, because she was soft-hearted; neither had I told my father, because he had not seen it. Therefore, beholding me still an innocent-looking young man, with fair curls on my forehead, and no store of bad language, John Fry thought this was the very first fight that ever had befallen me; and so when they let him at the gate, "with a message to the headmaster," as one of the monitors told Cop, and Peggy and Smiler were tied to the railings, till I should be through my business, John comes up to me with the tears in his eyes, and says, "Doon't thee goo for to do it, Jan; doon't thee do it, for gude now." But I told him that now it was much too late to cry off; so he said, "The Lord be with thee, Jan, and turn thy thumb-knuckle inwards."

It was not a very large piece of ground in the angle of the causeways, but quite big enough to fight upon, especially for Christians, who loved to be cheek by jowl at it. The great boys stood in a circle around, being gifted with strong privilege, and the little boys had leave to lie flat and look through the legs of the great boys. But while we were yet preparing, and the candles hissed in the fog-cloud, old Phoebe, of more than fourscore years, whose room was over the hall-porch, came hobbling out, as she always did, to mar the joy of the conflict. No one ever heeded her, neither did she expect it; but the evil was that two must always lose the first round of the fight, by having to lead her home again.

I marvel how Robin Snell felt. Very likely he thought nothing of it, always having been one of a hectoring and unruly sort. But I felt my heart go up and down as the others came round to strip me; and greatly fearing to be beaten, I blew hot upon my knuckles. Then pulled I off my jerkin, and laid it down on my head cap, and over that my waistcoat, and a boy was proud to take care of them. Thomas Hooper was his name, and I remember how he looked at me. My mother had made that jerkin, in the quiet winter evenings. And taken pride to loop it up in a fashionable way, and I was loth to soil it with blood, and good filberds were in the pocket. Then up to me came Robin Snell (mayor of Exeter thrice since that), and he stood very square, and looking at me, and I lacked not long to look at him. Round his waist he had a kerchief busking up his small-clothes, and on his feet light pumpkin shoes, and all his upper raiment off. And he danced about in a way that made my head swim on my shoulders, and he stood some inches over me. But I, being muddled with much doubt about John Fry and his errand, was only stripped of my jerkin and waistcoat, and not comfortable to begin.

"Come now, shake hands," cried one, jumping in joy of the spectacle, "shake hands. Keep your pluck up, and show good sport, and Lord love the better man of you."

Robin took me by the hand, and gazed at me disdainfully, and then smote me painfully in the face, ere I could get my fence up.

"Whutt be 'bout, lad?" cried John Fry; "hutt un again, Jan, wull 'e? Well done then, our Jan."

For I had replied to Robin now, with all the weight and cadence of penthemimeral caesura (a thing, the name of which I know, but could never make head nor tail of it), and the strife began in a serious style, and those looking on were not cheated. Although I could not collect their shouts when the blows were ringing upon me, it was no great loss; for John Fry told me afterwards that their oaths went up like a furnace fire. But to these we paid no heed or hap, being in the thick of swinging, and devoid of judgment. All I know is, I came to my corner, when the round was over, with very hard pumps in my chest, and a great desire to fall away.

"Time is up," cried head monitor. "If we count three before the come of thee, thwacked thou art, and must go to the women." I felt it hard upon me. He began to count, one, too, three—but before the "three" was out of his mouth, I was facing my foe, with both hands up, and my breath going rough and hot, and resolved to wait the turn of it. For I had found seat on the knee of one sage and skilled to tutor me, who knew how much the end very often differs from the beginning. A rare ripe scholar he was; and now he hath routed up the Germans in the matter of criticism. Sure the clever boys and men have most love towards the stupid ones.

"Finish him off, Bob," cried one, and that I noticed especially, because I thought it unkind of him, after eating of my toffee as he had that afternoon; "finish him off, neck and crop; he deserves it for sticking up to a man like you."

But I was not so to be finished off, though feeling in my knuckles now as if it were a blueness and a sense of chilblain. Nothing held except my legs, and they were good to help me. So this bout, or round, if you please, was foughten warily by me, with gentle recollection of what my tutor had told me, and some resolve to earn his praise before I came back to his knee again. And never, I think, in all my life, sounded sweeter words in my ears (except when my love loved me) than when my second and backer, who had made himself part of my doings now, and would have wept to see me beaten, said—

"Famously done, Jack, famously! Only keep your wind up, Jack, and you'll go right through him!"

Meanwhile John Fry was prowling about, asking what they thought of it, and whether I was like to be killed, because of my mother's trouble. But finding now that I had foughten three-score fights already, he came up to me woefully, in the quickness of my breathing, while I sat on the knee of my second, with a piece of spongious coralline to ease me of my bloodshed, and he says in my ears, as if he was clapping spurs into a horse—

"Never thee knack under, Jan, or never coom naigh Hexmoor no more."

With that it was all up with me. A simmering buzzed in my heavy brain, and a light came through my eyeplaces. At once I set both fists again, and my heart stuck to me like cobbler's wax. Either Robin Snell should kill me, or I would conquer Robin Snell. So I went in again with my courage up, and Bob came smiling for victory, and I hated him for smiling. He let at me with his left hand, and I gave him my right between his eyes, and he blinked, and was not pleased with it. I feared him not, and spared him not, neither spared myself. My breath came again, and my heart stood cool, and my eyes struck fire no longer. Only I knew that I would die sooner than shame my birthplace. How the rest of it was I know not; only that I had the end of it, and helped to put Robin in bed.

CHAPTER III

THE WAR-PATH OF THE DOONES

From Tiverton town to the town of Oare is a very long and painful road, and in good truth the traveller must make his way, as the saying is; for the way is still unmade, at least, on this side of Dulverton, although there is less danger now than in the time of my schooling; for now a good horse may go there without much cost of leaping, but when I was young the spurs would fail, when needed most, by reason of the slough-cake. It is to the credit of this age, and our advance upon fatherly ways, that now we have laid down rods and fagots, and even stump-oaks here and there, so that a man in good daylight need not sink, if he be quite sober. There is nothing I have striven at more than doing my duty, waywarden over Exmoor.

But in those days, when I came from school (and good times they were, too, full of a warmth and fine hearth-comfort, which now are dying out), it was a sad and sorry business to find where lay the highway. We are taking now to mark it off with a fence on either side, at least, when a town is handy; but to me this seems of a high pretence, and a sort of landmark, and channel for robbers, though well enough near London, where they have earned a race-course.

We left the town of the two fords, which they say is the meaning of it, very early in the morning, after lying one day to rest, as was demanded by the nags, sore of foot and foundered. For my part, too, I was glad to rest, having aches all over me, and very heavy bruises; and we lodged at the sign of the White Horse Inn, in the street called Gold Street, opposite where the souls are of John and Joan Greenway, set up in gold letters, because we must take the homeward way at cockcrow of the morning. Though still John Fry was dry with me of the reason of his coming, and only told lies about father, and could not keep them agreeable, I hoped for the best, as all young men will, especially after a victory. And I thought, perhaps father had sent for me because he had a good harvest, and the rats were bad in the corn-chamber.

It was high noon before we were got to Dulverton that day, near to which town the river Exe and its big brother Barle have union. My mother had an uncle living there, but we were not to visit his house this time, at which I was somewhat astonished, since we needs must stop for at least two hours, to bait our horses thorough well, before coming to the black bogway. The bogs are very good in frost, except where the hot-springs rise; but as yet there had been no frost this year, save just enough to make the blackbirds look big in the morning. In a hearty black-frost they look small, until the snow falls over them.

The road from Bampton to Dulverton had not been very delicate, yet nothing to complain of much—no deeper, indeed, than the hocks of a horse, except in the rotten places. The day was inclined to be mild and foggy, and both nags sweated freely; but Peggy carrying little weight (for my wardrobe was upon Smiler, and John Fry grumbling always), we could easily keep in front, as far as you may hear a laugh.

John had been rather bitter with me, which methought was a mark of ill taste at coming home for the holidays; and yet I made allowance for John, because he had never been at school, and never would have chance to eat fry upon condition of spelling it; therefore I rode on, thinking that he was hard-set, like a saw, for his dinner, and would soften after tooth-work. And yet at his most hungry times, when his mind was far gone upon bacon, certes he seemed to check himself and look at me as if he were sorry for little things coming over great.

But now, at Dulverton, we dined upon the rarest and choicest victuals that ever I did taste. Even now, at my time of life, to think of it gives me appetite, as once and awhile to think of my first love makes me love all goodness. Hot mutton pasty was a thing I had often heard of from very wealthy boys and men, who made a dessert of dinner; and to hear them talk of it made my lips smack, and my ribs come inwards.

And now John Fry strode into the hostel, with the air and grace of a short-legged man, and shouted as loud as if he was calling sheep upon Exmoor,—

"Hot mooton pasty for twoo trarv'lers, at number vaive, in vaive minnits! Dish un up in the tin with the grahvy, zame as I hardered last Tuesday."

Of course it did not come in five minutes, nor yet in ten or twenty; but that made it all the better when it came to the real presence; and the smell of it was enough to make an empty man thank God for the room there was inside him. Fifty years have passed me quicker than the taste of that gravy.

It is the manner of all good young men to be careless of apparel, and take no pride in adornment. Good lack, if I see a young man make to do about the fit of his crumpler, and the creasing of his breeches, and desire to be shod for comeliness rather than for use, I cannot 'scape the mark that God took thought to make a girl of him. Not so when they grow older, and court the regard of the maidens; then may the bravery pass from the inside to the outside of them; and no bigger fools are they, even then, than their fathers were before them. But God forbid any man to be a fool to love, and be loved, as I have been. Else would he have prevented it.

When the mutton pasty was done, and Peggy and Smiler had dined well also, out I went to wash at the pump, being a lover of soap and water, at all risk, except of my dinner. And John Fry, who cared very little to wash, save Sabbath days in his own soap, and who had kept me from the pump by threatening loss of the dish, out he came in a satisfied manner, with a piece of quill in his hand, to lean against a door-post, and listen to the horses feeding, and have his teeth ready for supper.

Then a lady's-maid came out, and the sun was on her face, and she turned round to go back again; but put a better face upon it, and gave a trip and hitched her dress, and looked at the sun full body, lest the hostlers should laugh that she was losing her complexion. With a long Italian glass in her fingers very daintily, she came up to the pump in the middle of the yard, where I was running the water off all my head and shoulders, and arms, and some of my breast even, and though I had glimpsed her through the sprinkle, it gave me quite a turn to see her. But she looked at me, no whit abashed, making a baby of me, no doubt, as a woman of thirty will do, even with a very big youth when they catch him on a hayrick, and she said to me in a brazen manner, as if I had been nobody, while I was shrinking behind the pump, and craving to get my shirt on, "Good leetle boy, come hither to me. Fine heaven! how blue your eyes are, and your skin like snow; but some naughty man has beaten it black. Oh, leetle boy, let me feel it. Ah, how then it must have hurt you! There now, and you shall love me."

All this time she was touching my breast, here and there, very lightly, with her delicate brown fingers, and with the slightest brush (a practised action which to any onlooker would have been missed—a mere sleight of hand—so that I wondered had it been an accident, though her arched eyebrow gave me hint of other thoughts) her hand dropped to the top of my trousers where curls of hair, neither fair as my scalp hair was still then, nor the black of later years, gave hint of the now-thickened thatch below, and I understood from her voice and manner that she was not of this country, but a foreigner by extraction. And then I was not so shy of her, because I could talk better English than she; and yet I longed for my jerkin, but liked not to be rude to her.

"If you please, madam, I must go. John Fry is waiting by the tapster's door, and Peggy neighing to me."

"There, there, you shall go, leetle dear, and perhaps I will go after you. I have taken much love of you. But the baroness is hard to me. How far you call it now to the bank of the sea at Wash—Wash—"

"At Watchett, likely you mean, madam. Oh, a very long way, and the roads as soft as the road to Oare."

"Oh-ah, oh-ah—I shall remember; that is the place where my leetle boy live, and some day I will come seek for him. Now make the pump to flow, my dear, and give me the good water. The baroness will not touch unless a nebule be formed outside the glass."

I did not know what she meant by that; yet I pumped for her very heartily, and marvelled to see her for fifty times throw the water away in the trough, as if it was not good enough. At last the water suited her, with a likeness of fog outside the glass, and the gleam of a crystal under it, and then she made a curtsey to me, in a sort of mocking manner, holding the long glass by the foot, not to take the cloud off; and then she wanted to kiss me; but I was out of breath, and have always been shy of that work, except when I come to offer it; and so I ducked under the pump-handle, and she knocked her chin on the knob of it; and the hostlers came out, and asked whether they would do as well.

Upon this, she retreated up the yard, with a certain dark dignity, and a foreign way of walking, which stopped them at once from going farther, because it was so different from the fashion of their sweethearts. One with another they hung back, where half a cart-load of hay was, and they looked to be sure that she would not turn round; and then each one laughed at the rest of them, one tracing in the air an outline as of a vase, so curved and full of promise of cushioning for a man atop was her figure, whilst another, looking wizened and worldlywise (probably a rantallion with his pouch sagging below his weapon but still planning on aiming it), put a hand to his shaft and thrust his hips forward feigning taking of the foreigner.

Insofar as my need for rest I slumbered well that night, having been spared the sharing of a room with John Fry's strident snores. I lay naked, dreaming of soothing hands caressing my bruises, the figure murmuring to me in a muffled, husky manner of throat. Yet my vacillation between quiet rest and awakening jolted into a moment of fear as my eyelids flew open to see the outline of a figure in white, and in those moments, believing I was confronted by one who had left this earth in mortal form, I could feel the blood pounding through my heart, though as soon as it spoke I knew I need have no such fear of the apparition (yet I was perturbed by its intent).

"Do not be afraid, for you surely knew that I would come to you before the sun steals the dark night?" My hand trembled as I realised that her hand had taken me to her and I was now touching a woman's breast—a gesture long yearned to suffer. No conscious thought prevailed as I closed my hand over her, fingers bending at the knuckles as my fingertips pressed into her, much as mother's fingers kneaded the dough for our bread. Yet no female flesh was I enjoying, but that she had taken my hands to feel her breasts through the smock of fine white linen. The giddy shiver of exploration into hitherto unknown territory flitted within the hollows of my body, darting from bough to bough, wings a-fluttering whilst this moth was drawn to its flame.

Without spoken word she gently took my hand from her body and placed it—my own girt hand—onto the bridge between the tops of my own thighs. I could already feel a hardening, as my blood stirred through my veins and more. My lids blinked rapidly over my watering eyes, now accustomed to the dark, and I failed to avert them (despite propriety long instilled in me by mother) as she crossed her arms in front of her (much as we were counselled at school we must lie in our dormitory beds with no hands permitted 'neath the cover). In a slow, deliberate manner, all the while below her thick brown eyebrows her eyes baiting mine (for I found that I could now observe such details by the silvered light straying through the window), she raised the garment aloft. As each moment uncurtained more of her naked body I could do naught but stare at her unbosoming. My breath rasped, scores of fancies scalding at my throat as I espied the dark triangle at the top of her legs and my eyes followed the hem of her gown arising to expose half of one nipple. This slightest peek at the tip of her breast excited me more, I am sure, than if she had revealed both breasts together, and I flicked my tongue over my dry lips.

My eyes widened as she slowly revealed both breasts to be framed atop and to the side by the white gown, captured in exquisite detail as a picture. Her twin mounds moved together as she took her crossed arms over her head, the garment fluttering with the slightest of sounds like a rustling of leaves as it slipped down her side to the floor. She slowly lowered herself to the edge of the bed and I dared not to move, verily not knowing what move a man should make. Her buttocks by my waist and sinking the coarse mattress lower, she lay down to face me, lifting her legs onto the bed, wrapping one on top of my leg nearest to her to catch me fast. Her fingers traced a path through the hair of my chest and over my abdomen (as a mother troubles a child in a playful rhyme leading to a tickling, though the butterfly sensations within could never be construed as those of my childhood—and this was no troublesome pursuit). My breath held within my throat as her hand caressed the hair around my manhood now standing proud of my body and as long and broad as ever I myself had seen it.

"Ah, John," she said, her voice low and beguiling. "You have the hair of a man in this place and so you are an adult. Now you have to make your choice as an adult, most defeeneetly not a boy—and I will not force you eether way. You should be proud of your size,

John, for many a man would want such as this tool. I know that you will make virgin maids gasp with surprise, or perhaps even fear you a leetle, for you are so big. But for now if you weesh I can help you learn how to use it as a man should. My leetle John is not so leetle, no?" (For such is the nearest I can describe the words she used.) "Do you want me, John?" She gently pulled at the hair at the root of my throbbing member, kindling my fire such that it was erect with no assistance from finger or hand. She twisted a tiny curl of my hair around her finger as a coquettish girl plays with the hair on her head and slowly ran her tongue across her upper lip, her mouth slightly open, looking as though she desired to devour me.

In earnest, this was a moment of reckoning for me, though 'twas innocent enough in me that I knew not what this meant nor what form of carnal desire this could possibly take. I lay not knowing what would happen, nor objecting when she slid my hand between her own legs. I could feel a bristling of hair tickling beneath my palm, and she placed her hand on top of mine to encourage me to flex my fingers over her. A warm wetness there gave me great surprise—and being always mindful of my mother's cautions on not giving a lady cause to feel uncomfortable, and being hugely confounded, I pulled my hand away lest I should embarrass her at finding this affliction. Her low laugh was handsome in its richness, and she returned my hand (needing now but little bidding) to the nest between her plump thighs.

"Do not worry about the water. It is only my, how do you say, juices? It is a good sign—it means I am ready for you—thees is your first time, no? Do not worry, I will guide you—we have leetle time now and there is much I could geeve to you but it is no good for a first time. I am practeesed in the art and you will find me a discreet friend, as I know you weel be to me."

I felt a stirring to a point I had never believed could happen, stood to attention with a fullness and throbbing I had not before known in my own explorations, be they inept fumblings in my darkened chamber at home or the frantic frigging at school. Her mouth, lips dark and full, closed over mine and her tongue parted my lips for me (for as yet I did not know the dance expected of my own lips), tracing around my tongue as if licking the froth from a cup of milk taken fresh from a cow, rolling her tongue around mine then sucking on it as it folded upwards, and drawing it into her own mouth (tasting of the wine at home brought out for special occasions or guests). The drawing upon my tongue (which found me bemused though it were not distasteful) ceased and for a moment I was in disorder and doubted if there were more a man and woman can do.

But in one swift movement she slid further up the bed, her breast almost level with my mouth, and she pushed down upon my head to guide my lips onto her nipple. "Now, my John, suck on me as I have just done with your tongue, as an infant does to hees mother. Suck softly or hard as you weesh."

Greedily and without need of further urging I opened my mouth around the tip of her breast and some base memory imprinted from the most natural of times as a baby arose within me. I could not help but utter a low moan—nay a groan, somewhere betwixt pleasure and surprise. "Now John," she whispered, "you can take my other breast eenstead and drink of it as you weesh. You can use your tongue to teekle across me." I needed no further urging to move my head to the other mound of fullness pressed against my face, bringing both hands to hold it fast inside my mouth.

I flicked my tongue across the peak as a cat lapping at a treat of milk served up for it, and she groaned from deep within her soul. "That is so good, John, I know you are going to be so good eenside me. But first I must show you more, so that when I find you again—as I will in Oh-ah, did you say?—you can pleasure me further."

She put her hands to each side of my face and gently pushed me from her breast, her nipple now elongated, caught between my teeth. She slid down the bed, her heated body against my skin, kissing gently my neck, my chest, my stomach with muscles taut, catching my erect member within her breasts, pushing them together to rub on it and then playing its tip across each of her nipples, rigid with her lust. I had the curiosity to ask for more, and her mouth nuzzled the hair with which she had played earlier afore I found my baleen enveloped in warmth and wet, and for a moment I knew not (nor cared, such was the heat in my breast) where it had gone. I was within her lips, working up and down the rigid shaft, her tongue playing across the tip as the froth atop a wave at Porlock. Nature herself gave me the knowledge that this was a mirror to my sucking and flicking on her breasts. The pleasure plumbed to my pelvis and she pulled back from cossetting me inside her mouth.

"I must not do thees more, John, for it will be too soon for you and you will spend without having been within me. Though now you know how it can be. You have had but a few tastes from the table. Now I will serve up the meal for you, and it will be well worth the wait and the pangs of your hunger." In a move of which any wrestler would have been proud, she rolled onto her back and pulled at me at each side of my waist. "Lie on top of me, my John," she urged with a mounting in her voice. I followed her instructions willingly, as a lamb follows a sheep, and rolled onto her, though instinctively mindful of my great weight upon her, and I raised myself up on my arms, elbows slightly bent, as though preparing my body to exercise afore wrestling.

Once more her hand found me and she slid it until the point of my member was between her legs, looking for all its worth as if it were to pierce her as a lance. Her practised hand guided me to her, all the while her sharp little eyes gazing deep into mine in the half-light. "Now, John, put it eenside me. Occupy me now. I can please you well, as you have never imagined."

Perchance out of politeness I should have felt to be gentle in the way I insheathed, but I cannot say but that I wanted her most earnestly. A natural instinct wrought its work and I thrust myself into the warmest, wettest, most welcoming place a man can be. Still holding myself above her I pushed fore and back in a rocking motion as she moved my hips to guide me before grasping at my buttocks, huge and heaving.

How wont was I to wish it never to end and yet I had need of relief from the pressure of rubbing up and down within her body, the blood pounding in my temples and ears as a blanket of bestiality wrapped its claws around me and I pummelled into her. Too soon I was spent, soaked with the sweat of a run ten miles over the Exmoor hills, and I fell upon her heaving body. "Oh yes, John, that was a very fine first time. You learn very queekly and you are so strong. And so very beeg. That is good for a woman. She has need to feel a fullness. And now you are defeeneetly a man." She smiled into my eyes as she nudged me off her body to her side. "My leetle boy is no more. He is my John. Go to sleep now, my man. I could not excuse it to myself if I should not have been with you, and you me, for such opportunity is the rarest of times. Though I feel it in my heart that I will visit Oh-ah some day.

"But remember, you must be discreet and not betray me by telling others that you received favour from me, and so will I be for you."

Raising herself on her elbow she swung her legs over the edge of the bed, with covers now wrinkled and rubbing, stooping to pick up her nightgown and draw it over her head. Though I had not sight of it as her face was turned away, I knew she was smiling broadly. Nothing save Paradise could have satisfied me more that night: I do not think I even heard her leave the room as stealthily as she had crept in, for even though I was lying in moistness, more than I could have imagined, I fell into a slumber as deep as a grave (and as I now know sating natural desire can blanket over a body) and such that I had to be awakened of the morn by John Fry to resume our journey home.

Now, up to the end of Dulverton town, on the northward side of it, where the two new pig-sties be, the Oare folk and the Watchett folk must trudge on together, until we come to a broken cross, where a murdered man lies buried. Peggy and Smiler went up the hill, as if nothing could be too much for them, after the beans they had eaten, and suddenly turning a corner of trees, we happened upon a great coach and six horses labouring very heavily. John Fry rode on with his hat in his hand, as became him towards the quality; but I was amazed to that degree, that I left my cap on my head, and drew bridle without knowing it.

For in the front seat of the coach, which was half-way open, being of the city-make, and the day in want of air, sate the foreign lady, who had met me at the pump and offered to salute me and unbeknown to others, had delivered a wondrous lesson in life, giving me my first taste of Eden's garden and filling her belly full of my seed. By her side was a little girl, dark-haired and very wonderful, with a wealthy softness on her, as if she must have her own way. I could not look at her for two glances, and she did not look at me for one, being such a little child, and busy with the hedges. But in the honourable place sate a handsome lady, very warmly dressed, and sweetly delicate of colour. And close to her was a lively child, two or it may be three years old, bearing a white cockade in his hat, and staring at all and everybody. Now, he saw Peggy, and took such a liking to her, that the lady his mother—if so she were—was forced to look at my pony and me. And, to tell the truth, although I am not of those who adore the high folk, she looked at us very kindly, and with a sweetness rarely found in the women who milk the cows for us.

Then I took off my cap to the beautiful lady, without asking wherefore; and she put up her hand and kissed it to me, thinking, perhaps, that I looked like a gentle and good young man; for folk always called me innocent, though God knows I never was that and of certainty no longer after the event (methinks the most fortifying of character) which had just befallen me. But now the foreign lady, or lady's maid, as it might be, who had been busy with little dark eyes, turned upon all this going-on, and looked me straight in the face. I was about to salute her, at a distance, indeed, and not with the nicety she had offered to me, but, strange to say, she stared at my eyes as if she had never seen me before, neither wished to see me again. At this I was so startled, such things beings out of my knowledge, that I startled Peggy also with the muscle of my legs, and she being fresh from stable, and the mire scraped off with cask-hoop, broke away so suddenly that I could do no more than turn round and lower my cap, now five months old, to the beautiful lady. Soon I overtook John Fry, and asked him all about them, and how it was that we had missed their starting from the hostel. But John would never talk much till after a gallon of cider; and all that I could win out of him was that they were "murdering Papishers," and little he cared to do with them, or the devil, as they came from. And a good thing for me, and a providence, that I was gone down Dulverton town to buy sweetstuff for Annie, else my stupid head would have gone astray with their great out-coming.

We saw no more of them after that, but turned into the sideway; and soon had the fill of our hands and eyes to look to our own going. For the road got worse and worse, until there was none at all, and perhaps the purest thing it could do was to be ashamed to show itself. But we pushed on as best we might, with doubt of reaching home any time, except by special grace of God.

The fog came down upon the moors as thick as ever I saw it; and there was no sound of any sort, nor a breath of wind to guide us. The little stubby trees that stand here and there, like bushes with a wooden leg to them, were drizzled with a mess of wet, and hung their points with dropping. Wherever the butt-end of a hedgerow came up from the hollow ground, like the withers of a horse, holes of splash were pocked and pimpled in the yellow sand of coneys, or under the dwarf tree's ovens. But soon it was too dark to see that, or anything else, I may say, except the creases in the dusk, where prisoned light crept up the valleys.

After awhile even that was gone, and no other comfort left us except to see our horses' heads jogging to their footsteps, and the dark ground pass below us, lighter where the wet was; and then the splash, foot after foot, more clever than we can do it, and the orderly jerk of the tail, and the smell of what a horse is.

John Fry was bowing forward with sleep upon his saddle, and now I could no longer see the frizzle of wet upon his beard—for he had a very brave one, of a bright red colour, and trimmed into a whale-oil knot, because he was newly married—although that comb of hair had been a subject of some wonder to me, whether I, in God's good time, should have the like of that, handsomely set with shining beads, small above and large below, from the weeping of the heaven. But still I could see the jog of his hat—a Sunday hat with a top to it—and some of his shoulder bowed out in the mist, so that one could say "Hold up, John," when Smiler put his foot in. "Mercy of God! where be us now?" said John Fry, waking suddenly; "us ought to have passed hold hash, Jan. Zeen it on the road, have 'ee?"

"No indeed, John; no old ash. Nor nothing else to my knowing; nor heard nothing, save thee snoring."

"Watt a vule thee must be then, Jan; and me myzell no better. Harken, lad, harken!"

We drew our horses up and listened, through the thickness of the air, and with our hands laid to our ears. At first there was nothing to hear, except the panting of the horses and the trickle of the eaving drops from our head-covers and clothing, and the soft sounds of the lonely night, that make us feel, and try not to think. Then there came a mellow noise, very low and mournsome, not a sound to be afraid of, but to long to know the meaning, with a soft rise of the hair. Three times it came and went again, as the shaking of a thread might pass away into the distance; and then I touched John Fry to know that there was something near me.

"Doon't 'e be a vule, Jan! Vaine moozick as iver I 'eer. God bless the man as made un doo it."

"Have they hanged one of the Doones then, John?"

"Hush, lad; niver talk laike o' thiccy. Hang a Doone! God knoweth, the King would hang pretty quick if her did."

"Then who is it in the chains, John?"

I felt my spirit rise as I asked; for now I had crossed Exmoor so often as to hope that the people sometimes deserved it, and think that it might be a lesson to the rogues who unjustly loved the mutton they were never born to. But, of course, they were born to hanging, when they set themselves so high.

"It be nawbody," said John, "vor us to make a fush about. Belong to t'other zide o' the moor, and come staling shape to our zide. Red Jem Hannaford his name. Thank God for him to be hanged, lad; and good cess to his soul for craikin' zo."

So the sound of the quiet swinging led us very modestly, as it came and went on the wind, loud and low pretty regularly, even as far as the foot of the gibbet where the four cross-ways are.

"Vamous job this here," cried John, looking up to be sure of it, because there were so many; "here be my own nick on the post. Red Jem, too, and no doubt of him; he do hang so handsome like, and his ribs up laike a horse a'most. God bless them as discoovered the way to make a rogue so useful. Good-naight to thee, Jem, my lad; and not break thy drames with the craikin'."

John Fry shook his bridle-arm, and smote upon Smiler merrily, as he jogged into the homeward track from the guiding of the body. But I was sorry for Red Jem, and wanted to know more about him, and whether he might not have avoided this miserable end, and what his wife and children thought of it, if, indeed, he had any.

But John would talk no more about it; and perhaps he was moved with a lonesome feeling, as the creaking sound came after us.

"Hould thee tongue, lad,' he said sharply; 'us be naigh the Doone-track now, two maile from Dunkery Beacon hill, the haighest place of Hexmoor. So happen they be abroad to-naight, us must crawl on our belly-places."

I knew at once what he meant—those bloody Doones of Bagworthy, the awe of all Devon and Somerset, outlaws, traitors, murderers. My legs began to tremble to and fro upon Peggy's sides, as I heard the dead robber in chains behind us, and thought of the live ones still in front.

"But, John," I whispered warily, sidling close to his saddle-bow; "dear John, you don't think they will see us in such a fog as this?"

"Never God made vog as could stop their eyesen," he whispered in answer, fearfully; "here us be by the hollow ground. Zober, lad, goo zober now, if thee wish to see thy moother."

For I was inclined to make a run of the danger, and cross the Doone-track at full speed; to rush for it, and be done with it. But even then I wondered why he talked of my mother so, and said not a word of father.

We were come to a long deep "goyal," as they call it on Exmoor, a word whose fountain and origin I have nothing to do with. Only I know that when some laughed at me at Tiverton, for talking about a "goyal," another clouted them on the head, and said that it was in Homer, and meant the hollow of the hand. And another time a Welshman told me that it must be something like the thing they call a "pant" in those parts. Still I know what it means well enough—to wit, a long trough among wild hills, falling towards the plain country, rounded at the bottom, perhaps, and stiff, more than steep, at the sides of it. Whether it be straight or crooked, makes no difference to it.

We rode very carefully down our side, and through the soft grass at the bottom, and all the while we listened as if the air was a speaking-trumpet. Then gladly we breasted our nags to the rise, and were coming to the comb of it, when I heard something, and caught John's arm, and he bent his hand to the shape of his ear. It was the sound of horses' feet knocking up through splashy ground, as if the bottom sucked them. Then a grunting of weary men, and the lifting noise of stirrups, and sometimes the clank of iron mixed with the wheezy croning of leather and the blowing of hairy nostrils.

"God's sake, Jack, slip round her belly, and let her go where she wull."

As John Fry whispered, so I did, for he was off Smiler by this time; but our two pads were too fagged to go far, and began to nose about and crop, sniffing more than they need have done. I crept to John's side very softly, with the bridle on my arm.

"Let goo braidle; let goo, lad. Plaise God they take them for forest-ponies, or they'll zend a bullet through us."

I saw what he meant, and let go the bridle; for now the mist was rolling off, and we were against the sky-line to the dark cavalcade below us. John lay on the ground by a barrow of heather, where a little gullet was, and I crept to him, afraid of the noise I made in dragging my legs along, and the creak of my cord breeches. John bleated like a sheep to cover it—a sheep very cold and trembling.

Then just as the foremost horseman passed, scarce twenty yards below us, a puff of wind came up the glen, and the fog rolled off before it. And suddenly a strong red light, cast by the cloud-weight downwards, spread like fingers over the moorland, opened the alleys of darkness, and hung on the steel of the riders.

"Dunkery Beacon," whispered John, so close into my ear, that I felt his lips and teeth ashake; "dursn't fire it now except to show the Doones way home again, since the naight as they went up and throwed the watchmen atop of it. Why, wutt be 'bout, lad? God's sake—"

For I could keep still no longer, but wriggled away from his arm, and along the little gullet, still going flat on my breast and thighs, until I was under a grey patch of stone, with a fringe of dry fern round it; there I lay, scarce twenty feet above the heads of the riders, and I feared to draw my breath, though prone to do it with wonder.

For now the beacon was rushing up, in a fiery storm to heaven, and the form of its flame came and went in the folds, and the heavy sky was hovering. All around it was hung with red, deep in twisted columns, and then a giant beard of fire streamed throughout the darkness. The sullen hills were flanked with light, and the valleys chined with shadow, and all the sombrous moors between awoke in furrowed anger.

But most of all the flinging fire leaped into the rocky mouth of the glen below me, where the horsemen passed in silence, scarcely deigning to look round. Heavy men and large of stature, reckless how they bore their guns, or how they sate their horses, with leathern jerkins, and long boots, and iron plates on breast and head, plunder heaped behind their saddles, and flagons slung in front of them; I counted more than thirty pass, like clouds upon red sunset. Some had carcasses of sheep swinging with their skins on, others had deer, and one had a child flung across his saddle-bow. Whether the child were dead, or alive, was more than I could tell, only it hung head downwards there, and must take the chance of it. They had got the child, a very young one, for the sake of the dress, no doubt, which they could not stop to pull off from it; for the dress shone bright, where the fire struck it, as if with gold and jewels. I longed in my heart to know most sadly what they would do with the little thing, and whether they would eat it.

It touched me so to see that child, a prey among those vultures, that in my foolish rage and burning I stood up and shouted to them leaping on a rock, and raving out of all possession. Two of them turned round, and one set his carbine at me, but the other said it was but a pixie, and bade him keep his powder. Little they knew, and less thought I, that the pixie then before them would dance their castle down one day.

John Fry, who in the spring of fright had brought himself down from Smiler's side, as if he were dipped in oil, now came up to me, all risk being over, cross, and stiff, and aching sorely from his wet couch of heather.

"Small thanks to thee, Jan, as my new waife bain't a widder. And who be you to zupport of her, and her son, if she have one? Zarve thee right if I was to chuck thee down into the Doone-track. Zim thee'll come to un, zooner or later, if this be the zample of thee."

And that was all he had to say, instead of thanking God! For if ever born man was in a fright, and ready to thank God for anything, the name of that man was John Fry not more than five minutes agone.

However, I answered nothing at all, except to be ashamed of myself; and soon we found Peggy and Smiler in company, well embarked on the homeward road, and victualling where the grass was good. Right glad they were to see us again—not for the pleasure of carrying, but because a horse (like a woman) lacks, and is better without, self-reliance.

My father never came to meet us, at either side of the telling-house, neither at the crooked post, nor even at home-linhay although the dogs kept such a noise that he must have heard us. Home-side of the linhay, and under the ashen hedge-row, where father taught me to catch blackbirds, all at once my heart went down, and all my breast was hollow. There was not even the lanthorn light on the peg against the cow's house, and nobody said "Hold your noise!" to the dogs, or shouted "Here our Jack is!"

I looked at the posts of the gate, in the dark, because they were tall, like father, and then at the door of the harness-room, where he used to smoke his pipe and sing. Then I thought he had guests perhaps—people lost upon the moors—whom he could not leave unkindly, even for his son's sake. And yet about that I was jealous, and ready to be vexed with him, when he should begin to make much of me. And I felt in my pocket for the new pipe which I had brought him from Tiverton, and said to myself, "He shall not have it until to-morrow morning."

Woe is me! I cannot tell. How I knew I know not now—only that I slunk away, without a tear, or thought of weeping, and hid me in a saw-pit. There the timber, over-head, came like streaks across me; and all I wanted was to lack, and none to tell me anything.

By-and-by, a noise came down, as of woman's weeping; and there my mother and sister were, choking and holding together. Although they were my dearest loves, I could not bear to look at them, until they seemed to want my help, and put their hands before their eyes.

CHAPTER IV

A VERY RASH VISIT

My dear father had been killed by the Doones of Bagworthy, while riding home from Porlock market, on the Saturday evening. With him were six brother-farmers, all of them very sober; for father would have no company with any man who went beyond half a gallon of beer, or a single gallon of cider. The robbers had no grudge against him; for he had never flouted them, neither made overmuch of outcry, because they robbed other people. For he was a man of such strict honesty, and due parish feeling, that he knew it to be every man's own business to defend himself and his goods; unless he belonged to our parish, and then we must look after him.

These seven good farmers were jogging along, helping one another in the troubles of the road, and singing goodly hymns and songs to keep their courage moving, when suddenly a horseman stopped in the starlight full across them.

By dress and arms they knew him well, and by his size and stature, shown against the glimmer of the evening star; and though he seemed one man to seven, it was in truth one man to one. Of the six who had been singing songs and psalms about the power of God, and their own regeneration—such psalms as went the round, in those days, of the public-houses—there was not one but pulled out his money, and sang small beer to a Doone.

But father had been used to think that any man who was comfortable inside his own coat and waistcoat deserved to have no other set, unless he would strike a blow for them. And so, while his gossips doffed their hats, and shook with what was left of them, he set his staff above his head, and rode at the Doone robber. With a trick of his horse, the wild man escaped the sudden onset, although it must have amazed him sadly that any durst resist him. Then when Smiler was carried away with the dash and the weight of my father (not being brought up to battle, nor used to turn, save in plough harness), the outlaw whistled upon his thumb, and plundered the rest of the yeomen. But father, drawing at Smiler's head, to try to come back and help them, was in the midst of a dozen men, who seemed to come out of a turf-rick, some on horse, and some a-foot. Nevertheless, he smote lustily, so far as he could see; and being of great size and strength, and his blood well up, they had no easy job with him. With the play of his wrist, he cracked three or four crowns, being always famous at single-stick; until the rest drew their horses away, and he thought that he was master, and would tell his wife about it.

But a man beyond the range of staff was crouching by the peat-stack, with a long gun set to his shoulder, and he got poor father against the sky, and I cannot tell the rest of it. Only they knew that Smiler came home, with blood upon his withers, and father was found in the morning dead on the moor, with his ivy-twisted cudgel lying broken under him. Now, whether this were an honest fight, God judge betwixt the Doones and me.

It was more of woe than wonder, being such days of violence, that mother knew herself a widow, and her children fatherless. Of children there were only three. I, John Ridd, was the eldest, and felt it a heavy thing on me; next came sister Annie, and then the little Eliza.

Now, before I got home and found my sad loss—and no one ever loved his father more than I loved mine—mother had done a most wondrous thing, which made all the neighbours say that she must be mad, at least. Upon the Monday morning, while her husband lay unburied, she cast a white hood over her hair, and gathered a black cloak round her, and, taking counsel of no one, set off on foot for the Doone-gate.

In the early afternoon she came to the hollow and barren entrance, where in truth there was no gate, only darkness to go through. If I get on with this story, I shall have to tell of it by-and-by, as I saw it afterwards; and will not dwell there now. Enough that no gun was fired at her, only her eyes were covered over, and somebody led her by the hand, without any wish to hurt her.

A very rough and headstrong road was all that she remembered, for she could not think as she wished to do, with the cold iron pushed against her. At the end of this road they delivered her eyes, and she could scarce believe them.

For she stood at the head of a deep green valley, carved from out the mountains in a perfect oval, with a fence of sheer rock standing round it, eighty feet or a hundred high; from whose brink black wooded hills swept up to the sky-line. By her side a little river glided out from underground with a soft dark babble, unawares of daylight; then growing brighter, lapsed away, and fell into the valley. Then, as it ran down the meadow, alders stood on either marge, and grass was blading out upon it, and yellow tufts of rushes gathered, looking at the hurry. But further down, on either bank, were covered houses built of stone, square and roughly cornered, set as if the brook were meant to be the street between them. Only one room high they were, and not placed opposite each other, but in and out as skittles are; only that the first of all, which proved to be the captain's, was a sort of double house, or rather two houses joined together by a plank-bridge, over the river.

Fourteen cots my mother counted, all very much of a pattern, and nothing to choose between them, unless it were the captain's. Deep in the quiet valley there, away from noise, and violence, and brawl, save that of the rivulet, any man would have deemed them homes of simple mind and innocence. Yet not a single house stood there but was the home of murder.

Two men led my mother down a steep and gliddery stair-way, like the ladder of a hay-mow; and thence from the break of the falling water as far as the house of the captain. And there at the door they left her trembling, strung as she was, to speak her mind.

Now, after all, what right had she, a common farmer's widow, to take it amiss that men of birth thought fit to kill her husband. And the Doones were of very high birth, as all we clods of Exmoor knew; and we had enough of good teaching now—let any man say the contrary—to feel that all we had belonged of right to those above us. Therefore my mother was half-ashamed that she could not help complaining.

But after a little while, as she said, remembrance of her husband came, and the way he used to stand by her side and put his strong arm round her, and how he liked his bacon fried, and praised her kindly for it—and so the tears were in her eyes, and nothing should gainsay them.

A tall old man, Sir Ensor Doone, came out with a bill-hook in his hand, hedger's gloves going up his arms, as if he were no better than a labourer at ditch-work. Only in his mouth and eyes, his gait, and most of all his voice, even a child could know and feel that here was no ditch-labourer. Good cause he has found since then, perhaps, to wish that he had been one.

With his white locks moving upon his coat, he stopped and looked down at my mother, and she could not help herself but curtsey under the fixed black gazing.

"Good woman, you are none of us. Who has brought you hither? Young men must be young—but I have had too much of this work."

And he scowled at my mother, for her comeliness; and yet looked under his eyelids as if he liked her for it. But as for her, in her depth of love-grief, it struck scorn upon her womanhood; and in the flash she spoke.

"What you mean I know not. Traitors! cut-throats! cowards! I am here to ask for my husband." She could not say any more, because her heart was now too much for her, coming hard in her throat and mouth; but she opened up her eyes at him.

"Madam," said Sir Ensor Doone—being born a gentleman, although a very bad one—"I crave pardon of you. My eyes are old, or I might have known. Now, if we have your husband prisoner, he shall go free without ransoms, because I have insulted you."

"Sir," said my mother, being suddenly taken away with sorrow, because of his gracious manner, "please to let me cry a bit."

He stood away, and seemed to know that women want no help for that. And by the way she cried he knew that they had killed her husband. Then, having felt of grief himself, he was not angry with her, but left her to begin again.

"Loth would I be," said mother, sobbing with her new red handkerchief, and looking at the pattern of it, "loth indeed, Sir Ensor Doone, to accuse any one unfairly. But I have lost the very best husband God ever gave to a woman; and I knew him when he was to your belt, and I not up to your knee, sir; and never an unkind word he spoke, nor stopped me short in speaking. All the herbs he left to me, and all the bacon-curing, and when it was best to kill a pig, and how to treat the maidens. Not that I would ever wish—oh, John, it seems so strange to me, and last week you were everything."

Here mother burst out crying again, not loudly, but turning quietly, because she knew that no one now would ever care to wipe the tears. And fifty or a hundred things, of weekly and daily happening, came across my mother, so that her spirit fell like slackening lime.

"This matter must be seen to; it shall be seen to at once," the old man answered, moved a little in spite of all his knowledge. "Madam, if any wrong has been done, trust the honour of a Doone; I will redress it to my utmost. Come inside and rest yourself, while

I ask about it. What was your good husband's name, and when and where fell this mishap?"

"Deary me," said mother, as he set a chair for her very polite, but she would not sit upon it; "Saturday morning I was a wife, sir; and Saturday night I was a widow, and my children fatherless. My husband's name was John Ridd, sir, as everybody knows; and there was not a finer or better man in Somerset or Devon. He was coming home from Porlock market, and a new gown for me on the crupper, and a shell to put my hair up—oh, John, how good you were to me!"

Of that she began to think again, and not to believe her sorrow, except as a dream from the evil one, because it was too bad upon her, and perhaps she would awake in a minute, and her husband would have the laugh of her. And so she wiped her eyes and smiled, and looked for something.

"Madam, this is a serious thing," Sir Ensor Doone said graciously, and showing grave concern: "my boys are a little wild, I know. And yet I cannot think that they would willingly harm any one. And yet—and yet, you do look wronged. Send Counsellor to me," he shouted, from the door of his house; and down the valley went the call, "Send Counsellor to Captain."

Counsellor Doone came in ere yet my mother was herself again; and if any sight could astonish her when all her sense of right and wrong was gone astray with the force of things, it was the sight of the Counsellor. A square-built man of enormous strength, but a foot below the Doone stature (which I shall describe hereafter), he carried a long grey beard descending to the leather of his belt. Great eyebrows overhung his face, like ivy on a pollard oak, and under them two large brown eyes, as of an owl when muting. And he had a power of hiding his eyes, or showing them bright, like a blazing fire. He stood there with his beaver off, and mother tried to look at him, but he seemed not to descry her.

"Counsellor," said Sir Ensor Doone, standing back in his height from him, "here is a lady of good repute—"

"Oh, no, sir; only a woman."

"Allow me, madam, by your good leave. Here is a lady, Counsellor, of great repute in this part of the country, who charges the Doones with having unjustly slain her husband—"

"Murdered him! murdered him!" cried my mother, "if ever there was a murder. Oh, sir! oh, sir! you know it."

"The perfect rights and truth of the case is all I wish to know," said the old man, very loftily: "and justice shall be done, madam."

"Oh, I pray you—pray you, sirs, make no matter of business of it. God from Heaven, look on me!"

"Put the case," said the Counsellor.

"The case is this," replied Sir Ensor, holding one hand up to mother: "This lady's worthy husband was slain, it seems, upon his return from the market at Porlock, no longer ago than last Saturday night. Madam, amend me if I am wrong."

"No longer, indeed, indeed, sir. Sometimes it seems a twelvemonth, and sometimes it seems an hour."

"Cite his name," said the Counsellor, with his eyes still rolling inwards.

"Master John Ridd, as I understand. Counsellor, we have heard of him often; a worthy man and a peaceful one, who meddled not with our duties. Now, if any of our boys have been rough, they shall answer it dearly. And yet I can scarce believe it. For the folk about these parts are apt to misconceive of our sufferings, and to have no feeling for us. Counsellor, you are our record, and very stern against us; tell us how this matter was."

"Oh, Counsellor!" my mother cried; "Sir Counsellor, you will be fair: I see it in your countenance. Only tell me who it was, and set me face to face with him, and I will bless you, sir, and God shall bless you, and my children."

The square man with the long grey beard, quite unmoved by anything, drew back to the door and spoke, and his voice was like a fall of stones in the bottom of a mine.

"Few words will be enow for this. Four or five of our best-behaved and most peaceful gentlemen went to the little market at Porlock with a lump of money. They bought some household stores and comforts at a very high price, and pricked upon the homeward road, away from vulgar revellers. When they drew bridle to rest their horses, in the shelter of a peat-rick, the night being dark and sudden, a robber of great size and strength rode into the midst of them, thinking to kill or terrify. His arrogance and hardihood at the first amazed them, but they would not give up without a blow goods which were on trust with them. He had smitten three of them senseless, for the power of his arm was terrible; whereupon the last man tried to ward his blow with a pistol. Carver, sir, it was, our brave and noble Carver, who saved the lives of his brethren and his own; and glad enow they were to escape. Notwithstanding, we hoped it might be only a flesh-wound, and not to speed him in his sins."

As this atrocious tale of lies turned up joint by joint before her, like a "devil's coach-horse," mother was too much amazed to do any more than look at him, as if the earth must open. But the only thing that opened was the great brown eyes of the Counsellor, which rested on my mother's face with a dew of sorrow, as he spoke of sins.

She, unable to bear them, turned suddenly on Sir Ensor, and caught (as she fancied) a smile on his lips, and a sense of quiet enjoyment.

"All the Doones are gentlemen," answered the old man gravely, and looking as if he had never smiled since he was a baby. "We are always glad to explain, madam, any mistake which the rustic people may fall upon about us; and we wish you clearly to conceive that we do not charge your poor husband with any set purpose of robbery, neither will we bring suit for any attainder of his property. Is it not so, Counsellor?"

"Without doubt his land is attainted; unless in mercy you forbear, sir."

"Counsellor, we will forbear. Madam, we will forgive him. Like enough he knew not right from wrong, at that time of night. The waters are strong at Porlock, and even an honest man may use his staff unjustly in this unchartered age of violence and rapine."

The Doones to talk of rapine! Mother's head went round so that she curtseyed to them both, scarcely knowing where she was, but calling to mind her manners. All the time she felt a warmth, as if the right was with her, and yet she could not see the way to spread it out before them. With that, she dried her tears in haste and went into the cold air, for fear of speaking mischief.

But when she was on the homeward road, and the sentinels had charge of her, blinding her eyes, as if she were not blind enough with weeping, some one came in haste behind her, and thrust a heavy leathern bag into the limp weight of her hand.

"Captain sends you this," he whispered; "take it to your family."

But mother let it fall in a heap, as if it had been a blind worm; and then for the first time crouched before God, that even the Doones should pity her.

CHAPTER V

AN ILLEGAL SETTLEMENT

Good folk who dwell in a lawful land, if any such there be, may for want of exploration, judge our neighbourhood harshly, unless the whole truth is set before them. In bar of such prejudice, many of us ask leave to explain how and why it was the robbers came to that head in the midst of us. We would rather not have had it so, God knows as well as anybody; but it grew upon us gently, in the following manner. Only let all who read observe that here I enter many things which came to my knowledge in later years.

In or about the year of our Lord 1640, when all the troubles of England were swelling to an outburst, great estates in the North country were suddenly confiscated, through some feud of families and strong influence at Court, and the owners were turned upon the world, and might think themselves lucky to save their necks. These estates were in co-heirship, joint tenancy I think they called it, although I know not the meaning, only so that if either tenant died, the other living, all would come to the live one in spite of any testament.

One of the joint owners was Sir Ensor Doone, a gentleman of brisk intellect; and the other owner was his cousin, the Earl of Lorne and Dykemont.

Lord Lorne was some years the elder of his cousin, Ensor Doone, and was making suit to gain severance of the cumbersome joint tenancy by any fair apportionment, when suddenly this blow fell on them by wiles and woman's meddling; and instead of dividing the land, they were divided from it.

The nobleman was still well-to-do, though crippled in his expenditure; but as for the cousin, he was left a beggar, with many to beg from him. He thought that the other had wronged him, and that all the trouble of law befell through his unjust petition. Many friends advised him to make interest at Court; for having done no harm whatever, and being a good Catholic, which Lord Lorne was not, he would be sure to find hearing there, and probably some favour. But he, like a very hot-brained man, although he had long been married to the daughter of his cousin (whom he liked none the more for that), would have nothing to say to any attempt at making a patch of it, but drove away with his wife and sons, and the relics of his money, swearing hard at everybody. In this he may have been quite wrong; probably, perhaps, he was so; but I am not convinced at all but what most of us would have done the same.

Some say that, in the bitterness of that wrong and outrage, he slew a gentleman of the Court, whom he supposed to have borne a hand in the plundering of his fortunes. Others say that he bearded King Charles the First himself, in a manner beyond forgiveness. One thing, at any rate, is sure—Sir Ensor was attainted, and made a felon outlaw, through some violent deed ensuing upon his dispossession.

He had searched in many quarters for somebody to help him, and with good warrant for hoping it, inasmuch as he, in lucky days, had been open-handed and cousinly to all who begged advice of him. But now all these provided him with plenty of good advice indeed, and great assurance of feeling, but not a movement of leg, or lip, or purse-string in his favour. All good people of either persuasion, royalty or commonalty, knowing his kitchen-range to be cold, no longer would play turnspit. And this, it may be, seared his heart more than loss of land and fame.

In great despair at last, he resolved to settle in some outlandish part, where none could be found to know him; and so, in an evil day for us, he came to the West of England. Not that our part of the world is at all outlandish, according to my view of it (for I never found a better one), but that it was known to be rugged, and large, and desolate. And here, when he had discovered a place which seemed almost to be made for him, so withdrawn, so self-defended, and uneasy of access, some of the country-folk around brought him little offerings—a side of bacon, a keg of cider, hung mutton, or a brisket of venison; so that for a little while he was very honest. But when the newness of his coming began to wear away, and our good folk were apt to think that even a gentleman ought to work or pay other men for doing it, and many farmers were grown weary of manners without discourse to them, and all cried out to one another how unfair it was that owning such a fertile valley young men would not spade or plough by reason of noble lineage—then the young Doones growing up took things they would not ask for.

And here let me, as a solid man, owner of five hundred acres (whether fenced or otherwise, and that is my own business), churchwarden also of this parish (until I go to the churchyard), and proud to be called the parson's friend—for a better man I never knew with tobacco and strong waters, nor one who could read the lessons so well and he has been at Blundell's too—once for all let me declare, that I am a thorough-going Church-and-State man, and Royalist, without any mistake about it. And this I lay down, because some people judging a sausage by the skin, may take in evil part my little glosses of style and glibness, and the mottled nature of my remarks and cracks now and then on the frying-pan. I assure them I am good inside, and not a bit of rue in me; only queer knots, as of marjoram, and a stupid manner of bursting.

There was not more than a dozen of them, counting a few retainers who still held by Sir Ensor; but soon they grew and multiplied in a manner surprising to think of. Whether it was the venison, which we call a strengthening victual, or whether it was the Exmoor mutton, or the keen soft air of the moorlands, anyhow the Doones increased much faster than their honesty. At first they had brought some ladies with them, of good repute with charity; and then, as time went on, they added to their stock by carrying. They carried off many good farmers' daughters, who were sadly displeased at first; but took to them kindly after awhile, and made a new home in their babies. For women, as it seems to me, like strong men more than weak ones, feeling that they need some staunchness, something to hold fast by.

And of all the men in our country, although we are of a thick-set breed, you scarce could find one in three-score fit to be placed among the Doones, without looking no more than a tailor. Like enough, we could meet them man for man (if we chose all around the crown and the skirts of Exmoor), and show them what a cross-buttock means, because we are so stuggy; but in regard of stature, comeliness, and bearing, no woman would look twice at us. Not but what I myself, John Ridd, and one or two I know of—but it becomes me best not to talk of that, although my hair is gray.

Perhaps their den might well have been stormed, and themselves driven out of the forest, if honest people had only agreed to begin with them at once when first they took to plundering. But having respect for their good birth, and pity for their misfortunes, and perhaps a little admiration at the justice of God, that robbed men now were robbers, the squires, and farmers, and shepherds, at first did nothing more than grumble gently, or even make a laugh of it, each in the case of others. After awhile they found the matter gone too far for laughter, as violence and deadly outrage stained the hand of robbery, until every woman clutched her child, and every man turned pale at the very name of Doone. For the sons and grandsons of Sir Ensor grew up in foul liberty, and haughtiness, and hatred, to utter scorn of God and man, and brutality towards dumb animals. There was only one good thing about them, if indeed it were good, to wit, their faith to one another, and truth to their wild eyry. But this only made them feared the more, so certain was the revenge they wreaked upon any who dared to strike a Doone. One night, some ten years ere I was born, when they were sacking a rich man's house not very far from Minehead, a shot was fired at them in the dark, of which they took little notice, and only one of them knew that any harm was done. But when they were well on the homeward road, not having slain either man or woman, or even burned a house down, one of their number fell from his saddle, and died without so much as a groan. The youth had been struck, but would not complain, and perhaps took little heed of the wound, while he was bleeding inwardly. His brothers and cousins laid him softly on a bank of whortle-berries, and just rode back to the lonely hamlet where he had taken his death-wound. No man nor woman was left in the morning, nor house for any to dwell in, only a child with its reason gone.

This affair made prudent people find more reason to let them alone than to meddle with them; and now they had so entrenched themselves, and waxed so strong in number, that nothing less than a troop of soldiers could wisely enter their premises; and even so it might turn out ill, as perchance we shall see by-and-by.

For not to mention the strength of the place, which I shall describe in its proper order when I come to visit it, there was not one among them but was a mighty man, straight and tall, and wide, and fit to lift four hundredweight. If son or grandson of old Doone, or one of the northern retainers, failed at the age of twenty, while standing on his naked feet to touch with his forehead the lintel of Sir Ensor's door, and to fill the door frame with his shoulders from sidepost even to sidepost, he was led away to the narrow pass which made their valley so desperate, and thrust from the crown with ignominy, to get his own living honestly. Now, the measure of that doorway is, or rather was, I ought to say, six feet and one inch lengthwise, and two feet all but two inches taken crossways in the clear. Yet I not only have heard but know, being so closely mixed with them, that no descendant of old Sir Ensor, neither relative of his (except, indeed, the Counsellor, who was kept by them for his wisdom), and no more than two of their following ever failed of that test, and relapsed to the difficult ways of honesty.

Not that I think anything great of a standard the like of that: for if they had set me in that door-frame at the age of twenty, it is like enough that I should have walked away with it on my shoulders, though I was not come to my full strength then: only I am speaking now of the average size of our neighbourhood, and the Doones were far beyond that. Moreover, they were taught to shoot with a heavy carbine so delicately and wisely, that even a boy could pass a ball through a rabbit's head at the distance of fourscore yards. Some people may think nought of this, being in practice with longer shots from the tongue than from the shoulder; nevertheless, to do as above is, to my ignorance, very good work, if you can be sure to do it. Not one word do I believe of Robin Hood splitting peeled wands at seven-score yards, and such like. Whoever wrote such stories knew not how slippery a peeled wand is, even if one could hit it, and how it gives to the onset. Now, let him stick one in the ground, and take his bow and arrow at it, ten yards away, or even five.

Now, after all this which I have written, and all the rest which a reader will see, being quicker of mind than I am (who leave more than half behind me, like a man sowing wheat, with his dinner laid in the ditch too near his dog), it is much but what you will understand the Doones far better than I did, or do even to this moment; and therefore none will doubt when I tell them that our good justiciaries feared to make an ado, or hold any public inquiry about my dear father's death. They would all have had to ride home that night, and who could say what might betide them. Least said soonest mended, because less chance of breaking.

So we buried him quietly—all except my mother, indeed, for she could not keep silence—in the sloping little churchyard of Oare, as meek a place as need be, with the Lynn brook down below it. There is not much of company there for anybody's tombstone, because the parish spreads so far in woods and moors without dwelling-house. If we bury one man in three years, or even a woman or child, we talk about it for three months, and say it must be our turn next, and scarcely grow accustomed to it until another goes.

Annie was not allowed to come, because she cried so terribly; but she ran to the window, and saw it all, mooing there like a little calf, so frightened and so left alone. As for Eliza, she came with me, one on each side of mother, and not a tear was in her eyes, but sudden starts of wonder, and a new thing to be looked at unwillingly, yet curiously. Poor little thing! she was very clever, the only one of our family—thank God for the same—but none the more for that guessed she what it is to lose a father.

CHAPTER VI

NECESSARY PRACTICE

About the rest of all that winter I remember very little, missing my father most out of doors, as when it came to the bird-catching, or the tracking of hares in the snow, or the training of a sheep-dog. Oftentimes I looked at his gun, an ancient piece found in the sea, a little below Glenthorne, and of which he was mighty proud, although it was only a match-lock; and I thought of the times I had held the fuse, while he got his aim at a rabbit, and once even at a red deer rubbing among the hazels. But nothing came of my looking at it, so far as I remember, save foolish tears of my own perhaps, till John Fry took it down one day from the hooks where father's hand had laid it; and it hurt me to see how John handled it, as if he had no memory.

"Bad job for he as her had not got thiccy the naight as her coom acrass them Doones. Rackon Varmer Jan 'ood a-zhown them the wai to kingdom come, 'stead of gooin' herzel zo aisy. And a maight have been gooin' to market now, 'stead of laying banked up over yanner. Maister Jan, thee can zee the grave if thee look alang this here goon-barryel. Buy now, whutt be blubberin' at? Wish I had never told thee."

"John Fry, I am not blubbering; you make a great mistake, John. You are thinking of Annie. I cough sometimes in the winter-weather, and father gives me lickerish—I mean—I mean—he used to. Now let me have the gun, John."

"Thee have the goon, Jan! Thee isn't fit to putt un to thy zhoulder. What a weight her be, for sure!"

"Me not hold it, John! That shows how much you know about it. Get out of the way, John; you are opposite the mouth of it, and likely it is loaded."

John Fry jumped in a livelier manner than when he was doing day-work; and I rested the mouth on a cross rack-piece, and felt a warm sort of surety that I could hit the door over opposite, or, at least, the cobwall alongside of it, and do no harm in the orchard. But John would not give me link or fuse, and, on the whole, I was glad of it, because I had heard my father say that the Spanish gun kicked like a horse, and because the load in it came from his hand, and I did not like to undo it. But I never found it kick very hard, and firmly set to the shoulder, unless it was badly loaded. In truth, the thickness of the metal was enough almost to astonish one; and what our people said about it may have been true enough, although most of them are such liars—at least, I mean, they make mistakes, as all mankind must do. Perchance it was no mistake at all to say that this ancient gun had belonged to a noble Spaniard, the captain of a fine large ship in the "Invincible Armada," which we of England managed to conquer, with God and the weather helping us, a hundred years ago or more—I can't say to a month or so.

After a little while, when John had fired away at a rat the charge I held so sacred, it came to me as a natural thing to practise shooting with that great gun, instead of John Fry's blunderbuss, which looked like a bell with a stalk to it. There is nothing better than a good windmill to shoot at, as I have seen them in flat countries; but we have no windmills upon the great moorland, yet here and there a few barn-doors, where shelter is, and a way up the hollows. And up those hollows you can shoot, with the help of the sides to lead your aim, and there is a fair chance of hitting the door, if you lay your cheek to the barrel, and try not to be afraid of it.

Gradually I won such skill, that I sent nearly all the lead gutter from the north porch of our little church through our best barn-door, a thing which has often repented me since, especially as churchwarden, and made me pardon many bad boys; but father was not buried on that side of the church.

To say truth, some other reason prevailed to frequent the churchyard, and it spares not my blushes to say that it was not for the paying of my respects to my father, nor for the practising of shooting. For there was a couple from the village who were known to be enamoured of each other but not yet betrothed, who, I discovered, also found the quiet of the souls of the graveyard to be their allies in discretion. Being of a curious nature and as with any young man of increasing desire to explore the art of conjoinment—a subject I would be more learned in—I had found a memorial behind which I could hide in advance of their arrival, its design being such that a cross carved into its soft, golden Ham stone provided a hole at the centre, through which they could be observed in their secret tryst.

I had learned that at the time of an evening afore dusk dies into dark, they would both by happenstance be visiting the same grave, though I suspect it was one of someone long-forgotten by, or even unknown to, them. (Even in these parts where it is so rare to have to lay someone here.) I watched as their assignations grew from a furtive kiss snatched from a full red mouth to further discoveries. This one evening, though my own experience in such matters were not as yet great, some sense of happening needled and I found my hand sliding down (with never a thought of intent) to rest lightly upon myself as the couple became entwined in a passionate embrace.

'Twas not hard to see this maid (as homely a young creature as I have seen though her face was enlivened this eve), her hand between his legs, bestowing her pleasure by fondling his stones through his clothing whilst his hand clasped over her breast with a squeeze none too soft in its intensity. He pulled away from her afore his right hand in some haste spun her to face away; methought for a moment he was sending her on her way, or perhaps turning her to look at something of import he had espied. But as she turned she bent at her ample waist, bowing her head towards the ground. I durst not but believe that he may be about to spank her for some wrong-doing and made to consider creeping away, but though care killed a cat I had second thought and pressed the bones around my right orb hard against the cold gravestone.

He lifted her coat up over her shoulders, in so doing covering her head now almost wedged between her own legs, urging her to hold the layers of outer covering and skirts, which she did with one hand whilst the other held onto the stone in front of her. In full view of me was her slit, its trail of dark hair spread to her buttocks, which were of such substance that the cheeks vacillated as she steadied herself. He dropped his breeches, and I could see him send saliva into his hand like a spittoon before encircling it around his tarse, moving the sheath swiftly up and down some dozen times, and then, palm upright, inserting his fingers into her, rubbing as though polishing below a mantel-shelf, before he removed his fingers and wiped them across the side of his coat. Then he placed his length, now proud and stiff, between her legs outstretched, rubbing its tip, red and shiny like a newly lit lanthorn in the dusk, against her—though, as I espied, not yet inside her. He nudged her legs further apart with his knees and pushed himself into her from behind—in the manner of a dog (backwards), shafting upwards and forwards, his buttocks now gleaming white half moons in the dimming light and the sound of slapping flesh on flesh filling the silence the birds had left as they thought it time to roost.

My breath caught in my throat. Though I had visited the churchyard but three or four times, there had been surety in my resolve that some deeper action would take place and thus instruct me more greatly in the fine arts of love and lust. Although I now had some little experience of such desires, I could not believe that he was taking her in a fashion no better than a farm animal from behind, and I gasped, though they could not have heard. Would to God I had not acted in any better fashion than a voyeur, and with the great benefit of hindsight (always the best master and one who may chide me with authority) would I fain avoid such encounters, for a case of conscience arose. She began to cry out with each thrust; from its heartfelt intensity and pitch was not she in some pain or fear? (For otherwise why would she have risked betraying her presence there so?) I knew that though she had shown alacrity until then, I must now speak a good word for her or act in some manner to prevent him making himself sport with her further (for I have always felt it a duty to protect others).

I had hardly time for a decision and though bound to discover my presence to them, I leapt up from behind my viewing place and fired at the church gutter, the sound rebounding around the tomb-stones and sending a flurry of birds already stilled in the half-light screeching from the tree branches and scuttling feathers and leaves to the ground, as I drew myself down ahind the grave once more, leaning my back against the stone, as cold and unwelcoming as the grave itself. In an instant he withdrew from her and made to pull up his breeches over his sticky shaft. The maid so roughly dealt with cast down her skirts most unhandsomely and swivelled round, though instead of making her escape as I had intended to so give her the opportunity, she clung to him, her hands grasping at his clothes, her head darting side to side like a bird. I was now sensible that she was steeped in fury.

"What be that? A shot? Where be that gun to? No one 'as followed me, I zwear."

"I don't know. I caan't see nuttin' nor any 'ere smoke nor anyone runnin' away. But we 'ad better be leavin' now though don't ee make haste as though ee 'ave somethin' to 'ide—purtend 'ee was visitin' one nat so full o' life as I be."

She, discomforted still, sighed deeply and agreed 'twas time to leave separately. "I were enjoyin' that, I were. I caan't wait 'til next time an' will be thinkin' on you tonight as I pleasure mysel' once I 'ave taken to my bed. But we 'ad best find zumwhere else to meet."

They gave each to the other one furtive little kiss before leaving the churchyard separately as if their paths had never crossed. I had this evening learned several lessons: that such contrarieties could take place between man and woman; that such entertainments are in many more a place than I had so far learned (and though I agreed not with swiving in such a holy place—for it should not have been that carnal desires were satisfied in full sight of God— fear of our Lord had not frighted me so that I had desisted from watching); and that she had indeed been furious, though not at the youth, but at having her great pleasure be interrupted thus their swiving unfinished.

But all this time, while I was visiting the churchyard or roving over the hills or about the farm, and even listening to John Fry, my mother, being so much older and feeling trouble longer, went about inside the house, or among the maids and fowls, not caring to talk to the best of them, except when she broke out sometimes about the good master they had lost, all and every one of us. But the fowls would take no notice of it, except to cluck for barley; and the maidens, though they had liked him well, were thinking of their sweethearts as the spring came on. Mother thought it wrong of them, selfish and ungrateful; and yet sometimes she was proud that none had such call as herself to grieve for him.

Though she had deep in her heart known well enough of her husband having taken his pleasure of at least one special sweetheart, and I myself had seen as such, once more being the seer unseen. I had been lying at the back of a hay-barn chewing on an apple fresh from our trees and not destined for the making of cider, which I had cleaved in half with a small knife carried in my pocket. For though I value as much as anybody hard work and it was not in my nature to shirk my duties, I had yearned for brief respite.

I stopped chewing and my breath hitched as I realised that others had entered the barn and I could hear whispering ("Come hither—you are like to have an excellent time of me") and the giggling of a female. Slowly I shifted my position so as to observe which maids were also abroad from their duties, to see the woman (her face unhandsome) sitting on the edge of the hay piled up, her smock and skirts and apron already up about her waist (her chief virtue being a haste which amazed me) and her legs spread wide, feet dangling down to the ground. In front of her I could see only the back and outstretched legs of a figure kneeling between her legs. By my own folly I was trapped within the barn, and I realised with such a jolt as ran through my entire body that there were two things amiss. The figure kneeling was greedily devouring of her between her thighs, and I knew well both the willing parties in this act.

Filling the barn were the sounds of sucking and slurping as a man eating good capon or mutton or Annie's best soup, his deep voice murmuring approval of his feast as she eased herself back onto her elbows, still watching him intently with a look of power over a man which many a woman knoweth she can have if only during venery. He held fast to her thighs (not firm enough for my liking), pushing them further apart as his head ducked in and out as at a game of apple-bobbing. He pulled his head away to look up at her, wiping the back of his hand across his mouth, then asking of her in sober earnest, "Be that good, my lovely?" She nodded her assent, grasping his head between her hands and shoving it back to where it pleased her best, saying, "Don't 'ee stop. Tickle me more wi' yer tongue then work it inside me, for I do so enjoy you bein' inside my body wi' more than yer gristle, though that be what I loves best, it be."

You cannot imagine how close I found myself to them and I held myself most still, quelling the heavy breathing about to brim within me. I could see his tongue protruding from his mouth and licking at her—long, upward, slow licks as a horse licks at some treat held in the hand. I found myself in imitation of his action and protruded the tip of my tongue to lick at the apple I was holding, with a wondering as to the taste of a woman being anything as sweet.

She leaned back further into the gentle prickles of the hay, moaning at first, then with a whispered urgency coaxing him to do more. "It be such gentle nibblin' but today I wants 'ee to bite at me." He leaned back over his heels and used his huge thumbs to open up her large, swollen, red lips hanging low beneath the wiry hair, so as to find what I now know is the mound which can take a woman to the heights of heaven. "Oh yes, maister" (with more than a slice of mockery in her country brogue, not much to respect nor hardly civil): "that be the place."

She rubbed at her large breasts in a circular fashion over her tight, begrimed bodice, pushing them together and up towards her broad chin as she slid her hands up over them and round again, fondling her nipples between finger and thumb. Her teeth bit down on her lower lip as her lids closed over her watery eyes. Clutching at his hair and pulling his head tighter into the darkness between her legs as if he could be lost within her, her hips began to shunt towards him in a regular rhythmic manner, pulsing, until the movements became shorter and faster and with a cry stifled by one fist taken up to her mouth, she tore at the hair of the figure revering her, half whispering and half groaning, "Yes, arrr, yes," sinking her head fast to the hay as if ready to take to bed.

With a movement fluid in its swiftness and belying his bulk, the figure raised his head (once again wiping his hand across his lips, which I could see were with fresh moisture issued from her), and stood upright, pulling down his clothing to reveal his excitement.

His legs bent at the knees, he quickly ploughed into her; swift movements in and out (and what an age 'twas to me); a shudder as though drawing warmth to himself afore a cold hearth, and he slumped forward o'er her lardy white belly before withdrawing from her, a deep sigh of satisfaction through his lips, slightly parted (though still silent in word). She was telling him how good this time had been. "I loves this, I does. An' today is e'en better than laazt time when mistress, she were away in Taun'on."

She lay back with a smile; her satisfaction had wrought a change to her pie-dough face; eyes aflame; cheeks scarlet as the skin of my apple; triumphant smirk to her lips; and taking up a handful of hay she swept it over the spot where the figure had burrowed, discarding it before using her skirt to dry further the wetness.

"You are still a welcoming woman, and I care for you greatly as thou knowest I have done for many a year, but you must not give yourself over to thinking we can do this too often. And never forget—keep your counsel."

"I knows where butter lies upon bread, Maister Jan."

My father—for I say true that was the man—strode out of the barn as if he had done nought but checked the fodder, and she—Betty, long rumoured to be his mistress—arose to lower her smock and outer skirts and waited some minutes before leaving, singing a merry tune to herself.

I pondered over what I had seen and you cannot imagine how I was surpris'd. I had heard the men talk (in whispers when they thought I was not listening and should be insensible of his activities) about what a good man my father was but how he was "acquainted" with others. (As many a man or woman chooses to have a "fucking friend" such as they say, especially should they be married; for if an accident should occur and a child be born, the spouse will oft never know that the seed came from another.) I lay back once more, much troubled, and tears traversed my cheeks to berain the dry hay.

I formed my thoughts into a neat square in my head, sure that mother was knowing of the nature of the master-servant friendship; that it suited both mother and father, for reasons of difference, to retain the services of Betty; and my father had a real affection for Betty even though she be visited by plainness. And as they say: suum cuique pulchrum est ("to each his own is beautiful").

I resumed eating my apple, teasing it with my tongue and sucking on the edge of it to release the juice, then nibbling at the edge with my front teeth without biting too hard within the core of the fruit, as I had just seen my father do with fruit more forbidden.

Knowing I had to wait a few moments before I left lest my audience become known, I picked up the handful of hay she had used between her legs and brought it to my nostrils, my curiosity being whetted to know how it would now smell. The familiar scent now mixed with a sharper, heavier odour—the incense of lust, and a smell I found exciting. I made sure it would not be given to the animals, for I did not want our livestock to be eating of such an act as I had witnessed. Though I should have preferred not to have seen my father much before any other person, I was not enough concerned in't to further think on it greatly, even though I would not have mother to know more of it—for it would have been painful to have delivered her of such news. Now that I have many years marched upon me since then, I cannot but conclude it be naught but normal and I should not now dwell and weary myself on thought of such lechery to besmirch the memory of my father, a goodly man—and only Annie seemed to go softly in and out, and cry, with nobody along of her, chiefly in the corner where the bees are and the grindstone. But somehow she would never let anybody behold her; being set, as you may say, to think it over by herself, and season it with weeping. Many times I caught her, and many times she turned upon me, and then I could not look at her, but asked how long to dinner-time.

Now in the depth of the winter month, such as we call December, father being dead and quiet in his grave a fortnight, it happened me to be out of powder for practice against his enemies. I had never fired a shot without thinking, "This for father's murderer"; and John Fry said that I made such faces it was a wonder the gun went off. But though I could hardly hold the gun, unless with my back against a bar, it did me good to hear it go off, and hope to have hitten his enemies.

In very quick time I left with a shilling in my pocket, and got Peggy out on the Porlock road without my mother knowing it. I was very bold, having John Fry's blunderbuss, and keeping a sharp look-out wherever any lurking place was. However, I saw only sheep and small red cattle, and the common deer of the forest, until I was nigh to Porlock town, and then rode straight to Mr. Pooke's, at the sign of the Spit and Gridiron.

Mr. Pooke was asleep, as it happened, not having much to do that day; and so I fastened Peggy by the handle of a warming-pan, at which she had no better manners than to snort and blow her breath; and in I walked with a manful style, bearing John Fry's blunderbuss. Now Timothy Pooke was a peaceful man, glad to live without any enjoyment of mind at danger, and I was tall and large already as most lads of a riper age. Mr. Pooke, as soon as he opened his eyes, dropped suddenly under the counting-board, and drew a great frying-pan over his head, as if the Doones were come to rob him, as their custom was, mostly after the fair-time. It made me feel rather hot and queer to be taken for a robber; and yet methinks I was proud of it.

"Gadzooks, Master Pooke," said I, having learned fine words at Tiverton; "do you suppose that I know not then the way to carry firearms? An it were the old Spanish match-lock in the lieu of this good flint-engine, which may be borne ten miles or more and never once go off, scarcely couldst thou seem more scared. I might point at thee muzzle on—just so as I do now—even for an hour or more, and like enough it would never shoot thee, unless I pulled the trigger hard, with a crock upon my finger; so you see; just so, Master Pooke, only a trifle harder."

"God sake, John Ridd, God sake," cried Pooke, knowing me by this time; "don't 'e, for good love now, don't 'e show it to me as if I was to suck it. Put 'un down, for good, now; and thee shall have the very best of all is in the shop."

"Ho!" I replied with much contempt, and swinging round the gun so that it fetched his hoop of candles down, all unkindled as they were: "Ho! as if I had not attained to the handling of a gun yet! My hands are cold coming over the moors, else would I go bail to point the mouth at you for an hour, sir, and no cause for uneasiness."

But in spite of all assurances, he showed himself desirous only to see the last of my gun and me. I dare say "villainous saltpetre," as the great playwright calls it, was never so cheap before nor since. For my shilling Master Pooke afforded me two great packages over-large to go into my pockets, as well as a mighty chunk of lead, which I bound upon Peggy's withers. And as if all this had not been enough, he presented me with a roll of comfits for my sister Annie, whose gentle face and pretty manners won the love of everybody.

There was still some daylight here and there as I rose the hill above Porlock, wondering whether my mother would be in a fright, or would not know it. The two great packages of powder, slung behind my back, knocked so hard against one another that I feared they must either spill or blow up, and hurry me over Peggy's ears from the woollen cloth I rode upon. For father always liked a horse to have some wool upon his loins whenever he went far from home, and had to stand about, where one pleased, hot, and wet, and panting. And father always said that saddles were meant for men full-grown and heavy, and losing their activity; and no boy or young man on our farm durst ever get into a saddle, because they all knew that the master would chuck them out pretty quickly. As for me, I had tried it once, from a kind of curiosity; and I could not walk for two or three days, the leather galled my knees so. But now, as Peggy bore me bravely, snorting every now and then into a cloud of air, for the night was growing frosty, presently the moon arose over the shoulder of a hill, and the pony and I were half glad to see her, and half afraid of the shadows she threw, and the images all around us. I was ready at any moment to shoot at anybody, having great faith in my blunderbuss, but hoping not to prove it. And as I passed the narrow place where the Doones had killed my father, such a fear broke out upon me that I leaned upon the neck of Peggy, and shut my eyes, and was cold all over. However, there was not a soul to be seen, until we came home to the old farmyard, and there was my mother crying sadly, and Betty Muxworthy scolding.

"Come along, now," I whispered to Annie, the moment supper was over; "and if you can hold your tongue, Annie, I will show you something."

She lifted herself on the bench so quickly, and flushed so rich with pleasure, that I was obliged to stare hard away, and make Betty look beyond us. Betty thought I had something hid in the closet beyond the clock-case, and she was the more convinced of it by reason of my denial. Not that Betty Muxworthy, or any one else, for that matter, ever found me in a falsehood, because I never told one, not even to my mother—or, which is still a stronger thing, not even to my sweetheart—but that Betty being wronged in the matter of marriage, a generation or two agone, by a man who came hedging and ditching, had now no mercy, except to believe that men from cradle to grave are liars, and women fools to look at them. Though it was talked about that she did not spend her time barren and empty.

When Betty could find no crime of mine, she knocked me out of the way in a minute, as if I had been nobody; and then she began to coax "Mistress Annie," as she always called her, and draw the soft hair down her hands, and whisper into her ears. Meanwhile, dear mother was falling asleep, having been troubled so much about me; and Watch, my father's pet dog, was nodding closer and closer up into her lap.

"Now, Annie, will you come?" I said, for I wanted her to hold the ladle for melting of the lead; "will you come at once, Annie? or must I go for Lizzie, and let her see the whole of it?"

"Indeed, then, you won't do that," said Annie; "Lizzie to come before me, John; and she can't stir a pot of brewis, and scarce knows a tongue from a ham, John, and says it makes no difference, because both are good to eat! Oh, Betty, what do you think of that to come of all her book-learning?"

"Thank God he can't say that of me," Betty answered shortly, for she never cared about argument, except on her own side; "thank he, I says, every marning a'most, never to lead me astray so. Men is desaving and so is galanies; but the most desaving of all is books, with their heads and tails, and the speckots in 'em, lik a peg as have taken the maisles. Some folk purtends to laugh and cry over them. God forgive them for liars!"

It was part of Betty's obstinacy that she never would believe in reading or the possibility of it, but stoutly maintained to the very last that people first learned things by heart, and then pretended to make them out from patterns done upon paper, for the sake of astonishing honest folk just as do the conjurers. And even to see the parson and clerk was not enough to convince her; all she said was, "It made no odds, they were all the same as the rest of us." And now that she had been on the farm nigh upon forty years, and had nursed my father, and made his clothes, and all that he had to eat, and loved him in a fashion as I had seen, and then put him in his coffin, she was come to such authority, that it was not worth the wages of the best man on the place to say a word in answer to Betty, even if he would face the risk to have ten for one, or twenty.

Annie was her love and joy. For Annie she would do anything, even so far as to try to smile, when the maid laughed and danced to her. And in truth I know not how it was, but every one was taken with Annie at the very first time of seeing her. She had such pretty ways and manners, and such a look of kindness, and a sweet soft light in her long blue eyes full of trustful gladness. Everybody who looked at her seemed to grow the better for it, because she knew no evil. And then the turn she had for cooking, you never would have expected it; and how it was her richest mirth to see that she had pleased you. I have been out on the world a vast deal as you will own hereafter, and yet have I never seen Annie's equal for making a weary man comfortable.

CHAPTER VII

HARD IT IS TO CLIMB

So many a winter night went by in a hopeful and pleasant manner, with the hissing of the bright round bullets, cast into the water, and the spluttering of the great red apples which Annie was roasting for me. We always managed our evening's work in the chimney of the back-kitchen, where there was room to set chairs and table, in spite of the fire burning. On the right-hand side was a mighty oven, where Betty threatened to bake us; and on the left, long sides of bacon, made of favoured pigs, and growing very brown and comely. Annie knew the names of all, and ran up through the wood-smoke, every now and then, when a gentle memory moved her, and asked them how they were getting on, and when they would like to be eaten. Then she came back with foolish tears, at thinking of that necessity; and I, being soft in a different way, would make up my mind against bacon.

But, Lord bless you! it was no good. Whenever it came to breakfast-time, after three hours upon the moors, I regularly forgot the pigs, but paid good heed to the rashers. For ours is a hungry county, if such there be in England; a place, I mean, where men must eat, and are quick to discharge the duty. The air of the moors is so shrewd and wholesome, stirring a man's recollection of the good things which have betided him, as the taste of another's lips or the taking of a good woman, and whetting his hope of something still better in the future, that by the time he sits down to a cloth, his heart and stomach are tuned too well to say "nay" to one another.

Almost everybody knows, in our part of the world at least, how pleasant and soft the fall of the land is round about Plover's

Barrows farm. All above it is strong dark mountain, spread with heath, and desolate, but near our house the valleys cove, and open warmth and shelter. Here are trees, and bright green grass, and orchards full of contentment, and a man may scarce espy the brook, although he hears it everywhere. And indeed a stout good piece of it comes through our farm-yard, and swells sometimes to a rush of waves, when the clouds are on the hill-tops. But all below, where the valley bends, and the Lynn stream comes along with it, pretty meadows slope their breast, and the sun spreads on the water. And nearly all of this is ours, till you come to Nicholas Snowe's land.

But about two miles below our farm, the Bagworthy water runs into the Lynn, and makes a real river of it. Thence it hurries away, with strength and a force of wilful waters, under the foot of a barefaced hill, and so to rocks and woods again, where the stream is covered over, and dark, heavy pools delay it. There are plenty of fish all down this way, and the farther you go the larger they get, having deeper grounds to feed in; and sometimes in the summer months, when mother could spare me off the farm, I came down here, with Annie to help (because it was so lonely), and caught well-nigh a basketful of little trout and minnows, with a hook and a bit of worm on it, or a fern-web, or a blow-fly, hung from a hazel pulse-stick. For of all the things I learned at Blundell's, only two abode with me, and one of these was the knack of fishing, and the other the art of swimming. And indeed they have a very rude manner of teaching children to swim there; for the big boys take the little boys, and put them through a certain process, which they grimly call "sheep-washing." In the third meadow from the gate of the school, going up the river, there is a fine pool in the Lowman, where the Taunton brook comes in, and they call it the Taunton Pool. The water runs down with a strong sharp stickle, and then has a sudden elbow in it, where the small brook trickles in; and on that side the bank is steep, four or it may be five feet high, overhanging loamily; but on the other side it is flat, pebbly, and fit to land upon. Now the large boys take the small boys, crying sadly for mercy, and thinking mayhap, of their mothers, with hands laid well at the back of their necks, they bring them up to the crest of the bank upon the eastern side, and make them strip their clothes off. Then the little boys, falling on their naked knees, blubber upwards piteously; but the large boys know what is good for them, and will not be entreated. So they cast them down, one after other into the splash of the water, and watch them go to the bottom first, and then come up and fight for it, with a blowing and a bubbling. It is a very fair sight to watch when you know there is little danger, because, although the pool is deep, the current is sure to wash a boy up on the stones, where the end of the depth is. As for me, they had no need to throw me more than once, because I jumped of my own accord, thinking small things of the Lowman, after the violent Lynn. Nevertheless, I learnt to swim there, as all the other boys did; for the greatest point in learning that is to find that you must do it. I loved the water naturally, and could not long be out of it; but even the boys who hated it most, came to swim in some fashion or other, after they had been flung for a year or two into the Taunton pool.

But now, although my sister Annie came to keep me company, and was not to be parted from me by the tricks of the Lynn stream, because I put her on my back and carried her across, whenever she could not leap it, or tuck up her things and take the stones; yet so it happened that neither of us had been up the Bagworthy water. We knew that it brought a good stream down, as full of fish as of pebbles; and we thought that it must be very pretty to make a way where no way was, nor even a bullock came down to drink. But whether we were afraid or not, I am sure I cannot tell, because it is so long ago; but I think that had something to do with it. For Bagworthy water ran out of Doone valley, a mile or so from the mouth of it.

It happened to me without choice, I may say, to explore the Bagworthy water. And it came about in this wise.

My mother had long been ailing, and not well able to eat much; and there is nothing that frightens us so much as for people to have no love of their victuals. Now I chanced to remember that once at the time of the holidays I had brought dear mother from Tiverton a jar of pickled loaches, caught by myself in the Lowman river, and baked in the kitchen oven, with vinegar, a few leaves of bay, and about a dozen pepper-corns. And mother had said that in all her life she had never tasted anything fit to be compared with them. Whether she said so good a thing out of compliment to my skill in catching the fish and cooking them, or whether she really meant it, is more than I can tell, though I quite believe the latter, and so would most people who tasted them; at any rate, I now resolved to get some loaches for her, and do them in the self-same manner, just to make her eat a bit.

There are many people, even now, who have not come to the right knowledge what a loach is, and where he lives, and how to catch and pickle him. And I will not tell them all about it, because if I did, very likely there would be no loaches left ten or twenty years after the appearance of this book. A pickled minnow is very good if you catch him in a stickle, with the scarlet fingers upon him; but I count him no more than the ropes in beer compared with a loach done properly.

Being resolved to catch some loaches, whatever trouble it cost me, I set forth without a word to any one, in the forenoon of St. Valentine's day. Annie should not come with me, because the water was too cold; for the winter had been long, and snow lay here and there in patches in the hollow of the banks, like a lady's gloves forgotten. And yet the spring was breaking forth, as it always does in Devonshire, when the turn of the days is over; and though there was little to see of it, the air was full of feeling.

It puzzles me now, that I remember all those young impressions so, because I took no heed of them at the time whatever; and yet they come upon me bright, when nothing else is evident in the gray fog of experience. I am like an old man gazing at the outside of his spectacles, and seeing, as he rubs the dust, the image of his grandson playing at bo-peep with him.

But let me be of any age, I never could forget that day, and how bitter cold the water was. For I doffed my shoes and hose, and put them into a bag about my neck; and left my coat at home, and tied my shirt-sleeves back to my shoulders. Then I took a three-pronged fork firmly bound to a rod with cord, and a piece of canvas kerchief, with a lump of bread inside it; and so went into the pebbly water, trying to think how warm it was. For more than a mile all down the Lynn stream, scarcely a stone I left unturned, being thoroughly skilled in the tricks of the loach, and knowing how he hides himself. For being gray-spotted, and clear to see through, and something like a cuttle-fish, only more substantial, he will stay quite still where a streak of weed is in the rapid water, hoping to be overlooked, not caring even to wag his tail. Then being disturbed he flips away, like whalebone from the finger, and hies to a shelf of stone, and lies with his sharp head poked in under it; or sometimes he bellies him into the mud, and only shows his back-ridge. And that is the time to spear him nicely, holding the fork very gingerly, and allowing for the bent of it, which comes to pass, I know not how, at the tickle of air and water.

Or if your loach should not be abroad when first you come to look for him, but keeping snug in his little home, then you may see him come forth amazed at the quivering of the shingles, and oar himself and look at you, and then dart up-stream, like a little grey streak; and then you must try to mark him in, and follow very daintily. So after that, in a sandy place, you steal up behind his tail to him, so that he cannot set eyes on you, for his head is up-stream always, and there you see him abiding still, clear, and mild, and affable. Then, as he looks so innocent, you make full sure to prog him well, in spite of the wry of the water, and the sun making elbows to everything, and the trembling of your fingers. But when you gird at him lovingly, and have as good as gotten him, lo! in the go-by of the river he is gone as a shadow goes, and only a little cloud of mud curls away from the points of the fork.

A long way down that limpid water, chill and bright as an iceberg, went myself that day on man's choice errand—destruction. All the young fish seemed to know that I was one who had taken out God's certificate, and meant to have the value of it; every one of them was aware that we desolate more than replenish the earth. For a cow might come and look into the water, and put her yellow lips down; a kingfisher, like a blue arrow, might shoot through the dark alleys over the channel, or sit on a dipping withy-bough with his beak sunk into his breast-feathers; even an otter might float downstream likening himself to a log of wood, with his flat head flush with the water-top, and his oily eyes peering quietly; and yet no panic would seize other life, as it does when a sample of man comes.

Now let not any one suppose that I thought of these things when I was young, for I knew not the way to do it. And proud enough in truth I was at the universal fear I spread in all those lonely places, where I myself must have been afraid, if anything had come up to me. It is all very pretty to see the trees big with their hopes of another year, though dumb as yet on the subject, and the waters murmuring gaiety, and the banks spread out with comfort; but a boy takes none of this to heart; unless he be meant for a poet (which God can never charge upon me), and he would liefer have a good apple, or even a bad one, if he stole it.

When I had travelled two miles or so, conquered now and then with cold, and coming out to rub my legs into a lively friction, and only fishing here and there, because of the tumbling water; suddenly, in an open space, where meadows spread about it, I found a good stream flowing softly into the body of our brook. And it brought, so far as I could guess by the sweep of it under my knee-caps, a larger power of clear water than the Lynn itself had; only it came more quietly down, not being troubled with stairs and steps, as the fortune of the Lynn is, but gliding smoothly and forcibly, as if upon some set purpose.

Hereupon I drew up and thought, and reason was much inside me; because the water was bitter cold, and my toes were aching. So on the bank I rubbed them well with a sprout of young sting-nettle, and was kindly inclined to eat a bit.

Now all the turn of all my life hung upon that moment. But as I sat there munching a crust of Betty Muxworthy's sweet brown bread, and a bit of cold bacon along with it, and kicking my red heels against the dry loam to keep them warm, I knew no more than fish under the fork what was going on over me. It seemed a sad business to go back now and tell Annie there were no loaches; and yet it was a frightful thing, knowing what I did of it, to venture, where no man durst, up the Bagworthy water.

As I ate more and more, my spirit arose within me, and I thought of what my father had been, and how he had told me a hundred times never to be a coward. And then I grew warm, and my heart was ashamed of its pit-a-patting, and I said to myself, "now if father looks, he shall see that I obey him." So I put the bag round my back again, and buckled my breeches far up from the knee, expecting deeper water, and crossing the Lynn, went stoutly up under the branches which hang so dark on the Bagworthy river.

I found it strongly over-woven, turned, and torn with thicket-wood, but not so rocky as the Lynn, and more inclined to go evenly. There were bars of chafed stakes stretched from the sides half-way across the current, and light outriders of pithy weed, and blades of last year's water-grass trembling in the quiet places, like a spider's threads, on the transparent stillness, with a tint of olive moving it. And here and there the sun came in, as if his light was sifted, making dance upon the waves, and shadowing the pebbles.

Here, although affrighted often by the deep, dark places, and feeling that every step I took might never be taken backward, on the whole I had very comely sport of loaches, trout, and minnows, forking some, and tickling some, and driving others to shallow nooks, whence I could bail them ashore. Now, if you have ever been fishing, you will not wonder that I was led on, forgetting all about danger, and taking no heed of the time, and in sooth there were very fine loaches here, having more lie and harbourage than in the rough Lynn stream, though not quite so large as in the Lowman, where I have even taken them to the weight of half a pound.

There never was any sound at all, except of a rocky echo, or a scared bird hustling away, or the sudden dive of a water-vole; and the place grew thicker and thicker, and the covert grew darker above me, until I thought that the fishes might have good chance of eating me, instead of my eating the fishes.

For now the day was falling fast behind the brown of the hill-tops, and the trees, being void of leaf and hard, seemed giants ready to beat me. And every moment as the sky was clearing up for a white frost, the cold of the water got worse and worse, until I was fit to cry with it. And so, in a sorry plight, I came to an opening in the bushes, where a great black pool lay in front of me, whitened with snow (as I thought) at the sides, till I saw it was only foam-froth.

Now, though I could swim with great ease and comfort, and feared no depth of water, when I could fairly come to it, yet I had no desire to go over head and ears into this great pool, being so cramped and weary, and cold enough in all conscience, though wet only up to the middle, not counting my arms and shoulders. And the look of this black pit was enough to stop one from diving into it, even on a hot summer's day with sunshine on the water; I mean, if the sun ever shone there. As it was, I shuddered and drew back; not alone at the pool itself and the black air there was about it, but also at the whirling manner, and wisping of white threads upon it in stripy circles round and round; and the centre still as jet.

But soon I saw the reason of the stir and depth of that great pit, as well as of the roaring sound which long had made me wonder. For skirting round one side, with very little comfort, because the rocks were high and steep, and the ledge at the foot so narrow, I came to a sudden sight and marvel, such as I never dreamed of. For, lo! I stood at the foot of a long pale slide of water, coming smoothly to me, without any break or hindrance, for a hundred yards or more, and fenced on either side with cliff, sheer, and straight, and shining. The water neither ran nor fell, nor leaped with any spouting, but made one even slope of it, as if it had been combed or planed, and looking like a plank of deal laid down a deep black staircase. However, there was no side-rail, nor any place to walk upon, only the channel a fathom wide, and the perpendicular walls of crag shutting out the evening.

The look of this place had a sad effect, scaring me very greatly, and making me feel that I would give something only to be at home again, with Annie cooking my supper, and our dog Watch sniffing upward. But nothing would come of wishing; that I had long found out; and it only made one the less inclined to work without white feather. So I laid the case before me in a little council; not for loss of time, but only that I wanted rest, and to see things truly.

Then says I to myself—"John Ridd, these trees, and pools, and lonesome rocks, and setting of the sunlight are making a gruesome coward of thee. Shall I go back to my mother so, and be called fearless?"

Nevertheless, I am free to own that it was not any fine sense of shame which settled my decision; for indeed there was nearly as much of danger in going back as in going on, and perhaps even more of labour, the journey being so roundabout. But that which saved me from turning back was a strange inquisitive desire; in a word, I would risk a great deal to know what made the water come down like that, and what there was at the top of it.

Therefore, seeing hard strife before me, I girt up my breeches anew, with each buckle one hole tighter, for the sodden straps were stretching and giving, and mayhap my legs were grown smaller from the coldness of it. Then I bestowed my fish around my neck more tightly, and not stopping to look much, for fear of fear, crawled along over the fork of rocks, where the water had scooped the stone out, and shunning thus the ledge from whence it rose like the mane of a white horse into the broad black pool, softly I let my feet into the dip and rush of the torrent.

And here I had reckoned without my host, although (as I thought) so clever; and it was much but that I went down into the great black pool, and had never been heard of more; and this must have been the end of me, except for my trusty loach-fork. For the green wave came down like great bottles upon me, and my legs were gone off in a moment, and I had not time to cry out with wonder, only to think of my mother and Annie, and knock my head very sadly, which made it go round so that brains were no good, even if I had any. But all in a moment, before I knew aught, except that I must die out of the way, with a roar of water upon me, my fork, praise God stuck fast in the rock, and I was borne up upon it. I felt nothing except that here was another matter to begin upon; and it might be worth while, or again it might not, to have another fight for it. But presently the dash of the water upon my face revived me, and my mind grew used to the roar of it, and meseemed I had been worse off than this, when first flung into the Lowman.

Therefore I gathered my legs back slowly, as if they were fish to be landed, stopping whenever the water flew too strongly off my shin-bones, and coming along without sticking out to let the wave get hold of me. And in this manner I won a footing, leaning well forward like a draught-horse, and balancing on my strength as it were, with the ashen stake set behind me. Then I said to my self, "John Ridd, the sooner you get yourself out by the way you came, the better it will be for you." But to my great dismay and affright, I saw that no choice was left me now, except that I must climb somehow up that hill of water, or else be washed down into the pool and whirl around it till it drowned me. For there was no chance of fetching back by the way I had gone down into it, and further up was a hedge of rock on either side of the waterway, rising a hundred yards in height, and for all I could tell five hundred, and no place to set a foot in.

Having said the Lord's Prayer (which was all I knew), and made a very bad job of it, I grasped the good loach-stick under a knot, and steadied me with my left hand, and so with a sigh of despair began my course up the fearful torrent-way. To me it seemed half a mile at least of sliding water above me, but in truth it was little more than a furlong, as I came to know afterwards. It would have been a hard ascent even without the slippery slime and the force of the river over it, and I had scanty hope indeed of ever winning the summit. Nevertheless, my terror left me, now I was face to face with it, and had to meet the worst; and I set myself to do my best with a vigour and sort of hardness which did not then surprise me, but have done so ever since.

The water was only six inches deep, or from that to nine at the utmost, and all the way up I could see my feet looking white in the gloom of the hollow, and here and there I found resting-place, to hold on by the cliff and pant awhile. And gradually as I went on, a warmth of courage breathed in me, to think that perhaps no other had dared to try that pass before me, and to wonder what mother would say to it. And then came thought of my father also, and the pain of my feet abated.

How I went carefully, step by step, keeping my arms in front of me, and never daring to straighten my knees is more than I can tell clearly, or even like now to think of, because it makes me dream of it. Only I must acknowledge that the greatest danger of all was just where I saw no jeopardy, but ran up a patch of black ooze-weed in a very boastful manner, being now not far from the summit.

Here I fell very piteously, and was like to have broken my knee-cap, and the torrent got hold of my other leg while I was indulging the bruised one. And then a vile knotting of cramp disabled me, and for awhile I could only roar, till my mouth was full of water, and all of my body was sliding. But the fright of that brought me to again, and my elbow caught in a rock-hole; and so I managed to start again, with the help of more humility.

Now being in the most dreadful fright, because I was so near the top, and hope was beating within me, I laboured hard with both legs and arms, going like a mill and grunting. At last the rush of forked water, where first it came over the lips of the fall, drove me into the middle, and I stuck awhile with my toe-balls on the slippery links of the pop-weed, and the world was green and gliddery, and I durst not look behind me. Then I made up my mind to die at last; for so my legs would ache no more, and my breath not pain my heart so; only it did seem such a pity after fighting so long to give in, and the light was coming upon me, and again I fought towards it; then suddenly I felt fresh air, and fell into it headlong.

CHAPTER VIII

A BOY AND A GIRL

When I came to myself again, my hands were full of young grass and mould, and a girl kneeling at my side was rubbing my forehead tenderly with a dock-leaf and a handkerchief.

"Oh, I am so glad," she whispered softly, as I opened my eyes and looked at her; "now you will try to be better, won't you?"

I had never heard so sweet a sound as came from between her bright red lips, while there she knelt and gazed at me; neither had I ever seen anything so beautiful as the large dark eyes intent upon me, full of pity and wonder. And then, my nature being slow, and perhaps, for that matter, heavy, I wandered with my hazy eyes down the black shower of her hair, as to my jaded gaze it seemed; and where it fell on the turf, among it (like an early star) was the first primrose of the season. And since that day I think of her, through all the rough storms of my life, when I see an early primrose. Perhaps she liked my countenance, and indeed I know she did, because she said so afterwards; although at the time she was too young to know what made her take to me. Not that I had any beauty, or ever pretended to have any, only a solid healthy face, which many girls have laughed at.

Thereupon I sate upright, with my trident still in one hand, and was much afraid to speak to her, being conscious of my country-brogue, lest she should cease to like me. But she clapped her hands, and made a trifling dance around my back, and came to me on the other side, as if I were a great plaything.

"What is your name?" she said, as if she had every right to ask me; "and how did you come here, and what are these wet things in this great bag?"

"You had better let them alone," I said; "they are loaches for my mother. But I will give you some, if you like."

"Dear me, how much you think of them! Why, they are only fish. But how your feet are bleeding! oh, I must tie them up for you. And no shoes nor stockings! Are you very poor?"

"No," I said, being vexed at this; "we are rich enough to buy all this great meadow, if we chose; and here my shoes and stockings be."

"Why, they are quite as wet as your feet; and I cannot bear to see your feet. Oh, please to let me manage them; I will do it very softly."

"Oh, I don't think much of that," I replied; "I shall put some goose-grease to them. But how you are looking at me! I never saw any one like you before. My name is John Ridd. What is your name?"

"Lorna Doone," she answered, in a low voice, as if afraid of it, and hanging her head so that I could see only her forehead and eyelashes; "if you please, my name is Lorna Doone; and I thought you must have known it."

Then I stood up and touched her hand, and tried to make her look at me; but she only turned away the more. Young and harmless as she was, her name alone made guilt of her. Nevertheless I could not help looking at her tenderly, and the more when her blushes turned into tears, and her tears to long, low sobs.

"Don't cry," I said, "whatever you do. I am sure you have never done any harm. I will give you all my fish Lorna, and catch some more for mother; only don't be angry with me."

She flung her soft arms up in the passion of her tears, and looked at me so piteously, that what did I do but kiss her. It seemed to be a very odd thing, when I came to think of it, but she touched my heart with a sudden delight, like a cowslip-blossom (although there were none to be seen yet), and the sweetest flowers of spring.

She gave me no encouragement, as my mother in her place would have done; nay, she even wiped her lips (which methought was rather rude of her), and drew away, and smoothed her dress, as if I had used a freedom. Then I felt my cheeks grow burning red, and I gazed at my legs and was sorry. For although she was not at all proud (at any rate in her countenance), yet I knew that she was by birth a thousand years in front of me. They might have taken and framed me, or (which would be more to the purpose) my sisters, until it was time for us to die, and then have trained our children after us, for many generations; yet never could we have gotten that look upon our faces which Lorna Doone had naturally, as if she had been born to it.

Here was I, a yeoman's son, a yeoman every inch of me, even where I was naked; and there was she, a lady born, and thoroughly aware of it, and dressed by people of rank and taste, who took pride in her beauty and set it to advantage. For though her hair was fallen down by reason of her wildness, and some of her frock was touched with wet where she had tended me so, behold her dress was pretty enough for the queen of all the angels. The colours were bright and rich indeed, and the substance very sumptuous, yet simple and free from tinsel stuff, and matching most harmoniously. All from her waist to her neck was white, plaited in close like a curtain, and the dark soft weeping of her hair, and the shadowy light of her eyes (like a wood rayed through with sunset), made it seem yet whiter, as if it were done on purpose. As for the rest, she knew what it was a great deal better than I did, for I never could look far away from her eyes when they were opened upon me.

Now, seeing how I heeded her, and feeling that I had kissed her, she turned to the stream in a bashful manner, and began to watch the water, and rubbed one leg against the other.

I, for my part, being vexed at her behaviour to me, took up all my things to go, and made a fuss about it; to let her know I was going. But she did not call me back at all, as I had made sure she would do; moreover, I knew that to try the descent was almost certain death to me, and it looked as dark as pitch; and so at the mouth I turned round again, and came back to her, and said, "Lorna."

"Oh, I thought you were gone," she answered; "why did you ever come here? Do you know what they would do to us, if they found you here with me?"

"Beat us, I dare say, very hard; or me, at least. They could never beat you."

"No. They would kill us both outright, and bury us here by the water; and the water often tells me that I must come to that."

"But what should they kill me for?"

"Because you have found the way up here, and they never could believe it. Now, please to go; oh, please to go. They will kill us both in a moment. Yes, I like you very much"—for I was teasing her to say it—"very much indeed, and I will call you John Ridd, if you like; only please to go, John. And when your feet are well, you know, you can come and tell me how they are."

"But I tell you, Lorna, I like you very much indeed—nearly as much as Annie, and a great deal more than Lizzie. And I never saw any one like you, and I must come back again to-morrow, and so must you, to see me; and I will bring you such lots of things—there are apples still, and a thrush I caught with only one leg broken, and our dog has just had puppies—"

"Oh, dear, they won't let me have a dog. There is not a dog in the valley. They say they are such noisy things—"

"Only put your hand in mine—what little things they are, Lorna! And I will bring you the loveliest dog; I will show you just how long he is."

"Hush!" A shout came down the valley, and all my heart was trembling, like water after sunset, and Lorna's face was altered from pleasant play to terror. She shrank to me, and looked up at me, with such a power of weakness, that I at once made up my mind to save her or to die with her. A tingle went through all my bones, and I only longed for my carbine. Lorna took courage from me, and put her cheek quite close to mine.

"Come with me down the waterfall. I can carry you easily; and mother will take care of you."

"No, no," she cried, as I took her up: "I will tell you what to do. They are only looking for me. You see that hole, that hole there?"

She pointed to a little niche in the rock which verged the meadow, about fifty yards away from us. In the fading of the twilight I could just descry it.

"Yes, I see it; but they will see me crossing the grass to get there."

"Look! look!" She could hardly speak. "There is a way out from the top of it; they would kill me if I told it. Oh, here they come, I can see them."

The maid turned as white as the snow which hung on the rocks above her, and she looked at the water and then at me, and she cried, "Oh dear! oh dear!" And then she began to sob aloud. But I drew her behind the withy-bushes, and close down to the water, where it was quiet and shelving deep, ere it came to the lip of the chasm. Here they could not see either of us from the upper valley, and might have sought a long time for us, even when they came quite near, if the trees had been clad with their summer clothes. Luckily I had picked up my fish and taken my three-pronged fork away.

Crouching in that hollow nest, I saw a dozen fierce men come down, on the other side of the water, not bearing any fire-arms, but looking lax and jovial, as if they were come from riding and a dinner taken hungrily. "Queen, queen!" they were shouting, here and there, and now and then: "where the pest is our little queen gone?"

"They always call me 'queen,' and I am to be queen by-and-by," Lorna whispered to me, with her soft cheek on my rough one, and her little heart beating against me: "oh, they are crossing by the timber there, and then they are sure to see us."

"Stop," said I; "now I see what to do. I must get into the water, and you must go to sleep."

"To be sure, yes, away in the meadow there. But how bitter cold it will be for you!"

She saw in a moment the way to do it, sooner than I could tell her; and there was no time to lose.

"Now mind you never come again," she whispered over her shoulder, as she crept away, "only I shall come sometimes—oh, here they are, Madonna!"

Daring scarce to peep, I crept into the water, and lay down bodily in it, with my head between two blocks of stone, and some flood-drift combing over me. The dusk was deepening between the hills, and a white mist lay on the river; but I, being in the channel of it, could see every ripple, and twig, and rush, and glazing of twilight above it, as bright as in a picture; so that to my ignorance there seemed no chance at all but what the men must find me. For all this time they were shouting and swearing, and keeping such a hullabaloo, that the rocks all round the valley rang, and my heart quaked, so (what with this and the cold) that the water began to gurgle round me, and to lap upon the pebbles.

Neither in truth did I try to stop it, being now so desperate, between the fear and the wretchedness; till I caught a glimpse of the maid, whose beauty and whose kindliness had made me yearn to be with her. And then I knew that for her sake I was bound to be brave and hide myself. She was lying beneath a rock, thirty or forty yards from me, feigning to be fast asleep, with her dress spread beautifully, and her hair drawn over her.

Presently one of the great rough men came round a corner upon her; and there he stopped and gazed awhile at her fairness and her innocence. Then he caught her up in his arms, and kissed her so that I heard him; and if I had only brought my gun, I would have tried to shoot him.

"Here our queen is! Here's the queen, here's the captain's daughter!" he shouted to his comrades; "fast asleep, by God, and hearty! Now I have first claim to her; and no one else shall touch her. Back to the bottle, all of you!"

He set her dainty form upon his great square shoulder, and her narrow feet in one broad hand; and so in triumph marched away, with the purple velvet of her skirt ruffling in his long black beard, and the silken length of her hair fetched out, like a cloud by the wind behind her. This way of her going vexed me so, that I leaped upright in the water, and must have been spied by some of them, but for their haste to the wine-bottle. Of their little queen they took small notice, being in this urgency; although they had thought to find her drowned; but trooped away after one another with kindly challenge to gambling, so far as I could make them out; and I kept sharp watch, I assure you.

Going up that darkened glen, Lorna, riding still the largest and most fierce of them, turned and put up a hand to me, and I put up a hand to her, in the thick of the mist and the willows.

She was gone; and when I got over my thriftless fright, I longed to have more to say to her. Her voice to me was so different from all I had ever heard before, as might be a sweet silver bell intoned to the small chords of a harp. But I had no time to think about this, if I hoped to have any supper.

I crept into a bush for warmth, and rubbed my shivering legs on bark and longed for mother's fagot. Then as daylight sank below the forget-me-not of stars, with a sorrow to be quit, I knew that now must be my time to get away, if there were any.

Therefore, wringing my sodden breaches, I managed to crawl from the bank to the niche in the cliff which Lorna had shown me.

Through the dusk I had trouble to see the mouth, at even the five land-yards of distance; nevertheless, I entered well, and held on by some dead fern-stems, and did hope that no one would shoot me.

But while I was hugging myself like this, my joy was like to have ended in sad grief both to myself and my mother, and haply to all honest folk who shall love to read this history. For hearing a noise in front of me, and like a coward not knowing where, but afraid to turn round or think of it, I felt myself going down some deep passage into a pit of darkness. It was no good to catch the sides, the whole thing seemed to go with me. Then, without knowing how, I was leaning over a night of water.

This water was of black radiance, as are certain diamonds, spanned across with vaults of rock, and carrying no image, neither showing marge nor end, but centred (as it might be) with a bottomless indrawal.

With that chill and dread upon me, and the sheer rock all around, and the faint light heaving wavily on the silence of this gulf, I must have lost my wits and gone to the bottom, if there were any.

But suddenly a robin sang (as they will do after dark, towards spring) in the brown fern and ivy behind me. I took it for our Annie's voice (for she could call any robin), and gathering quick warm comfort, sprang up the steep way towards the starlight. Climbing back, as the stones glid down, I heard the cold greedy wave go japping, like a blind black dog, into the distance of arches and hollow depths of darkness.

CHAPTER IX

THERE IS NO PLACE LIKE HOME

I can assure you, and tell no lie (as John Fry always used to say, when telling his very largest), that I scrambled back to the mouth of that pit as if the evil one had been after me. And sorely I repented now of all my folly, or madness it might well be termed, in venturing, with none to help, and nothing to compel me, into that accursed valley. Once let me get out, thinks I, and if ever I get in again, without being cast in by neck and by crop, I will give our new-born donkey leave to set up for my schoolmaster.

How I kept that resolution we shall see hereafter. It is enough for me now to tell how I escaped from the den that night. First I sat down in the little opening which Lorna had pointed out to me, and wondered whether she had meant, as bitterly occurred to me, that I should run down into the pit, and be drowned, and give no more trouble. But in less than half a minute I was ashamed of that idea, and remembered how she was vexed to think that even a loach should lose his life. And then I said to myself, "Now surely she would value me more than a thousand loaches; and what she said must be quite true about the way out of this horrible place."

Therefore I began to search with the utmost care and diligence, although my teeth were chattering, and all my bones beginning to ache with the chilliness and the wetness. Before very long the moon appeared, over the edge of the mountain, and among the trees at the top of it; and then I espied rough steps, and rocky, made as if with a sledge-hammer, narrow, steep, and far asunder, scooped here and there in the side of the entrance, and then round a bulge of the cliff, like the marks upon a great brown loaf, where a hungry child has picked at it. And higher up, where the light of the moon shone broader upon the precipice, there seemed to be a rude broken track, like the shadow of a crooked stick thrown upon a house-wall.

Herein was small encouragement; and at first I was minded to lie down and die; but it seemed to come amiss to me. God has His time for all of us; but He seems to advertise us when He does not mean to do it. Moreover, I saw a movement of lights at the head of the valley, as if lanthorns were coming after me, and the nimbleness given thereon to my heels was in front of all meditation.

Straightway I set foot in the lowest stirrup (as I might almost call it), and clung to the rock with my nails, and worked to make a jump into the second stirrup. And I compassed that too, with the aid of my stick; but the third step-hole was the hardest of all, and the rock swelled out on me over my breast, and there seemed to be no attempting it, until I espied a good stout rope hanging in a groove of shadow, and just managed to reach the end of it.

How I clomb up, and across the clearing, and found my way home through the Bagworthy forest, is more than I can remember now, for I took all the rest of it then as a dream, by reason of perfect weariness. And indeed it was quite beyond my hopes to tell so much as I have told, for at first beginning to set it down, it was all like a mist before me. Nevertheless, some parts grew clearer, as one by one I remembered them, having taken a little soft cordial, because the memory frightens me.

For the toil of the water, and danger of labouring up the long cascade or rapids, and then the surprise of the fair maid, and terror of the murderers, and desperation of getting away—all these are much to me even now, when I am a stout churchwarden, and sit by the side of my fire, after going through many far worse adventures, which I will tell, God willing. Only the labour of writing is such (especially so as to construe, and challenge a reader on parts of speech, and hope to be even with him); that by this pipe which I hold in my hand I ever expect to be beaten, as in the days when old Doctor Twiggs, if I made a bad stroke in my exercise, shouted aloud with a sour joy, "John Ridd, sirrah, down with your small-clothes!"

When I got home, all the supper was in, and the men sitting at the white table, and mother and Annie and Lizzie near by, all eager, and offering to begin (except, indeed, my mother, who was looking out at the doorway), and by the fire was Betty Muxworthy, scolding, and cooking, and tasting her work, all in a breath, as a man would say. I looked through the door from the dark by the wood-stack, and was half of a mind to stay out like a dog, for fear of the rating and reckoning; but the way my dear mother was looking about and the browning of the sausages got the better of me.

But nobody could get out of me where I had been all the day and evening; although they worried me never so much, and longed to shake me to pieces, especially Betty Muxworthy, who never could learn to let well alone. Not that they made me tell any lies, although it would have served them right almost for intruding on other people's business; but that I just held my tongue, and ate my supper rarely, and let them try their taunts and jibes, and drove them almost wild after supper, by smiling exceeding knowingly. And indeed I could have told them things, as I hinted once or twice; and then poor Betty and our little Lizzie were so mad with eagerness, that between them I went into the fire, being thoroughly overcome with laughter and my own importance.

Now what the working of my mind was (if, indeed it worked at all, and did not rather follow suit of body) it is not in my power to say; only that the result of my adventure in the Doone Glen was to make me dream a good deal of nights, which I had never done much before, and to drive me, with tenfold zeal and purpose, to the practice of bullet-shooting. Not that I ever expected to shoot the Doone family, one by one, or even desired to do so, for my nature is not revengeful; but that it seemed to be somehow my business to understand the gun, as a thing I must be at home with.

I could hit the barn-door now capitally well with the Spanish match-lock, and even with John Fry's blunderbuss, at ten good land-yards distance, without any rest for my fusil. And what was very wrong of me, though I did not see it then, I kept John Fry there, to praise my shots, from dinner-time often until the grey dusk, while he all the time should have been at work spring-ploughing upon the farm. And for that matter so should I have been, or at any rate driving the horses; but John was by no means loath to be there, instead of holding the plough-tail. And indeed, one of our old sayings is,—

> "For pleasure's sake I would liefer wet,
> Than ha' ten lumps of gold for each one of my sweat."

And again, which is not a bad proverb, though unthrifty and unlike a Scotsman's,—

> "God makes the wheat grow greener,
> While farmer be at his dinner."

And no Devonshire man, or Somerset either (and I belong to both of them), ever thinks of working harder than God likes to see him.

Nevertheless, I worked hard at the gun, and by the time that I had sent all the church-roof gutters, so far as I honestly could cut them, through the red pine-door, I began to long for a better tool that would make less noise and throw straighter. But the sheep-shearing came and the hay-season next, and then the harvest of small corn, and the digging of the root called "batata" (a new but good thing in our neighbourhood, which our folk have made into "taties"), and then the sweating of the apples, and the turning of the cider-press, and the stacking of the firewood, and netting of the woodcocks, and the springles to be minded in the garden and by the hedgerows, where blackbirds hop to the molehills in the white October mornings, and grey birds come to look for snails at the time when the sun is rising.

It is wonderful how time runs away, when all these things and a great many others come in to load him down the hill and prevent him from stopping to look about. And I for my part can never conceive how people who live in towns and cities, where neither lambs nor birds are (except in some shop windows), nor growing corn, nor meadow-grass, nor even so much as a stick to cut or a stile to climb and sit down upon—how these poor folk get through their lives without being utterly weary of them, and dying from pure indolence, is a thing God only knows, if His mercy allows Him to think of it.

How the year went by I know not, only that I was abroad all day, shooting, or fishing, or minding the farm, or riding after some stray beast, or away by the seaside below Glenthorne, wondering at the great waters, and resolving to go for a sailor. For in those days I had a firm belief, as many other strong men have, of being born for a seaman.

Yet in truth it was neither sea nor thought of becoming a sailor which took me to frequent the beach. I have a story to tell you of a maid of the sea. Who she was or whence she came I know not to this day, as I sit here a God-fearing churchwarden, and it may be that I had taken a heathen rather than a Christian; though thought now turns to doubt that I had suborned.

It was known that pirates—barbarians from Algeria, I had heard it told—had not ten years afore captured a man from Exeter. Therefore not beyond reason was it that she be from a ship poised to plunder our people or goods, though such may have given rise in my imaginings. I had no good reason to be on the beach other than my yearning for sailing to lands of uncommon sights and odours. Idly gazing over the waves ribbed with silvered foam, the sleep of laziness overcame me and I lay my head on the sand to better dream.

What made me awake I know not; perchance the faint sweet smell mingling in the salt air, perchance the shadow of one standing close by me, but so startled was I upon awakening to find a shape outlined against the sun, strands of unkempt raven hair lucent as she took a hand through it brushing it off her face, her bodice dipped over one shoulder, body arched back against the rock face, hips thrust forward, and one bare foot, toes pointing toward the ground, rubbing slowly up and down the other leg.

I could not at that time see her eyes, dark as the richest of soil sown with black, yet I knew that there was therein them some semblance of a smile.

The beach was deserted other than three birds soaring above, their wings extended as they peered into the caliginous water below them, an occasional plangent, piercing screech prickling the air in which I now, too, felt elevated as though I had taken of too much small-beer, such were my thoughts unformed and unsettled. Slowly she lowered herself to the ensalted sand by my side, speaking to me in a language of which I had no knowledge, my experience being so limited to driblets of Greek and Latin (and of course the dialect of hereabouts, which to some would appear to be a language within itself).

With harsh sounds disconcerting and beguiling in equal measure, and a husking which made me want to place my fingers on her thin brown throat (above square shoulders like two brown chapiters atop the sturdy columns of her arms), to feel how this sound was made, she gently traced my jawline with a black-tipped gull's feather freed from its host's muscle and fallen to the sand, holding the bare calamus and moving the barbs across my lips with a tickling as soft as the clouds it once had touched and which pulled my belly up at my very rib-cage. I took her hand in mine, not with intent to still it but to feel my flesh against hers of abstruse texture and colour; curiosity being the victor over goosey disquiet. Why should not her hands have been as soft as the skin on her body I knew not; they were calloused and harsh, parched skin and small cracks like earth deprived of nature's nourishment, the like I have seen on the men who work the fields, yet as she dropped the feather and ran her hands through my hair, the roughness stirred in me a longing to feel her make rough with my manhood.

Heat washed over me and for sure the blood rushed to my cheeks as I wondered what she might next do, this exotic beauty with a skin more dusk than daylight but none the less becoming for it, though I had not afore thought to find other than the winter whitest of skin so enticing. Slowly she arose, not once taking her eyes from mine, her gaze of an intensity to have lit a moonless night.

I rubbed at the side of my forehead with my fingertips as I watched, captivated as her slave yet unbound, as she slowly moved her hips from side to side, raising each to its waist at the end of its arc, yet not moving the rest of her body. In splendid isolation the hips, wrapped round with a ragged fringed shawl which once had boasted a gold thread of finery, began to inscribe a shape in the air as if she were writing the number eight with them; her entire body, her shoulders, a pendulum to the right as her hips (as if in leisure) swayed to the left, once again her body rolling rhythmically about its axis.

Slowly she raised one hand, fingers pointing to the ground, tracing a line from her navel up between her breasts and to her proud chin (as though she were drawing a thread), the back of her hand skimming her jaw as she outlined it afore raising her hand above her head in the most becoming of manners; then as her hips continued their own description of a figure, she turned her hand as if to beckon me, letting it float down by her face once more.

No music, and yet it were as if she were dancing for me—though surely no such dance had ever existed on our shores, for we are bound to use our feet; and usually (for men) after having imbibed well the cider—drawing me into her with an invisible thread as a spider into her web and, entranced by the slowness and deliberacy of her limbs, imbued with a grace unbeknown to me, the music of arousal played in my head.

Her eyes entrapped me as a net catches fish and, in earnest, she was at that moment the handsomest thing that could be looked upon. As her skirt and begrimed laced bodice obeyed her touch and fell to the centuries of sand, God saw it fit to gift to me sight of her firm breasts with nipples surrounded by the largest irregular and darkest circular smutches I had ever seen on a woman. Some moments passed afore I wrenched my eyes a little downward, their curious path over her navel to the soft mound of her belly and her legs, firm and of fine muscle, dark as though long fingered by the sun. Lo! how I gasped to see no interruption of her burnished skin at her thighs. For I had expected to see the blackest of curly hair, the mirrored colour of her heavy eyebrows, but instead saw only flesh as smooth and unblemished as a child's. I found my brain a little troubled till I had accustomed to it, my lower lip dropping over my chin as I gave studious attention to her mons veneris; for I was now learning that, shorn of the coarse hair which normally conceals it, the area was most delicately rounded—a soft hill on the horizon of sex, below which her crevice was clearly visible. Once recovered from my disquiet, I found it most inviting.

Slowly she shook her head from side to side, one eyebrow raised as a question, the smile playing on her lips once more, and she took my hand in hers to guide it to the area bereft of hair. Bemusement begat pleasure as my fingers savoured the feel of purest silk, smoother than Annie's finest butter. Still she stood above me, and I raised my other hand to rub over her stomach and the skin between her pronounced hips, relishing the softness as an infant's skin, and with my thumbs I played—parting, opening, and closing—at her claret lips, with clarity for the first time of what fruits lay there to be plucked, not hidden betwixt a copse of wiry hair. I now knew of the inner gates to the oyster of love, flesh within the outer shell, brownish red and crowned by the pearl which I could see was swelling slightly and rendered harder, almost as does a man.

She took the back of my head in her hands and pulled it towards her, and I swiftly moved to my knees and ran my lips over the glabrous soft skin, my tongue now inserted between the two distinct lips (which I observed were as rounded as many a man's cods), tasting her muskiness (for so I had heard of late a spicy smell being called), and her saltiness, intensified by the sea water in which I now believed she must have bathed or swum. With no rough, indelicate hair around my mouth, my lips and tongue were unimpeded in their exploration and as I steadied myself by holding her firm thighs, the hue of coffee (used for medicinal purposes and which we now consume over conversation and commerce), I relished the proximity and texture of such tender skin, my shaft now throbbing with desire. A moan of lust escaped my lips as I inhaled her scent, she now mistress of my body.

Sighing deeply, in the way someone most satisfied draws in through their nostrils and sings a note in their throat as they breathe out, she kept me tight to her, kneading the back of my head in circles, grasping my hair (long to my broad shoulders) in her fingers (as I do when I clean with soap and water), and I drew back for air yet did not want to desist from our mutual pleasure. A willing scholar, I followed suit in the kneading movements. My thumb described an orb over her rounded nympha, now proud of the fleshy lips of ruddy-brown, the whole area having darkened with desire. I took my fingers first one way, then the other, the looking-glass to her own stroking of my head. As I lifted my chin to sup again of her she widened her legs to open the gate even further, then clasped them around my head as she moved her hips swiftly and rhythmically, tilting forward with her mound pressing against my teeth, which I found were (it must be said to my surprise) already nibbling at her, the flower opening to me as a bud to the sun.

Forsooth her words, had they been in any language, were to have told me of her pleasure. Words as dark and rich and soft and, I suspect, as base as the bogs on Exmoor; the sound changing to two deep gasps—nay, growls—as a rush of her juices spilled over my lips and the stubble of my chin, which she had urged me to brush so roughly over her pubis, hairless and now reddened. I drank from her greedily as if I had never before eaten, for indeed had I never tasted such exotic fare.

I drew back my head from her body and sank back, my pride in having pleasured this creature so much swelling me even further as I loosed my breeches and took myself in hand. (And can there be anything vainer than a young man held in high esteem for his prowess in love-making?) Yet as I did so she gently pushed me back to lie on the sharp sand, the grains of rock slithered over by waves and pounded by storms cushioning beneath the storm now in my body. She smoothly slid down, with the silent stealth of a cat stalking its prey, to lie upon me, her tongue probing mine now, tasting of her own juices, murmuring a deep throaty note of approval before slinking further with her sinuous body glistening (not with sweat but with an oil not washed off by the sea, the smell of which gave no familiarity yet further awakened my fancy), her tongue tracking down the line of black hair to my breeches. Sliding her thumbs into the waist band now below my protrusion, she slipped the cloth over my hips, which I found rising up of their own accord to make ease of this. As she moved them down over my thighs and knees she followed them down one leg with her mouth, nipping and nudging and nibbling at my skin, until she could eat her way up the other leg without hindrance.

Grasping me in one hand, she rubbed the loose skin up and down and yet she desisted for a moment, a look of puzzlement on her face as she regarded the skin traversing over my tarse and shielding the red tip as it was shifted upwards, like a hosen sheathing a kernel of grain. This was no English wench, innocent nor knowing only the ways of the countryside around here. Her brows met in a V over her sharp nose, until I now took her hand below mine and eased it up and down over me, so that she could see it was nothing of which she should be afraid, and indeed was the giver of much gratification to me. Though being of little education (as I surmised, though had naught on which to inform that other than her being as a woman), she proved a speedy scholar and took up the rubbing of me, her elbow stilled at her side and with hand fluid, and moving only at the wrist, much as I had seen in her dance.

(With the benefit of years gone by, I now believe that she was not accustomed to seeing this fold of skin overlying my penis, for I have heard that Jews and Turks (if common gossips be believed) have this removed, though I will never know her origins nor her destination.)

Looking up into my eyes with a fierce and challenging glint in hers, she stopped the feather-light moves of her fingertips drawing the hood up and down, and locked my gaze into hers before unlocking my well of joy: plunging her dark lips over me, taking me full into her mouth before moving her lips up and down my pulsating shaft; the contrast between this and the touch of her digits as if I had been plunged from a hot bowl of water into one of ice. Short breathings overcame me.

And surely I heard music now, not mere perceptions of the brain, but from her; as whilst still keeping me inside the warmth and wetness of her mouth she hummed some form of weird and wonderful notes I felt were not within my memory to recognise, nor in harmony with my ears, yet contrarily not unpleasant. The tingling and reverberation of her humming into me and over me delivered of me shots of pleasurable pain to my toes, as lightning in a storm. How I longed to plunge myself deep into her, but she was in control of me and I was her varlet, willing and wanting of her.

At the point that I felt that I would start on the journey to spending, the humming in her throat ceased and swiftly she slipped me out of her mouth, in one move clasping my body between her legs (much as I do in wrestling) and urging me over onto her so that she lay beneath me and my torso was pressed onto her, the firm breasts digging into my chest. I plunged deeply into her, my pelvis pressing onto her beautifully bare flesh. And if I had been permitted to desire any one thing at that time, wont that I myself had been shaven there so as to serve to make greater rubbing, smooth skin upon smooth skin, with each thrust.

By now the sea was gently teasing at our bodies, the tide having caught us unawares and with each seventh wave which lapped at us (for it is said that the sea surges more strongly after six times) I pushed myself deeper into her. Where the cold water should have eaten into our souls I felt nothing but hot desire, and as her inner muscles tightened and relaxed around me, stroking me from the inside out, I ebbed and flowed in time with her before conquering this outlandish beauty and pouring my English seed into her.

For some few moments we lay, the water now washing at where our bodies were still affixed to each other, until unbidden I slipped out from her. Standing, with some reluctance to leave her, it must be said, I retrieved my breeches from Neptune now threatening to claim them as his, and scooped up some water to cleanse myself, fully expecting her to do the same. Instead she unhurriedly arose and for some moments did naught other than stare out to the horizon, still as the rocks around us; the only sign of her presence upon the landscape her feet circumscribing their shape on the wet sand. Slowly she lowered her eyes—black stars in her heavenly face now clouded with a look of sorrow—below the veil of sweat-dampened lashes, wriggling her toes, and in so doing scattering the shape of her foot. Then, scooping up her garments, she placed one hand over my eyes, a gesture I took to mean to close them, and this I did (thinking this a time for feigned modesty as she dressed herself). Longing now to repair my own clothing to my body, I awaited some word or sign that she was ready for me to see her with her skin, the colour of some glorious woods, once again beclothed.

How long I stood there I know not, but when I durst risk a look (and I was quickly tired with waiting), she had gone from view. The outline of her feet in the sand tracked into the water and I could think only that she had swum out of sight around the rocks now meeting the sea, that 'twas only seabird or fish that could have sight of her. It was more than a degree perplexing and I felt a sadness at the way in which she had left me; and to this day I ponder on her name and her business on that beach.

Many was the day I returned in secret with high hopes of a repeat encounter, trusting that a little good fortune might match us in amour once more, for even without converse I learned much which was new from her, and I knew that this would stand in good stead with my Lorna when the day came for us to enter into such loving. (For a gallant who comes to his love lacking experience and ability to educate her is no good thing.)

Though she had been but a grain in the sands of time of my long life, yet e'en now I feel a stirring within me when I think on her.

Mother, still thinking it was purely a lust for her son to set sail, would oft wring her hands in despair over her apron, though she believed I had not ventured again to the shore. But Betty Muxworthy spoke her mind quite in a different way about it, the while she was wringing my hosen, and clattering to the drying-horse.

"Zailor, ees fai! ay and zarve un raight. Her can't kape out o' the watter here, whur a' must goo vor to vaind un, zame as a gurt to-ad squalloping, and mux up till I be wore out, I be, wi' the very saight of 's braiches. How wil un ever baide aboard zhip, wi' the watter zinging out under un, and comin' up splash when the wind blow. Latt un goo, missus, latt un goo, zay I for wan, and old Davy wash his clouts for un."

And this discourse of Betty's tended more than my mother's prayers, I fear, to keep me from going too often. But Betty, like many active women, was false by her crossness only; thinking it just for the moment perhaps, and rushing away with a bucket; ready to stick to it, like a clenched nail, if beaten the wrong way with argument; but melting over it, if you left her, as stinging soap, left along in a basin, spreads all abroad without bubbling.

But all this is beyond the children, and beyond me too for that matter, even now in ripe experience; for I never did know what women mean, and never shall except when they tell me, if that be in their power. Now let that question pass. For although I am now in a place of some authority, I have observed that no one ever listens to me, when I attempt to lay down the law; but all are waiting with open ears until I do enforce it. And so methinks he who reads a history cares not much for the wisdom or folly of the writer (knowing well that the former is far less than his own, and the latter vastly greater), but hurries to know what the people did, and how they got on about it. And this I can tell, if any one can, having been myself in the thick of it.

The fright I had taken that night in Glen Doone satisfied me for a long time thereafter; and I took good care not to venture even in the fields and woods of the outer farm, without John Fry for company. John was greatly surprised and pleased at the value I now set upon him; until, what betwixt the desire to vaunt and the longing to talk things over, I gradually laid bare to him nearly all that had befallen me; except, indeed, about Lorna (and certain other experiences which a sort of shame kept me from mentioning). Not that I did not think of Lorna, and wish very often to see her again. And yet my sister Annie was in truth a great deal more to me than all the men of the parish, and of Brendon, and Countisbury, put together; although at the time I never dreamed it, and would have laughed if told so. Annie was of a pleasing face, and very gentle manner, almost like a lady some people said; but without any airs whatever, only trying to give satisfaction. And if she failed, she would go and weep, without letting any one know it, believing the fault to be all her own, when mostly it was of others. But if she succeeded in pleasing you, it was beautiful to see her smile, and stroke her soft chin in a way of her own, which she always used when taking note how to do the right thing again for you. And then her cheeks had a bright clear pink, and her eyes were as blue as the sky in spring, and she stood as upright as a young apple-tree, and no one could help but smile at her, and pat her brown curls approvingly; whereupon she always curtseyed. For she never tried to look away when honest people gazed at her; and even in the court-yard she would come and help to take your saddle, and tell (without your asking her) what there was for dinner.

A very comely maiden, tall, and with a well-built neck, and very fair white shoulders, under a bright cloud of curling hair. Alas! poor Annie, like most of the gentle maidens—but tush, I am not come to that yet; and for the present she seemed to me little to look at, after the beauty of Lorna Doone.

CHAPTER X

A BRAVE RESCUE AND A ROUGH RIDE

It happened upon a November evening (a deal of rain having fallen, and all the troughs in the yard being flooded, and the bark from the wood-ricks washed down the gutters, and even our water-shoot going brown) that the ducks in the court made a terrible quacking, instead of marching off to their pen, one behind another. Thereupon Annie and I ran out to see what might be the sense of it. There were thirteen ducks, and ten lily-white (as the fashion then of ducks was), not I mean twenty-three in all, but ten white and three brown-striped ones; and without being nice about their colour, they all quacked very movingly. They pushed their gold-coloured bills here and there (yet dirty, as gold is apt to be), and they jumped on the triangles of their feet, and sounded out of their nostrils; and some of the over-excited ones ran along low on the ground, quacking grievously with their bills snapping and bending, and the roof of their mouths exhibited.

Annie began to cry "Dilly, dilly, einy, einy, ducksey," according to the burden of a tune they seem to have accepted as the national duck's anthem; but instead of being soothed by it, they only quacked three times as hard, and ran round till we were giddy. And then they shook their tails together, and looked grave, and went round and round again. Now I am uncommonly fond of ducks, both roasted and roasting and roystering; and it is a fine sight to behold them walk, poddling one after other, with their toes out, like soldiers drilling, and their little eyes cocked all ways at once, and the way that they dib with their bills, and dabble, and throw up their heads and enjoy something, and then tell the others about it. Therefore I knew at once, by the way they were carrying on, that there must be something or other gone wholly amiss in the duck-world. Sister Annie perceived it too, but with a greater quickness; for she counted them like a good duck-wife, and could only tell thirteen of them, when she knew there ought to be fourteen.

And so we began to search about, and the ducks ran to lead us aright, having come that far to fetch us; and when we got down to the foot of the court-yard where the two great ash-trees stand by the side of the little water, we found good reason for the urgency and melancholy of the duck-birds. Lo! the old white drake, the father of all, a bird of high manners and chivalry, always the last to help himself from the pan of barley-meal, and the first to show fight to a dog or cock intruding upon his family, this fine fellow, and pillar of the state, was now in a sad predicament, yet quacking very stoutly. For the brook, wherewith he had been familiar from his callow childhood, and wherein he was wont to quest for water-newts, and tadpoles, and caddis-worms, and other game, this brook, which afforded him very often scanty space to dabble in, and sometimes starved the cresses, was now coming down in a great brown flood, as if the banks never belonged to it. The foaming of it, and the noise, and the cresting of the corners, and the up and down, like a wave of the sea, were enough to frighten any duck, though bred upon stormy waters, which our ducks never had been.

There is always a hurdle six feet long and four and a half in depth, swung by a chain at either end from an oak laid across the channel. And the use of this hurdle is to keep our kine at milking time from straying away there drinking (for in truth they are very dainty) and to fence strange cattle, or Farmer Snowe's horses, from coming along the bed of the brook unknown, to steal our substance. But now this hurdle, which hung in the summer a foot above the trickle, would have been dipped more than two feet deep but for the power against it. For the torrent came down so vehemently that the chains at full stretch were creaking, and the hurdle buffeted almost flat, and thatched (so to say) with the drift-stuff, was going see-saw, with a sulky splash on the dirty red comb of the waters. But saddest to see was between two bars, where a fog was of rushes, and flood-wood, and wild-celery haulm, and dead crowsfoot, who but our venerable mallard jammed in by the joint of his shoulder, speaking aloud as he rose and fell, with his top-knot full of water, unable to comprehend it, with his tail washed far away from him, but often compelled to be silent, being ducked very harshly against his will by the choking fall-to of the hurdle.

For a moment I could not help laughing, because, being borne up high and dry by a tumult of the torrent, he gave me a look from his one little eye (having lost one in fight with the turkey-cock), a gaze of appealing sorrow, and then a loud quack to second it. But the quack came out of time, I suppose, for his throat got filled with water, as the hurdle carried him back again. And then there was scarcely the screw of his tail to be seen until he swung up again, and left small doubt by the way he sputtered, and failed to quack, and hung down his poor crest, but what he must drown in another minute, and frogs triumph over his body.

Annie was crying, and wringing her hands, and I was about to rush into the water, although I liked not the look of it, but hoped to hold on by the hurdle, when a man on horseback came suddenly round the corner of the great ash-hedge on the other side of the stream, and his horse's feet were in the water.

"Ho, there," he cried; "get thee back. The flood will carry thee down like a straw. I will do it for thee, and no trouble."

With that he leaned forward, and spoke to his mare—she was just of the tint of a strawberry, a young thing, very beautiful—and she arched up her neck, as misliking the job; yet, trusting him, would attempt it. She entered the flood, with her dainty fore-legs sloped further and further in front of her, and her delicate ears pricked forward, and the size of her great eyes increasing, but he kept her straight in the turbid rush, by the pressure of his knee on her. Then she looked back, and wondered at him, as the force of the torrent grew stronger, but he bade her go on; and on she went, and it foamed up over her shoulders; and she tossed up her lip and scorned it, for now her courage was waking. Then as the rush of it swept her away, and she struck with her forefeet down the stream, he leaned from his saddle in a manner which I never could have thought possible, and caught up old Tom with his left hand, and set him between his holsters, and smiled at his faint quack of gratitude. In a moment all these were carried downstream, and the rider lay flat on his horse, and tossed the hurdle clear from him, and made for the bend of smooth water.

They landed some thirty or forty yards lower, in the midst of our kitchen-garden, where the winter-cabbage was; but though Annie and I crept in through the hedge, and were full of our thanks and admiring him, he would answer us never a word, until he had spoken in full to the mare, as if explaining the whole to her.

"Sweetheart, I know thou couldst have leaped it," he said, as he patted her cheek, being on the ground by this time, and she was nudging up to him, with the water pattering off her; "but I had good reason, Winnie dear, for making thee go through it."

She answered him kindly with her soft eyes, and smiled at him very lovingly, and they understood one another. Then he took from his waistcoat two peppercorns, and made the old drake swallow them, and tried him softly upon his legs, where the leading gap in the hedge was. Old Tom stood up quite bravely, and clapped his wings, and shook off the wet from his tail-feathers; and then away into the court-yard, and his family gathered around him, and they all made a noise in their throats, and stood up, and put their bills together, to thank God for this great deliverance.

Having taken all this trouble, and watched the end of that adventure, the gentleman turned round to us with a pleasant smile on his face, as if he were lightly amused with himself; and we came up and looked at him. He was rather short, about John Fry's height, or may be a little taller, but very strongly built and springy, as his gait at every step showed plainly, although his legs were bowed with much riding, and he looked as if he lived on horseback. He was not more than four-and-twenty, fresh and ruddy looking, with a short nose and keen blue eyes, and a merry waggish jerk about him, as if the world were not in earnest. Yet he had a sharp, stern way, like the crack of a pistol, if anything misliked him; and we knew that it was safer to tickle than tackle him.

"Well, what be gaping at?" He gave pretty Annie a chuck on the chin, and took me all in without winking.

"Your mare," said I, standing stoutly up. "I never saw such a beauty, sir. Will you let me have a ride of her?"

"Think thou couldst ride her, lad? She will have no burden but mine. Thou couldst never ride her. Tut! I would be loath to kill thee."

"Ride her!" I cried with the bravest scorn, for she looked so kind and gentle; "there never was horse upon Exmoor foaled, but I could tackle in half an hour. Only I never ride upon saddle. Take them leathers off of her."

He looked at me with a dry little whistle, and thrust his hands into his breeches-pockets, and so grinned that I could not stand it. And Annie laid hold of me in such a way that I was almost mad with her. And he laughed, and approved her for doing so. And the worst of all was—he said nothing.

"Get away, Annie, will you? Do you think I'm a fool, good sir! Only trust me with her, and I will not override her."

"For that I will go bail. She is liker to override thee. But the ground is soft to fall upon, after all this rain. Now come out into the yard, young man, for the sake of your mother's cabbages. And the mellow straw-bed will be softer for thee, since pride must have its fall. I am thy mother's cousin, and am going up to house. Tom

Faggus is my name, as everybody knows; and this is my young mare, Winnie."

What a fool I must have been not to know it at once! Tom Faggus, the great highwayman, and his young blood-mare, the strawberry! Already her fame was noised abroad, nearly as much as her master's; and my longing to ride her grew tenfold, but fear came at the back of it. Not that I had the smallest fear of what the mare could do to me, by fair play and horse-trickery, but that the glory of sitting upon her seemed to be too great for me; especially as there were rumours abroad that she was not a mare after all, but a witch. However, she looked like a filly all over, and wonderfully beautiful, with her supple stride, and soft slope of shoulder, and glossy coat beaded with water, and prominent eyes full of docile fire. Whether this came from her Eastern blood of the Arabs newly imported, and whether the cream-colour, mixed with our bay, led to that bright strawberry tint, is certainly more than I can decide, being chiefly acquaint with farm-horses. And these come of any colour and form; you never can count what they will be, and are lucky to get four legs to them.

Mr. Faggus gave his mare a wink, and she walked demurely after him, a bright young thing, flowing over with life, yet dropping her soul to a higher one, and led by love to anything, as the manner is of females, when they know what is the best for them. Then Winnie trod lightly upon the straw, because it had soft muck under it, and her delicate feet came back again.

"Up for it still, be ye?" Tom Faggus stopped, and the mare stopped there; and they looked at me provokingly.

"Is she able to leap, sir? There is good take-off on this side of the brook."

Mr. Faggus laughed very quietly, turning round to Winnie so that she might enter into it. And she, for her part, seemed to know exactly where the fun lay.

"Good tumble-off, you mean. Well, there can be small harm to thee. I am akin to thy family, and know the substance of their skulls."

"Let me get up," said I, waxing wroth, for reasons I cannot tell you, because they are too manifold; "take off your saddle-bag things. I will try not to squeeze her ribs in, unless she plays nonsense with me."

Then Mr. Faggus was up on his mettle, at this proud speech of mine; and John Fry was running up all the while, and Bill Dadds, and half a dozen. Tom Faggus gave one glance around, and then dropped all regard for me. The high repute of his mare was at stake, and what was my life compared to it? Through my defiance, and stupid ways, here was I in a duello.

Something of this occurred to him even in his wrath with me, for he spoke very softly to the filly, who now could scarce subdue herself; but she drew in her nostrils, and breathed to his breath and did all she could to answer him.

"Not too hard, my dear," he said to the filly: "led him gently down on the mixen. That will be quite enough." Then he turned the saddle off, and I was up in a moment. She began at first so easily, and pricked her ears so lovingly, and minced about as if pleased to find so light a weight upon her, that I thought she knew I could ride a little, and feared to show any capers. "Gee wug, Polly!" cried I, for all the men were now looking on, being then at the leaving-off time: "Gee wug, Polly, and show what thou be'est made of." With that I plugged my heels into her, and Billy Dadds flung his hat up.

Nevertheless, she outraged not, though her eyes were frightening Annie, and John Fry took a pick to keep him safe; but she curbed to and fro with her strong forearms rising like springs ingathered, waiting and quivering grievously, and beginning to sweat about it. Then her master gave a shrill clear whistle, when her ears were bent towards him, and I felt her form beneath me gathering up like whalebone, and her hind-legs coming under her, and I knew that I was in for it.

First she reared upright in the air, and struck me full on the nose with her comb, till I bled worse than Robin Snell made me; and then down with her fore-feet deep in the straw, and her hind-feet going to heaven. Finding me stick to her still like wax, for my mettle was up as hers was, away she flew with me swifter than ever I went before, or since, I trow. She drove full-head at the cobwall—"Oh, Jack, slip off," screamed Annie—then she turned like light, when I thought to crush her, and ground my left knee against it. "Mux me," I cried, for my breeches were broken, and short words went the furthest—"if you kill me, you shall die with me." Then she took the court-yard gate at a leap, knocking my words between my teeth, and then right over a quick set hedge, as if the sky were a breath to her; and away for the water-meadows, while I lay on her neck like a child at the breast and wished I had never been born. Straight away, all in the front of the wind, and scattering clouds around her, all I knew of the speed we made was the frightful flash of her shoulders, and her mane like trees in a tempest. I felt the earth under us rushing away, and the air left far behind us, and my breath came and went, and I prayed to God, and was sorry to be so late of it.

All the long swift while, without power of thought, I clung to her crest and shoulders, and dug my nails into her creases, and my toes into her flank-part, and was proud of holding on so long, though sure of being beaten. Then in her fury at feeling me still, she rushed at another device for it, and leaped the wide water-trough sideways across, to and fro, till no breath was left in me. The hazel-boughs took me too hard in the face, and the tall dog-briers got hold of me, and the ache of my back was like crimping a fish; till I longed to give up, thoroughly beaten, and lie there and die in the cresses. But there came a shrill whistle from up the home-hill, where the people had hurried to watch us; and the mare stopped as if with a bullet, then set off for home with the speed of a swallow, and going as smoothly and silently. I never had dreamed of such delicate motion, fluent, and graceful, and ambient, soft as the breeze flitting over the flowers, but swift as the summer lightning. I sat up again, but my strength was all spent, and no time left to recover it, and though she rose at our gate like a bird, I tumbled off into the mixen.

CHAPTER XI

TOM DESERVES HIS SUPPER

"Well done, lad," Mr. Faggus said good-naturedly; for all were now gathered round me, as I rose from the ground, somewhat tottering, and miry, and crest-fallen, but otherwise none the worse (having fallen upon my head, which is of uncommon substance); nevertheless John Fry was laughing, so that I longed to clout his ears for him; "Not at all bad work; we may teach you to ride by-and-by, I see; I thought not to see you stick on so long—"

"I should have stuck on much longer, sir, if her sides had not been wet. She was so slippery—"

"Thou art right. She hath given many the slip. Ha, ha! Vex not, Jack, that I laugh at thee. She is like a sweetheart to me, and better, than any of them be. It would have gone to my heart if thou hadst conquered. None but I can ride my Winnie mare."

"Foul shame to thee then, Tom Faggus," cried mother, coming up suddenly, and speaking so that all were amazed, having never seen her wrathful; "to put my Jack across her, as if his life were no more than thine! The only son of his father, an honest man, and a quiet man, not a roystering drunken robber! Any other man would have taken thy mad horse and thee, and flung them both into horse-pond—ay, and what's more, I'll have it done now, if a hair of his head is injured. Oh, my boy, my boy! What could I do without thee? Put up the other arm, Johnny." All the time mother was scolding so, she was feeling me, and wiping me; while Faggus tried to look greatly ashamed, having sense of the ways of women.

"Only look at his jacket, mother!" cried Annie; "and a shillingsworth gone from his small-clothes!"

"What care I for his clothes, thou goose? Take that, and heed thine own a bit." And mother gave Annie a slap which sent her swinging up against Mr. Faggus, and he caught her, and kissed and protected her, and she looked at him very nicely, with great tears in her soft blue eyes. "Oh, fie upon thee, fie upon thee!" cried mother (being yet more vexed with him, because she had beaten Annie); "after all we have done for thee, and saved thy worthless neck—and to try to kill my son for me! Never more shall horse of thine enter stable here, since these be thy returns to me. Small thanks to you, John Fry, I say, and you Bill Dadds, and you Jem Slocomb, and all the rest of your coward lot; much you care for your master's son! Afraid of that ugly beast yourselves, and you put a man so much younger than you upon him!"

"Wull, missus, what could us do?" began John; "Jan wudd goo, now wudd't her, Jem? And how was us—"

"Jan indeed! Master John, if you please, to a lad of his years and stature. And now, Tom Faggus, be off, if you please, and think yourself lucky to go so; and if ever that horse comes into our yard, I'll hamstring him myself if none of my cowards dare do it."

Everybody looked at mother, to hear her talk like that, knowing how quiet she was day by day and how pleasant to be cheated. And the men began to shoulder their shovels, both so as to be away from her, and to go and tell their wives of it. Winnie too was looking at her, being pointed at so much, and wondering if she had done amiss. And then she came to me, and trembled, and stooped her head, and asked my pardon, if she had been too proud with me.

"Winnie shall stop here to-night," said I, for Tom Faggus still said never a word all the while; but began to buckle his things on, for he knew that women are to be met with wool, as the cannon-balls were at the siege of Tiverton Castle; "mother, I tell you, Winnie shall stop; else I will go away with her. I never knew what it was, till now, to ride a horse worth riding."

"Young man," said Tom Faggus, still preparing sternly to depart, "you know more about a horse than any man on Exmoor. Your mother may well be proud of you, but she need have had no fear. As if I, Tom Faggus, your father's cousin—and the only thing I am proud of—would ever have let you mount my mare, which dukes and princes have vainly sought, except for the courage in your eyes, and the look of your father about you. I knew you could ride when I saw you, and rarely you have conquered. But women don't understand us. Good-bye, John; I am proud of you, and I hoped to have done you pleasure. And indeed I came full of some courtly tales, that would have made your hair stand up. But though not a crust have I tasted since this time yesterday, having given my meat to a widow, I will go and starve on the moor far sooner than eat the best supper that ever was cooked, in a place that has forgotten me." With that he fetched a heavy sigh, as if it had been for my father; and feebly got upon Winnie's back, and she came to say farewell to me. He lifted his hat to my mother, with a glance of sorrow, but never a word; and to me he said, "Open the gate, Cousin John, if you please. You have beaten her so, that she cannot leap it, poor thing."

But before he was truly gone out of our yard, my mother came softly after him, with her afternoon apron across her eyes, and one hand ready to offer him. Nevertheless, he made as if he had not seen her, though he let his horse go slowly.

"Stop, Cousin Tom," my mother said, "a word with you, before you go."

"Why, bless my heart!" Tom Faggus cried, with the form of his countenance so changed, that I verily thought another man must have leaped into his clothes—"do I see my Cousin Sarah? I thought every one was ashamed of me, and afraid to offer me shelter, since I lost my best cousin, John Ridd. 'Come here,' he used to say, 'Tom, come here, when you are worried, and my wife shall take good care of you.' 'Yes, dear John,' I used to answer, 'I know she promised my mother so; but people have taken to think against me, and so might Cousin Sarah.' Ah, he was a man, a man! If you only heard how he answered me. But let that go, I am nothing now, since the day I lost Cousin Ridd." And with that he began to push on again; but mother would not have it so.

"Oh, Tom, that was a loss indeed. And I am nothing either. And you should try to allow for me; though I never found any one that did." And mother began to cry, though father had been dead so long; and I looked on with a stupid surprise, having stopped from crying long ago.

"I can tell you one that will," cried Tom, jumping off Winnie, in a trice, and looking kindly at mother; "I can allow for you, Cousin Sarah, in everything but one. I am in some ways a bad man myself; but I know the value of a good one; and if you gave me orders, by God—" And he shook his fists towards Bagworthy Wood, just heaving up black in the sundown.

"Hush, Tom, hush, for God's sake!" And mother meant me, without pointing at me; at least I thought she did. For she ever had weaned me from thoughts of revenge, and even from longings for judgment. "God knows best, boy," she used to say, "let us wait His time, without wishing it." And so, to tell the truth, I did; partly through her teaching, and partly through my own mild temper, and my knowledge that father, after all, was killed because he had thrashed them.

"Good-night, Cousin Sarah, good-night, Cousin Jack," cried Tom, taking to the mare again; "many a mile I have to ride, and not a bit inside of me. No food or shelter this side of Exeford, and the night will be black as pitch, I trow. But it serves me right for indulging the lad, being taken with his looks so."

"Cousin Tom," said mother, and trying to get so that Annie and I could not hear her; "it would be a sad and unkinlike thing for you to despise our dwelling-house. We cannot entertain you, as the lordly inns on the road do; and we have small change of victuals. But the men will go home, being Saturday; and so you will have the fireside all to yourself. There are some few collops of red deer's flesh, and a ham just down from the chimney, and some dried salmon from Lynmouth weir, and cold roast-pig, and some oysters. And if none of those be to your liking, we could roast two woodcocks in half an hour, and Annie would make the toast for them. And the good folk made some mistake last week, going up the country, and left a keg of old Holland cordial in the coving of the wood-rick, having borrowed our Smiler, without asking leave. I fear there is something unrighteous about it. But what can a poor widow do? John Fry would have taken it, but for our Jack. Our Jack was a little too sharp for him."

Ay, that I was; John Fry had got it, like a billet under his apron, going away in the gray of the morning, as if to kindle his fireplace. "Why, John," I said, "what a heavy log! Let me have one end of it." "Thank'e, Jan, no need of thiccy," he answered, turning his back to me; "waife wanteth a log as will last all day, to kape the crock a zimmerin." And he banged his gate upon my heels to make me stop and rub them. "Why, John," said I, "you'm got a log with round holes in the end of it. Who has been cutting gun-wads? Just lift your apron, or I will."

But, to return to Tom Faggus—he stopped to sup that night with us, and took a little of everything; a few oysters first, and then dried salmon, and then ham and eggs, done in small curled rashers, and then a few collops of venison toasted, and next to that a little cold roast-pig, and a woodcock on toast to finish with, before the Scheidam and hot water. And having changed his wet things first, he seemed to be in fair appetite, and praised Annie's cooking mightily, with a kind of noise like a smack of his lips, and a rubbing of his hands together, whenever he could spare them.

He had gotten John Fry's best small-clothes on, for he said he was not good enough to go into my father's (which mother kept to look at), nor man enough to fill them. And in truth my mother was very glad that he refused, when I offered them. But John was over-proud to have it in his power to say that such a famous man had ever dwelt in any clothes of his; and afterwards he made show of them. For Mr. Faggus's glory, then, though not so great as now it is, was spreading very fast indeed all about our neighbourhood, and even as far as Bridgwater.

Tom Faggus was a jovial soul, if ever there has been one, not making bones of little things, nor caring to seek evil. There was about him such a love of genuine human nature, that if a traveller said a good thing, he would give him back his purse again. It is true that he took people's money more by force than fraud; and the law (being used to the inverse method) was bitterly moved against him, although he could quote precedent. These things I do not understand; having seen so much of robbery (some legal, some illegal), that I scarcely know, as here we say, one crow's foot from the other. It is beyond me and above me, to discuss these subjects; and in truth I love the law right well, when it doth support me, and when I can lay it down to my liking, with prejudice to nobody. Loyal, too, to the King am I, as behoves churchwarden; and ready to make the best of him, as he generally requires. But after all, I could not see (until I grew much older, and came to have some property) why Tom Faggus, working hard, was called a robber and felon of great; while the King, doing nothing at all (as became his dignity), was liege-lord, and paramount owner; with everybody to thank him kindly for accepting tribute.

For the present, however, I learned nothing more as to what our cousin's profession was; only that mother seemed frightened, and whispered to him now and then not to talk of something, whereupon he always nodded with a sage expression, and applied himself to hollands.

"Now let us go and see Winnie, Jack," he said to me after supper; "for the most part I feed her before myself; but she was so hot from the way you drove her. Now she must be grieving for me, and I never let her grieve long."

I was too glad to go with him, and Annie came slyly after us. The filly was walking to and fro on the naked floor of the stable (for he would not let her have any straw, until he should make a bed for her), and without so much as a headstall on, for he would not have her fastened. "Do you take my mare for a dog?" he had said when John Fry brought him a halter. And now she ran to him like a child, and her great eyes shone at the lanthorn.

"Hit me, Jack, and see what she will do. I will not let her hurt thee." He was rubbing her ears all the time he spoke, and she was leaning against him. Then I made believe to strike him, and in a moment she caught me by the waistband, and lifted me clean from the ground, and was casting me down to trample upon me, when he stopped her suddenly.

"What think you of that? Have you horse or dog that would do that for you? Ay, and more than that she will do. If I were to whistle, by-and-by, in the tone that tells my danger, she would break this stable-door down, and rush into the room to me. Nothing will keep her from me then, stone-wall or church-tower. Ah, Winnie, Winnie, you little witch, we shall die together."

Then he turned away with a joke, and began to feed her nicely, for she was very dainty. Not a husk of oat would she touch that had been under the breath of another horse, however hungry she might be. And with her oats he mixed some powder, fetching it from his saddle-bags. What this was I could not guess, neither would he tell me, but laughed and called it "star-shavings." He watched her eat every morsel of it, with two or three drinks of pure water, ministered between whiles; and then he made her bed in a form I had never seen before, and so we said "Good-night" to her.

Afterwards by the fireside he kept us very merry, sitting in the great chimney-corner, and making us play games with him. And all the while he was smoking tobacco in a manner I never had seen before, not using any pipe for it, but having it rolled in little sticks about as long as my finger, blunt at one end and sharp at the other. The sharp end he would put in his mouth, and lay a brand of wood to the other, and then draw a white cloud of curling smoke, and we never tired of watching him. Then Annie put up her lips and asked, with both hands on his knees (for she had taken to him wonderfully), "Is it meant for girls then, Cousin Tom?" But she had better not have asked, for he gave it her to try, and she shut both eyes, and sucked at it. One breath, however, was quite enough, for it made her cough so violently that Lizzie and I must thump her back until she was almost crying. To atone for that, Cousin Tom set to, and told us whole pages of stories, not about his own doings at all, but strangely enough they seemed to concern almost every one else we had ever heard of. Without halting once for a word or a deed, his tales flowed onward as freely and brightly as the flames of the wood up the chimney, and with no smaller variety. For he spoke with the voices of twenty people, giving each person the proper manner, and the proper place to speak from; so that Annie and Lizzie ran all about, and searched the clock and the linen-press. And he changed his face every moment so, and with such power of mimicry that without so much as a smile of his own, he made even mother laugh so that she broke her new tenpenny waistband, and Betty Muxworthy roared in the wash-up.

CHAPTER XII

A MAN JUSTLY POPULAR

Now although Mr. Faggus was so clever, and generous, and celebrated, I know not whether, upon the whole, we were rather proud of him as a member of our family, or inclined to be ashamed of him. And indeed I think that the sway of the balance hung upon the company we were in. For instance, with the men at Brendon—for there is no village at Oare—I was exceeding proud to talk of him, and would freely brag of my Cousin Tom. But with the rich parsons of the neighbourhood, or the justices (who came round now and then, and were glad to ride up to a warm farm-house), or even the well-to-do tradesmen of Porlock—in a word, any settled power, which was afraid of losing things—with all of them we were very shy of claiming our kinship to that great outlaw.

And sure, I should pity, as well as condemn him though our ways in the world were so different, knowing as I do his story; which knowledge, methinks, would often lead us to let alone God's prerogative—judgment, and hold by man's privilege—pity. Not that I would find excuse for Tom's downright dishonesty, which was beyond doubt a disgrace to him, and no credit to his kinsfolk; only that it came about without his meaning any harm or seeing how he took to wrong; yet gradually knowing it. And now, to save any further trouble, and to meet those who disparage him (without allowance for the time or the crosses laid upon him), I will tell the history of him, just as if he were not my cousin, and hoping to be heeded. And I defy any man to say that a word of this is either false, or in any way coloured by family. Much cause he had to be harsh with the world; and yet all acknowledged him very pleasant, when a man gave up his money. And often and often he paid the toll for the carriage coming after him, because he had emptied their pockets, and would not add inconvenience. By trade he had been a blacksmith, in the town of Northmolton, in Devonshire, a rough rude place at the end of Exmoor, so that many people marvelled if such a man was bred there. Not only could he read and write, but he had solid substance; a piece of land worth a hundred pounds, and right of common for two hundred sheep, and a score and a half of beasts, lifting up or lying down. And being left an orphan (with all these cares upon him) he began to work right early, and made such a fame at the shoeing of horses, that the farriers of Barum were like to lose their custom. And indeed he won a golden Jacobus for the best-shod nag in the north of Devon, and some say that he never was forgiven.

As to that, I know no more, except that men are jealous. But whether it were that, or not, he fell into bitter trouble within a month of his victory; when his trade was growing upon him, and his sweetheart ready to marry him. For he loved a maid of Southmolton (a currier's daughter I think she was, and her name was Betsy Paramore), and her father had given consent; and Tom Faggus, wishing to look his best, and be clean of course, had a tailor at work upstairs for him, who had come all the way from Exeter. And Betsy's things were ready too—for which they accused him afterwards, as if he could help that—when suddenly, like a thunderbolt, a lawyer's writ fell upon him.

This was the beginning of a law-suit with Sir Robert Bampfylde, a gentleman of the neighbourhood, who tried to oust him from his common, and drove his cattle and harassed them. And by that suit of law poor Tom was ruined altogether, for Sir Robert could pay for much swearing; and then all his goods and his farm were sold up, and even his smithery taken. But he saddled his horse, before they could catch him, and rode away to Southmolton, looking more like a madman than a good farrier, as the people said who saw him. But when he arrived there, instead of comfort, they showed him the face of the door alone; for the news of his loss was before him, and Master Paramore was a sound, prudent man, and a high member of the town council. It is said that they even gave him notice to pay for Betsy's wedding-clothes, now that he was too poor to marry her. This may be false, and indeed I doubt it; in the first place, because Southmolton is a busy place for talking; and in the next, that I do not think the action would have lain at law, especially as the maid lost nothing, but used it all for her wedding next month with Dick Vellacott, of Mockham.

All this was very sore upon Tom; and he took it to heart so grievously, that he said, as a better man might have said, being loose of mind and property, "The world hath preyed on me like a wolf. God help me now to prey on the world."

And in sooth it did seem, for a while, as if Providence were with him; for he took rare toll on the highway, and his name was soon as good as gold anywhere this side of Bristowe. He studied his business by night and by day, with three horses all in hard work, until he had made a fine reputation; and then it was competent to him to rest, and he had plenty left for charity. And I ought to say for society too, for he truly loved high society, treating squires and noblemen (who much affected his company) to the very best fare of the hostel. And they say that once the King's Justitiaries, being upon circuit, accepted his invitation, declaring merrily that if never true bill had been found against him, mine host should now be qualified to draw one. And so the landlords did; and he always paid them handsomely, so that all of them were kind to him, and contended for his visits. Let it be known in any township that Mr. Faggus was taking his leisure at the inn, and straightway all the men flocked thither to drink his health without outlay, and all the women to admire him; while the children were set at the cross-roads to give warning of any officers. One of his earliest meetings was with Sir Robert Bampfylde himself, who was riding along the Barum road with only one serving-man after him. Tom

Faggus put a pistol to his head, being then obliged to be violent, through want of reputation; while the serving-man pretended to be a long way round the corner. Then the baronet pulled out his purse, quite trembling in the hurry of his politeness. Tom took the purse, and his ring, and time-piece, and then handed them back with a very low bow, saying that it was against all usage for him to rob a robber. Then he turned to the unfaithful knave, and trounced him right well for his cowardice, and stripped him of all his property.

But now Mr. Faggus kept only one horse, lest the Government should steal them; and that one was the young mare Winnie. How he came by her he never would tell, but I think that she was presented to him by a certain Colonel, a lover of sport, and very clever in horseflesh, whose life Tom had saved from some gamblers. When I have added that Faggus as yet had never been guilty of bloodshed (for his eyes, and the click of his pistol at first, and now his high reputation made all his wishes respected), and that he never robbed a poor man, neither insulted a woman, but was very good to the Church, and of hot patriotic opinions, and full of jest and jollity, I have said as much as is fair for him, and shown why he was so popular. Everybody cursed the Doones, who lived apart disdainfully. But all good people liked Mr. Faggus— when he had not robbed them—and many a poor sick man or woman blessed him for other people's money; and all the hostlers, stable-boys, and tapsters entirely worshipped him.

I have been rather long, and perhaps tedious, in my account of him, lest at any time hereafter his character should be misunderstood, and his good name disparaged; whereas he was my second cousin, and the lover of my—But let that bide. 'Tis a melancholy story.

He came again about three months afterwards, in the beginning of the spring-time, and brought me a beautiful new carbine, having learned my love of such things, and my great desire to shoot straight. But mother would not let me have the gun, until he averred upon his honour that he had bought it honestly. And so he had, no doubt, so far as it is honest to buy with money acquired rampantly. Scarce could I stop to make my bullets in the mould which came along with it, but must be off to the Quarry Hill, and new target I had made there. And he taught me then how to ride bright Winnie, who was grown since I had seen her, but remembered me most kindly. After making much of Annie, who had a wondrous liking for him—and he said he was her godfather, but God knows how he could have been, unless they confirmed him precociously—away he went, and young Winnie's sides shone like a cherry by candlelight.

Now I feel that of those days I have little more to tell, because everything went quietly, as the world for the most part does with us. I began to work at the farm in earnest, and tried to help my mother, and when I remembered Lorna Doone, it seemed no more than the thought of a dream, which I could hardly call to mind. Now who cares to know how many bushels of wheat we grew to the acre, or how the cattle milched till we ate them, or what the turn of the seasons was? But my stupid self seemed like to be the biggest of all the cattle; for having much to look after the sheep, and being always in kind appetite, , I grew wider until there was no man of my size to be seen elsewhere upon Exmoor. Let that pass: what odds to any how wide I be? There is no Doone's door at Plover's Barrows and if there were I could never go through it. They vexed me so much about my size, girding at me with paltry jokes whose wit was good only to stay at home, that I grew shamefaced about the matter, and feared to encounter a looking-glass. But mother was very proud, and said she never could have too much of me.

The worst of all to make me ashamed of bearing my head so high—a thing I saw no way to help, for I never could hang my chin down, and my back was like a gatepost whenever I tried to bend it—the worst of all was our little Eliza, who never could come to a size, though she had the wine from the Sacrament at Easter and Allhallowmas, only to be small and skinny, sharp, and clever crookedly. Not that her body was out of the straight (being too small for that perhaps), but that her wit was full of corners, jagged, and strange, and uncomfortable. You never could tell what she might say next; and I like not that kind of women. Now God forgive me for talking so of my own father's daughter, and so much the more by reason that my father could not help it. The right way is to face the matter, and then be sorry for every one. My mother fell grievously on a slide, which John Fry had made nigh the apple-room door, and hidden with straw from the stable, to cover his own great idleness. My father laid John's nose on the ice, and kept him warm in spite of it; but it was too late for Eliza. She was born next day with more mind than body—the worst thing that can befall a man.

But Annie, my other sister, was a fine fair girl, beautiful to behold. I could look at her by the fireside, for an hour together, when I was not too sleepy, and think of my dear father. And she would do the same thing by me, only wait the between of the blazes. Her hair was done up in a knot behind, but some would fall over her shoulders; and the dancing of the light was sweet to see through a man's eyelashes. There never was a face that showed the light or the shadow of feeling, as if the heart were sun to it, more than our dear Annie's did. To look at her carefully, you might think that she was not dwelling on anything; and then she would know you were looking at her, and those eyes would tell all about it. God knows that I try to be simple enough, to keep to His meaning in me, and not make the worst of His children. Yet often have I been put to shame, and ready to bite my tongue off, after speaking amiss of anybody, and letting out my littleness, when suddenly mine eyes have met the pure soft gaze of Annie.

Though as the reader of this story will no doubt now have awareness, it was not always of our father that Annie dreamt with a melancholy and wistfulness. With goodness in her heart and every bone of her loving body, this beautiful creature could not yet give of herself to Tom, though clearly she was enamoured of him and at times would appear pink of cheek and flustered afore confessing that she was deep in desire of him.

I chose not to think of my sweet sister lusting after this braggartly cousin, though it is said that each and every woman, whether she be virgin or encunted, has a need, when the desire so overcomes her (and some say this could be twice a day, though I think this excessive for a woman), to seek easement with Mother Nature.

But oft times, though may I chide myself, I pictured Lorna pleasuring of herself, and I cannot deny that it excited me to some degree, knowing that she was engaging in foeminam subagitare by her own hand (as my Latin masters may have described her activity). For I saw within my head (thick-skulled but nonetheless capable of fancy; and based upon, with the fullness of time, my own experiences) Lorna with her hands beneath the bedclothes, having already caressed her own breasts. Licking her fingers to spread saliva over her love-mound so as to ease the rubbing of it from side to side, then taking her female rod between first and second fingers as they point in a chevron (for so the French, skilled most finely in lovemaking, I have heard, have taught us that word) towards her slit, she brings her fingers together in the action of scissors used for mending cloths, so as to render it bolder. She gasps with delight as it hardens in mimicry of a man's penis, and she starts to work it against the bone of her pubis, such that the pressure creates pleasure in the seat of her womanly delight. And without need or opportunity to take my man's-yard, she finds most imaginative ways to sate her desire.

Wetting her fingers once more, digiting herself and using her other hand to press against her mound at the same time, her pleasure now so two-fold in degree that her lips part with a gasp. (Even if a maid and not yet my wife, she need have no concern of lacking in moral restraint or unchaste thought, for she is free to make her own music and dance to her own tune, while preserving her sanctified maidenhead.) And should she tire of such activity or desire augmentation of her sensual gratification within her own bed-chamber, she may devise other manner of fulfilment.

As for myself, I stroke loosely between my thumb and fingers, curved to accommodate my swelling shape, as I think of her without trouble of a mate less skilled in her satisfaction; having lubricated herself with her own watery saliva or her fingers dipped into a pot of pomatum and rubbed gently over her now pulsing pudenda and inserted into the neck of her gateway, smearing the path. Standing on her bed to gain height, and positioning herself over the smaller and lower bedpost, she slowly eases the tiny, smooth, ball-shaped finial into herself, her legs astride the wooden post and keeping her within balance as she works herself around it, savouring the tightness as it stretches the channel inside her.

But yet at other times (just as a woman may have an itching in her to enjoy a man of different size or shape, though may God forbid Lorna ever to follow this path), she chooses to use an ox-horn kept for the purpose, smooth and slightly curved, making up in length what it may lack in breadth (for so are the baleens of some men), and lies back to enjoy its insertion by her own hand, accommodating it with ease. Some say that the tip of the horn gives a woman the greater pleasure during her self-amors as it rubs against her upper, innermost wall, yet it is my belief (though I am not to be considered a man of the world) that it is her clitoris (for so I have now heard it named) which is her gateway to satisfaction and in fullness of time and effort leads her own seed to spill forth.

And I cannot deny that to see with mine own eyes (rather than have lascivious thought give sight) Lorna disposing herself to her own desires will lead me to grasp my own tarse in my hand; and if she is not to welcome me inside her (for some women do tease so, though they may encourage men to rub their tip over their temptation), then may I pump up and down the shaft, as pumping the water from a well, until its head shines as Dunkery Beacon on the hills, reddened and full of the fire of my loins. My thoughts see more: I hasten my pumping, using my free hand to fondle and caress my own nipples or cods, until I can slow my rubbing at its peak and spend over her body, as we both watch the viscid liquid, the colour of milk watered down, in Vesuvian spurts from the summit of my mountain of lust. (And Lorna by my side will be as fond on't as if my seed were as beauteous as her own form.)

And so went my thoughts at that time, representing Lorna to me as I imagined rather than as she was, consumed as I was by lust and love for her. As for Lorna's family, the Doones, they were thriving still, and no one to come against them; except indeed by word of mouth, to which they lent no heed whatever. Complaints were made from time to time, both in high and low quarters (as the rank might be of the people robbed), and once or twice in the highest of all, to wit, the King himself. But His Majesty made a good joke about it (not meaning any harm, I doubt), and was so much pleased with himself thereupon, that he quite forgave the mischief. Moreover, the main authorities were a long way off; and the Chancellor had no cattle on Exmoor; and as for my lord the Chief Justice, some rogue had taken his silver spoons; whereupon his lordship swore that never another man would he hang until he had that one by the neck. Therefore the Doones went on as they listed, and none saw fit to meddle with them. For the only man who would have dared to come to close quarters with them, that is to say Tom Faggus, himself was a quarry for the law, if ever it should be unhooded. Moreover, he had transferred his business to the neighbourhood of Wantage, in the county of Berks, where he found the climate drier, also good downs and commons excellent for galloping, and richer yeomen than ours be, and better roads to rob them on.

Some folk, who had wiser attended to their own affairs, said that I (being sizeable, and able to shoot not badly) ought to do something against those Doones, and show what I was made of. Though I loved my father still, and would fire at a word about him, I saw not how it would do him good for me to harm his injurers. Some races are of revengeful kind, and will for years pursue their wrong, and sacrifice this world and the next for a moment's foul satisfaction, but methinks this comes of some black blood, perverted and never purified. And I doubt but men of true English birth are stouter than so to be twisted, though some of the women may take that turn, if their own life runs unkindly.

Let that pass—I am never good at talking of things beyond me. All I know is, that if I had met the Doone who had killed my father, I would gladly have thrashed him black and blue, supposing I were able; but would never have fired a gun at him, unless he began that game with me, or fell upon more of my family, or were violent among women. And to do them justice, my mother and Annie were equally kind and gentle, but Eliza would flame and grow white with contempt, and not trust herself to speak to us.

Now a strange thing came to pass that winter, when I was twenty-one years old, a very strange thing, which affrighted the rest, and made me feel uncomfortable. Not that there was anything in it, to do harm to any one, only that none could explain it, except by attributing it to the devil. The weather was very mild and open, and scarcely any snow fell; at any rate, none lay on the ground, even for an hour, in the highest part of Exmoor; a thing which I knew not before nor since, as long as I can remember. But the nights were wonderfully dark, as though with no stars in the heaven; and all day long the mists were rolling upon the hills and down them, as if the whole land were a wash-house. The moorland was full of snipes and teal, and curlews flying and crying, and lapwings flapping heavily, and ravens hovering round dead sheep; yet no redshanks nor dottrell, and scarce any golden plovers (of which we have great store generally) but vast lonely birds, that cried at night, and moved the whole air with their pinions; yet no man ever saw them. It was dismal as well as dangerous now for any man to go fowling (which of late I loved much in the winter) because the fog would come down so thick that the pan of the gun was reeking, and the fowl out of sight ere the powder kindled, and then the sound of the piece was so dead, that the shooter feared harm, and glanced over his shoulder. But the danger of course was far less in this than in losing of the track, and falling into the mires, or over the brim of a precipice.

Nevertheless, I must needs go out, being young and very stupid, and feared of being afraid; a fear which a wise man has long cast by, having learned of the manifold dangers which ever and ever encompass us. And beside this folly and wildness of youth, perchance there was something, I know not what, of the joy we have in uncertainty. Mother, in fear of my missing home—though for that matter, I could smell supper, when hungry, through a hundred land-yards of fog—my dear mother, who thought of me ten times for one thought about herself, gave orders to ring the great sheep-bell, which hung above the pigeon-cote, every ten minutes of the day, and the sound came through the plaits of fog, and I was vexed about it, like the letters of a copy-book. It reminded me, too, of Blundell's bell, and the grief to go into school again.

But during those two months of fog (for we had it all the winter), the saddest and the heaviest thing was to stand beside the sea. To be upon the beach yourself, and see the long waves coming in; to know that they are long waves, but only see a piece of them; and to hear them lifting roundly, swelling over smooth green rocks, plashing down in the hollow corners, but bearing on all the same as ever, soft and sleek and sorrowful, till their little noise is over, and never to deliver to me once more the beautiful girl, perchance my very own siren.

One old man who lived at Lynmouth, seeking to be buried there, having been more than half over the world, though shy to speak about it, and fain to come home to his birthplace, this old Will Watcombe (who dwelt by the water) said that our strange winter arose from a thing he called the "Gulf-stream," rushing up channel suddenly. He said it was hot water, almost fit for a man to shave with, and it threw all our cold water out, and ruined the fish and the spawning-time, and a cold spring would come after it. I was fond of going to Lynmouth on Sunday to hear this old man talk, for sometimes he would discourse with me, when nobody else could move him. He told me that this powerful flood set in upon our west so hard sometimes once in ten years, and sometimes not for fifty, and the Lord only knew the sense of it; but that when it came, therewith came warmth and clouds, and fog, and moisture, and nuts, and fruit, and even shells; and all the tides were thrown abroad. As for nuts he winked awhile, and chewed a piece of tobacco; yet did I not comprehend him. Only afterwards I heard that nuts with liquid kernels came, travelling on the Gulf-stream; for never before was known so much foreign cordial landed upon our coast, floating ashore by mistake in the fog, and (what with the tossing and the mist) too much astray to learn its duty.

Folk, who are ever too prone to talk, said that Will Watcombe himself knew better than anybody else about this drift of the Gulf-stream, and the places where it would come ashore, and the caves that took the in-draught. But De Whichehalse, our great magistrate, certified that there was no proof of unlawful importation; neither good cause to suspect it, at a time of Christian charity. And we knew that it was a foul thing for some quarrymen to say that night after night they had been digging a new cellar at Ley Manor to hold the little marks of respect found in the caverns at high-water weed. Let that be, it is none of my business to speak evil of dignities; duly we common people joked of the "Gulp-stream," as we called it.

But the thing which astonished and frightened us so, was not, I do assure you, the landing of foreign spirits, nor the loom of a lugger at twilight in the gloom of the winter moonrise. That which made us crouch in by the fire, or draw the bed-clothes over us, and try to think of something else, was a strange mysterious sound.

At grey of night, when the sun was gone, and no red in the west remained, neither were stars forthcoming, suddenly a wailing voice rose along the valleys, and a sound in the air, as of people running. It mattered not whether you stood on the moor, or crouched behind rocks away from it, or down among reedy places; all as one the sound would come, now from the heart of the earth beneath, now overhead bearing down on you. And then there was rushing of something by, and melancholy laughter, and the hair of a man would stand on end before he could reason properly.

God, in His mercy, knows that I am stupid enough for any man, and very slow of impression, nor ever could bring myself to believe that our Father would let the evil one get the upper hand of us. But when I had heard that sound three times, in the lonely gloom of the evening fog, and the cold that followed the lines of air, I was loath to go abroad by night, even so far as the stables, and loved the light of a candle more, and the glow of a fire with company.

There were many stories about it, of course, all over the breadth of the moorland. But those who had heard it most often declared that it must be the wail of a woman's voice, and the rustle of robes fleeing horribly, and fiends in the fog going after her. To that, however, I paid no heed, when anybody was with me; only we drew more close together, and barred the doors at sunset.

CHAPTER XIII

MASTER HUCKABACK COMES IN

Mr. Reuben Huckaback, whom many good folk in Dulverton will remember long after my time, was my mother's uncle, being indeed her mother's brother. He owned the very best shop in the town, and did a fine trade in soft ware, especially when the pack-horses came safely in at Christmas-time. And we being now his only kindred (except indeed his granddaughter, little Ruth Huckaback, of whom no one took any heed), mother beheld it a Christian duty to keep as well as could be with him, both for love of a nice old man, and for the sake of her children. And truly, the Dulverton people said that he was the richest man in their town, and could buy up half the county armigers; 'ay, and if it came to that, they would like to see any man, at Bampton, or at Wivelscombe, and you might say almost Taunton, who could put down golden Jacobus and Carolus against him.

Now this old gentleman—so they called him, according to his money; and I have seen many worse ones, more violent and less wealthy—he must needs come away that time to spend the New Year-tide with us; not that he wanted to do it (for he hated country-life), but because my mother pressing, as mothers will do to a good bag of gold, had wrung a promise from him; and the only boast of his life was that never yet had he broken his word, at least since he opened business.

Now it pleased God that Christmas-time (in spite of all the fogs) to send safe home to Dulverton, and what was more, with their loads quite safe, a goodly string of packhorses. Nearly half of their charge was for Uncle Reuben, and he knew how to make the most of it. Then having balanced his debits and credits, and set the writs running against defaulters, as behoves a good Christian at Christmas-tide, he saddled his horse, and rode off towards Oare, with a good stout coat upon him, and leaving Ruth and his head man plenty to do, and little to eat, until they should see him again.

It had been settled between us that we should expect him soon after noon on the last day of December. For the Doones being lazy and fond of bed, as the manner is of dishonest folk, the surest way to escape them was to travel before they were up and about, to-wit, in the forenoon of the day. But herein we reckoned without our host: for being in high festivity, as became good Papists, the robbers were too lazy, it seems, to take the trouble of going to bed; and forth they rode on the Old Year-morning, not with any view of business, but purely in search of mischief.

We had put off our dinner till one o'clock (which to me was a sad foregoing), and there was to be a brave supper at six of the clock, upon New Year's-eve; and the singers to come with their lanthorns, and do it outside the parlour-window, and then have hot cup till their heads should go round, after making away with the victuals. For although there was nobody now in our family to be churchwarden of Oare, it was well admitted that we were the people entitled alone to that dignity; and though Nicholas Snowe was in office by name, he managed it only by mother's advice; and a pretty mess he made of it, so that every one longed for a Ridd again, soon as ever I should be old enough. This Nicholas Snowe was to come in the evening, with his three tall comely daughters, strapping girls, and well skilled in the dairy; and the story was all over the parish, on a stupid conceit of John Fry's, that I should have been in love with all three, if there had been but one of them. (Though had John Fry been appraised of my dealings with a Snowe girl of a later time, his gossipings would have had greater meat on the juicy bone of tittle-tattle, and much chewing over of it would he have made.) These Snowes were to come, and come they did, partly because Mr. Huckaback liked to see fine young maidens, and partly because none but Nicholas Snowe could smoke a pipe now all around our parts, except of the very high people, whom we durst never invite. And Uncle Ben, as we all knew well, was a great hand at his pipe, and would sit for hours over it, in our warm chimney-corner, and never want to say a word, unless it were inside him; only he liked to have somebody there over against him smoking.

Now when I came in, before one o'clock, after seeing to the cattle—for the day was thicker than ever, and we must keep the cattle close at home, if we wished to see any more of them—I fully expected to find Uncle Ben sitting in the fireplace, lifting one cover and then another, as his favourite manner was, and making sweet mouths over them; for he loved our bacon rarely, and they had no good leeks at Dulverton; and he was a man who always would see his business done himself. But there instead of my finding him with his quaint dry face pulled out at me, and then shut up sharp not to be cheated—who should run out but Betty Muxworthy, and poke me with a saucepan lid.

"Get out of that now, Betty," I said in my politest manner, for really Betty was now become a great domestic evil. She would have her own way so, and of all things the most distressful was for a man to try to reason.

"Zider-press," cried Betty again, for she thought it a fine joke to call me that, because of my size, and my hatred of it; "here be a rare get up, anyhow."

"A rare good dinner, you mean, Betty. Well, and I have a rare good appetite." With that I wanted to go and smell it, and not to stop for Betty.

"Troost thee for thiccy, Jan Ridd. But thee must keep it bit langer, I reckon. Her baint coom, Maister Ziderpress. Whatt'e mak of that now?"

"Do you mean to say that Uncle Ben has not arrived yet, Betty?"

"Raived! I knaws nout about that, whuther a hath of noo. Only I tell 'e, her baint coom. Rackon them Dooneses hath gat 'un."

And Betty, who hated Uncle Ben, because he never gave her a groat, and she was not allowed to dine with him, I am sorry to say that Betty Muxworthy grinned all across, and poked me again with the greasy saucepan cover. But I misliking so to be treated, strode through the kitchen indignantly, for Betty behaved to me even now, as if I were only Eliza.

"Oh, Johnny, Johnny," my mother cried, running out of the grand show-parlour, where the case of stuffed birds was, and peacock-feathers, and the white hare killed by grandfather; "I am so glad you are come at last. There is something sadly amiss, Johnny."

Mother had upon her wrists something very wonderful, of the nature of fal-lal as we say, and for which she had an inborn turn, being of good draper family, and polished above the yeomanry. Nevertheless I could never bear it, partly because I felt it to be out of place in our good farm-house, partly because I hate frippery, partly because it seemed to me to have nothing to do with father, and partly because I never could tell the reason of my hating it. And yet the poor soul had put them on, not to show her hands off (which were above her station) but simply for her children's sake, because Uncle Ben had given them. But another thing, I never could bear for man or woman to call me, "Johnny," "Jack," or "John," I cared not which; and that was honest enough, and no smallness of me there, I say.

"Well, mother, what is the matter, then?"

"I am sure you need not be angry, Johnny. I only hope it is nothing to grieve about, instead of being angry. You are very sweet-tempered, I know, John Ridd, and perhaps a little too sweet at times"—here she meant the Snowe girls, and I hanged my head, for it were known well that they liked me, though no one other than the girls themselves (I suppose) knew exactly how they loved to forward themselves unto me. "But what would you say if the people there"—she never would call them '*Doones*'—"had gotten your poor Uncle Reuben, horse, and Sunday coat, and all?"

"Why, mother, I should be sorry for them. He would set up a shop by the river-side, and come away with all their money."

"That all you have to say, John! And my dinner done to a very turn, and the supper all fit to go down, and no worry, only to eat and be done with it! And all the new plates come from Watchett, with the Watchett blue upon them, at the risk of the lives of everybody, and the capias from good Aunt Jane for stuffing a curlew with onion before he begins to get cold, and make a woodcock of him, and the way to turn the flap over in the inside of a roasting pig—"

"Well, mother dear, I am very sorry. But let us have our dinner. You know we promised not to wait for him after one o'clock; and you only make us hungry. Everything will be spoiled, mother, and what a pity to think of! After that I will go to seek for him in the thick of the fog, like a needle in a hay-band. That is to say, unless you think"—for she looked very grave about it—"unless you really think, mother, that I ought to go without dinner."

"Oh no, John, I never thought that, thank God! Bless Him for my children's appetites; and what is Uncle Ben to them?"

So we made a very good dinner indeed, though wishing that he could have some of it, and wondering how much to leave for him; and then, as no sound of his horse had been heard, I set out with my gun to look for him.

I followed the track on the side of the hill, from the farm-yard, where the sledd-marks are—for we have no wheels upon Exmoor yet, nor ever shall, I suppose; though a dunder-headed man tried it last winter, and broke his axle piteously, and was nigh to break his neck—and after that I went all along on the ridge of the rabbit-cleve, with the brook running thin in the bottom; and then down to the Lynn stream and leaped it, and so up the hill and the moor beyond. The fog hung close all around me then, when I turned the crest of the highland, and the gorse both before and behind me looked like a man crouching down in ambush. But still there was a good cloud of daylight, being scarce three of the clock yet, and when a lead of red deer came across, I could tell them from sheep even now. I was half inclined to shoot at them, for the children did love venison; but they drooped their heads so, and looked so faithful, that it seemed hard measure to do it. If one of them had bolted away, no doubt I had let go at him.

After that I kept on the track, trudging very stoutly, for nigh upon three miles, and my beard (now beginning to grow at some length) was full of great drops and prickly, whereat I was very proud. I had not so much as a dog with me, and the place was unkind and lonesome, and the rolling clouds very desolate; and now if a wild sheep ran across he was scared at me as an enemy; and I for my part could not tell the meaning of the marks on him. We called all this part Gibbet-moor, not being in our parish; but though there were gibbets enough upon it, most part of the bodies was gone for the value of the chains, they said, and the teaching of young chirurgeons.

But of all this I had little fear, being well-acquaint with Exmoor, and the wise art of the sign-posts, whereby a man, who barred the road, now opens it up both ways with his finger-bones, so far as rogues allow him. My carbine was loaded and freshly primed, and I knew myself to be even now a match in strength for any two men of the size around our neighbourhood, except in the Glen Doone. "Girt Jan Ridd," I was called already, and folk grew feared to wrestle with me; though I was tired of hearing about it, and often longed to be smaller. And most of all upon Sundays, when I had to make way up our little church, and the maidens tittered at me. For indeed they were the ones who called me girt, not abashed in marvelling at my size, and it were not how tall I stood next to a tree about which they talked (and them not even waiting until their womanish secret meetings to share their wonderings).

The soft white mist came thicker around me, as the evening fell; and the peat ricks here and there, and the furze-hucks of the summer-time, were all out of shape in the twist of it. By-and-by, I began to doubt where I was, or how come there, not having seen a gibbet lately; and then I heard the draught of the wind up a hollow place with rocks to it; and for the first time fear broke out (like cold sweat) upon me. And yet I knew what a fool I was, to fear nothing but a sound! But when I stopped to listen, there was no sound, more than a beating noise, and that was all inside me. Therefore I went on again, making company of myself, and keeping my gun quite ready.

Now when I came to an unknown place, where a stone was set up endwise, with a faint red cross upon it, and a polish from some conflict, I gathered my courage to stop and think, having sped on the way too hotly. Against that stone I set my gun, trying my spirit to leave it so, but keeping with half a hand for it; and then what to do next was the wonder. As for finding Uncle Ben that was his own business, or at any rate his executor's; first I had to find myself, and plentifully would thank God to find myself at home again, for the sake of all our family.

The volumes of the mist came rolling at me (like great logs of wood, pillowed out with sleepiness), and between them there was nothing more than waiting for the next one. Then everything went out of sight, and glad was I of the stone behind me, and view of mine own shoes. Then a distant noise went by me, as of many horses galloping, and in my fright I set my gun and said, "God send something to shoot at." Yet nothing came, and my gun fell back, without my will to lower it.

But presently, while I was thinking "What a fool I am!" arose as if from below my feet, so that the great stone trembled, that long, lamenting lonesome sound, as of an evil spirit not knowing what to do with it. For the moment I stood like a root, without either hand or foot to help me, and the hair of my head began to crawl, lifting my hat, as a snail lifts his house; and my heart like a shuttle went to and fro. But finding no harm to come of it, neither visible form approaching, I wiped my forehead, and hoped for the best, and resolved to run every step of the way, till I drew our own latch behind me.

Yet here again I was disappointed, for no sooner was I come to the cross-ways by the black pool in the hole, but I heard through the patter of my own feet a rough low sound very close in the fog, as of a hobbled sheep a-coughing. I listened, and feared, and yet listened again, though I wanted not to hear it. For being in haste of the homeward road, and all my heart having heels to it, loath I was to stop in the dusk for the sake of an aged wether. Yet partly my love of all animals, and partly my fear of the farmer's disgrace, compelled me to go to the succour, and the noise was coming nearer. A dry short wheezing sound it was, barred with coughs and want of breath; but thus I made the meaning of it.

"Lord have mercy upon me! O Lord, upon my soul have mercy! An' if I cheated Sam Hicks last week, Lord knowest how well he deserved it, and lied in every stocking's mouth—oh Lord, where be I a-going?"

These words, with many jogs between them, came to me through the darkness, and then a long groan and a choking. I made towards the sound, as nigh as ever I could guess, and presently was met, point-blank, by the head of a mountain-pony. Upon its back lay a man bound down, with his feet on the neck and his head to the tail, and his arms falling down like stirrups. The wild little nag was scared of its life by the unaccustomed burden, and had been tossing and rolling hard, in desire to get ease of it.

Before the little horse could turn, I caught him, jaded as he was, by his wet and grizzled forelock, and he saw that it was vain to struggle, but strove to bite me none the less, until I smote him upon the nose.

"Good and worthy sir," I said to the man who was riding so roughly; "fear nothing; no harm shall come to thee."

"Help, good friend, whoever thou art," he gasped, but could not look at me, because his neck was jerked so; "God hath sent thee, and not to rob me, because it is done already."

"What, Uncle Ben!" I cried, letting go the horse in amazement, that the richest man in Dulverton—"Uncle Ben here in this plight! What, Mr. Reuben Huckaback!"

"An honest hosier and draper, serge and longcloth warehouseman"—he groaned from rib to rib—"at the sign of the Gartered Kitten in the loyal town of Dulverton. For God's sake, let me down, good fellow, from this accursed marrow-bone; and a groat of good money will I pay thee, safe in my house to Dulverton; but take notice that the horse is mine, no less than the nag they robbed from me."

"What, Uncle Ben, dost thou not know me, thy dutiful nephew John Ridd?"

Not to make a long story of it, I cut the thongs that bound him, and set him astride on the little horse; but he was too weak to stay so. Therefore I mounted him on my back, turning the horse into horse-steps, and leading the pony by the cords which I fastened around his nose, set out for Plover's Barrows.

Uncle Ben went fast asleep on my back, being jaded and shaken beyond his strength, for a man of three-score and five; and as soon he felt assured of safety he would talk no more. And to tell the truth he snored so loudly, that I could almost believe that fearful noise in the fog every night came all the way from Dulverton.

Now as soon as ever I brought him in, we set him up in the chimney-corner, comfortable and handsome; and it was no little delight to me to get him off my back; for, like his own fortune, Uncle Ben was of a good round figure. He gave his long coat a shake or two, and he stamped about in the kitchen, until he was sure of his whereabouts, and then he fell asleep again until supper should be ready.

"He shall marry Ruth," he said by-and-by to himself, and not to me; "he shall marry Ruth for this, and have my little savings, soon as they be worth the having. Very little as yet, very little indeed; and ever so much gone to-day along of them rascal robbers."

My mother made a dreadful stir, of course, about Uncle Ben being in such a plight as this; so I left him to her care and Annie's, and soon they fed him rarely, while I went out to see to the comfort of the captured pony. And in truth he was worth the catching, and served us very well afterwards, though Uncle Ben was inclined to claim him for his business at Dulverton, where they have carts and that like. "But," I said, "you shall have him, sir, and welcome, if you will only ride him home as first I found you riding him." And with that he dropped it.

A very strange old man he was, short in his manner, though long of body, glad to do the contrary things to what any one expected of him, and always looking sharp at people, as if he feared to be cheated. This surprised me much at first, because it showed his ignorance of what we farmers are—an upright race, as you may find, scarcely ever cheating indeed, except upon market-day, and even then no more than may be helped by reason of buyers expecting it. Now our simple ways were a puzzle to him, as I told him very often; but he only laughed, and rubbed his mouth with the back of his dry shining hand, and I think he shortly began to languish for want of some one to higgle with. I had a great mind to give him the pony, because he thought himself cheated in that case; only he would conclude that I did it with some view to a legacy.

Of course, the Doones, and nobody else, had robbed good Uncle Reuben; and then they grew sportive, and took his horse, an especially sober nag, and bound the master upon the wild one, for a little change as they told him. For two or three hours they had fine enjoyment chasing him through the fog, and making much sport of his groanings; and then waxing hungry, they went their way, and left him to opportunity. Now Mr. Huckaback growing able to walk in a few days' time, became thereupon impatient, and could not be brought to understand why he should have been robbed at all.

"I have never deserved it," he said to himself, not knowing much of Providence, except with a small *p* to it; "I have never deserved it, and will not stand it in the name of our lord the King, not I!" At other times he would burst forth thus: "Three-score years and five have I lived an honest and laborious life, yet never was I robbed before. And now to be robbed in my old age, to be robbed for the first time now!"

Thereupon of course we would tell him how truly thankful he ought to be for never having been robbed before, in spite of living so long in this world, and that he was taking a very ungrateful, not to say ungracious, view, in thus repining, and feeling aggrieved; when anyone else would have knelt and thanked God for enjoying so long an immunity. But say what we would, it was all as one. Uncle Ben stuck fast to it, that he had nothing to thank God for.

CHAPTER XIV

A MOTION WHICH ENDS IN A MULL

Instead of minding his New-Year pudding, Master Huckaback carried on so about his mighty grievance, that at last we began to think there must be something in it, after all; especially as he assured us that choice and costly presents for the young people of our household were among the goods divested. But mother told him her children had plenty, and wanted no gold and silver, and little Eliza spoke up and said, "You can give us the pretty things, Uncle Ben, when we come in the summer to see you."

Our mother reproved Eliza for this, although it was the heel of her own foot; and then to satisfy our uncle, she promised to call Farmer Nicholas Snowe, to be of our council that evening, "And if the young maidens would kindly come, without taking thought to smoothe themselves, why it would be all the merrier, and who knew but what Uncle Huckaback might bless the day of his robbery, etc., etc.—and thorough good honest girls they were, fit helpmates either for shop or farm." All of which was meant for me; but I stuck to my platter and answered not.

In the evening Farmer Snowe came up, leading his daughters after him, like fillies trimmed for a fair; and Uncle Ben, who had not seen them on the night of his mishap (because word had been sent to stop them), was mightily pleased and very pleasant, according to his town-bred ways. The damsels had seen good company, and soon got over their fear of his wealth, and played him a number of merry pranks, which made our mother quite jealous for Annie, who was always shy and diffident. However, when the hot cup was done, and before the mulled wine was ready, we packed all the maidens in the parlour and turned the key upon them;

and then we drew near to the kitchen fire to hear Uncle Ben's proposal. Farmer Snowe sat up in the corner, caring little to hear about anything, but smoking slowly, and nodding backward like a sheep-dog dreaming. Mother was in the settle, of course, knitting hard, as usual; and Uncle Ben took to a three-legged stool, as if all but that had been thieved from him. Howsoever, he kept his breath from speech, giving privilege, as was due, to mother.

"Master Snowe, you are well assured," said mother, colouring like the furze as it took the flame and fell over, "that our kinsman here hath received rough harm on his peaceful journey from Dulverton. The times are bad, as we all know well, and there is no sign of bettering them, and if I could see our Lord the King I might say things to move him! nevertheless, I have had so much of my own account to vex for—"

"You are flying out of the subject, Sarah," said Uncle Ben, seeing tears in her eyes, and tired of that matter.

"Zettle the pralimbinaries," spoke Farmer Snowe, on appeal from us, "virst zettle the pralimbinaries; and then us knows what be drivin' at."

"Preliminaries be damned, sir," cried Uncle Ben, losing his temper. "What preliminaries were there when I was robbed; I should like to know? Robbed in this parish as I can prove, to the eternal disgrace of Oare and the scandal of all England. And I hold this parish to answer for it, sir; this parish shall make it good, being a nest of foul thieves as it is; ay, farmers, and yeomen, and all of you. I will beggar every man in this parish, if they be not beggars already, ay, and sell your old church up before your eyes, but what I will have back my tarlatan, time-piece, saddle, and dove-tailed nag."

Mother looked at me, and I looked at Farmer Snowe, and we all were sorry for Master Huckaback, putting our hands up one to another, that nobody should browbeat him; because we all knew what our parish was, and none the worse for strong language, however rich the man might be. But Uncle Ben took it in a different way. He thought that we all were afraid of him, and that Oare parish was but as Moab or Edom, for him to cast his shoe over.

"Nephew Jack," he cried, looking at me when I was thinking what to say, and finding only emptiness, "you are a heavy lout, sir; a bumpkin, a clodhopper; and I shall leave you nothing, unless it be my boots to grease."

"Well, uncle," I made answer, "I will grease your boots all the same for that, so long as you be our guest, sir."

Now, that answer, made without a thought, stood me for two thousand pounds, as you shall see, by-and-by, perhaps.

"As for the parish," my mother cried, being too hard set to contain herself, "the parish can defend itself, and we may leave it to do so. But our Jack is not like that, sir; and I will not have him spoken of. Leave him indeed! Who wants you to do more than to leave him alone, sir; as he might have done you the other night; and as no one else would have dared to do. And after that, to think so meanly of me, and of my children!"

"Hoity, toity, Sarah! Your children, I suppose, are the same as other people's."

"That they are not; and never will be; and you ought to know it, Uncle Reuben, if any one in the world ought. Other people's children!"

"Well, well!" Uncle Reuben answered, "I know very little of children; except my little Ruth, and she is nothing wonderful."

"I never said that my children were wonderful, Uncle Ben; nor did I ever think it. But as for being good—"

Here mother fetched out her handkerchief, being overcome by our goodness; and I told her, with my hand to my mouth, not to notice him; though he might be worth ten thousand times ten thousand pounds.

But Farmer Snowe came forward now, for he had some sense sometimes; and he thought it was high time for him to say a word for the parish.

"Maister Huckaback," he began, pointing with his pipe at him, the end that was done in sealing-wax, "tooching of what you was plaized to zay 'bout this here parish, and no oother, mind me no oother parish but thees, I use the vreedom, zur, for to tell 'e, that thee be a laiar."

Then Farmer Nicholas Snowe folded his arms across with the bowl of his pipe on the upper one, and gave me a nod, and then one to mother, to testify how he had done his duty, and recked not what might come of it. However, he got little thanks from us; for the parish was nothing at all to my mother, compared with her children's interests; and I thought it hard that an uncle of mine, and an old man too, should be called a liar, by a visitor at our fireplace. For we, in our rude part of the world, counted it one of the worst disgraces that could befall a man, to receive the lie from any one. But Uncle Ben, as it seems was used to it, in the way of trade, just as people of fashion are, by a style of courtesy.

Therefore the old man only looked with pity at Farmer Nicholas; and with a sort of sorrow, too, reflecting how much he might have made in a bargain with such a customer, so ignorant and hot-headed.

"Now let us bandy words no more," said mother, very sweetly; "nothing is easier than sharp words, except to wish them unspoken; as I do many and many's the time, when I think of my good husband. But now let us hear from Uncle Reuben what he would have us do to remove this disgrace from amongst us, and to satisfy him of his goods."

"I care not for my goods, woman," Master Huckaback answered grandly; "although they were of large value, about them I say nothing. But what I demand is this, the punishment of those scoundrels."

"Zober, man, zober!" cried Farmer Nicholas; "we be too naigh Badgery 'ood, to spake like that of they Dooneses."

"Pack of cowards!" said Uncle Reuben, looking first at the door, however; "much chance I see of getting redress from the valour of this Exmoor! And you, Master Snowe, the very man whom I looked to to raise the country, and take the lead as churchwarden—why, my youngest shopman would match his ell against you. Pack of cowards," cried Uncle Ben, rising and shaking his lappets at us; "don't pretend to answer me. Shake you all off, that I do—nothing more to do with you!"

We knew it useless to answer him, and conveyed our knowledge to one another, without anything to vex him. However, when the mulled wine was come, and a good deal of it gone (the season being Epiphany), Uncle Reuben began to think that he might have been too hard with us. Moreover, he was beginning now to respect Farmer Nicholas bravely, because of the way he had smoked his pipes, and the little noise made over them. And Lizzie and Annie were doing their best—for now we had let the girls out—to wake more lightsome uproar; also young Faith Snowe was toward to keep the old men's cups aflow, and hansel them to their liking.

So at the close of our entertainment, when the girls were gone away to fetch and light their lanthorns (over which they made rare noise, blowing each the other's out for counting of the sparks to come), Master Huckaback stood up, without much aid from the crock-saw, and looked at mother and all of us.

"Let no one leave this place," said he, "until I have said what I want to say; for saving of ill-will among us; and growth of cheer and comfort. May be I have carried things too far, even to the bounds of churlishness, and beyond the bounds of good manners. I will not unsay one word I have said, having never yet done so in my life; but I would alter the manner of it, and set it forth in this light. If you folks upon Exmoor here are loath and wary at fighting, yet you are brave at better stuff; the best and kindest I ever knew, in the matter of feeding."

Here he sat down with tears in his eyes, and called for a little mulled bastard. All the maids, who were now come back, raced to get it for him, but Annie of course was foremost. And herein ended the expedition, a perilous and a great one, against the Doones of Bagworthy; an enterprise over which we had all talked plainly more than was good for us. Though for Master Huckaback's part, his expedition venturing into unknown territory (into a snow-storm as it may be termed by one with more humour than I) was to keep him awake for some while. I will never know half this episode, 'twas so clandestine; but 'tis no matter, 'tis still a tale worth the telling. For Master Snowe, he too having made much of our mulled wine and being urged by my mother (though not, I feel sure, with the greatest of sincerity, but she being of courtesy through and through) to stay the night with us whilst the three girls were found space, though not fair commodious, with my sisters, furnished an opportunity for young Faith to provide a further hansel, perhaps the first of many to come.

She, though being younger in years than her two sisters, was not younger in pure thought (likely having been tutored well by the others, for what better way for a girl to learn than to seek instruction from those kin who may have been tickled sweetly). Dear, innocent Annie told me on the morrow that poor Faith, whilst greatly pleased at our welcome, had found the chamber too crowded for her liking and had been forced to venture awhile downstairs to ease out her legs. But I knew that her legs had been asunder for some different reason, and the itching in her foot was but an excuse.

My first indication of her deception by artifice was when I heard the door to the room next to mine creaking more slowly than would Master Huckaback have moved it had he had need to exit. Words followed, though I could not decipher them, though I did not need to stretch beyond proper limit my hearing to be aware of the laughter with repeated short catches of breath, interspersed with a sharp "shoosh"-ing sound with giggling bubbling over it as water gushes over a rock. Perhaps emboldened by their lustfulness, the two became louder and I prayed that my mother and Betty might not hear them (though the former, being of polite manner to visitors, would never have sought to question any activities, save but if she had thought it were her Annie).

For some short moment I thought I might provide some sort of sign to them that they were being overheard and that desist they must, but in truth I found more than a tittle of excitement rising through me, not in thinking of my uncle's carnal desires, but as I wondered which one of the three misses (and well I would soon know of their forwardness to would-be suitors) was providing him with his private epiphany, and as my baleen stirred I turned onto my stomach, sliding my pillow down below my belly, part of it gripped between my legs; rolling it up around me so as to press hard into the fold.

Snatches of conversation caught in the night air. "Ah, such commendable merit in the hand of a willing miss, for you take me in hand well, and there will be such pleasure in your turning to my cods that I may be heeded to reward you well tomorrow."

"Sirrah, I am delighted to sup of your experience." I heard from their speech, not soft enough for discretion, that she—whichever of the Snowe girls—must be sliding his stones over the palm of her hand and frigging them within her fingers, before grasping his stiff cock in both hands (as I heard him say), and gasp in delight (she being experienced in milking the dairy cows and employing such rhythmic, fluid action).

I pushed myself harder and faster into the bed cushion. A squeaking of the bed aside the other face of the wall followed as I heard a voice—that of the girl—bid him lie back down. "Hush, close your eyes. Let your head meet the pillow once more and I will sit astride your standing, for I am of a disposition to yearn to provide gratification to such a buxom shaft. It cannot be denied it entices me greatly and I have thought of your having of me your own pleasure."

Though I was not privy to direct observation of their postures, I knew that in her benevolence she was taking upon herself the labour of being atop his body, kneeling and trapping his thighs between her legs.

"Your youth greatly enhances my pleasure—you…are…so…taut…around…me. So very good—around me," I heard him say, his short breathings betwixt almost every word.

"Nay, Master Huckaback, it is you who are filling me such that I am stretched most pleasurably, and how can a girl disavow a man grown to such abundance as you?"

"Ride this between your legs," he urged with appetency thickening his voice, and, secure in her saddle, she quickened her pace so that I felt sure the bed would soon charge through the wall between us like a stallion maddened by a mare's teasing and squirting. I heard him start to groan as he filled her belly and she, being of less surprise than he, urged him to keep his silence: "Bite down on your cries, lest we be found, and so will it but intensify your pleasure."

I found myself following this advice clearly borne of experience, though it were some time afterwards that my own horsing galloped to its destination and I bit down into the bed-clothes, my teeth clamping on the cloth as the warm, sticky fluid gushed from me. For my part, I slept well that night once spent, having thought myself into excitement (though in truth those devious activities in the chamber aside mine appeared to be of a length likely to have satisfied Uncle Reuben in greater store than the Snowe maiden).

CHAPTER XV

QUO WARRANTO?

On the following day Master Huckaback, with some show of mystery, demanded from my mother an escort into a dangerous part of the world, to which his business compelled him. My mother made answer to this that he was kindly welcome to take our John Fry with him; at which the good clothier laughed, and said that John was nothing like big enough, but another John must serve his turn, not only for his size, but because if he were carried away, no stone would be left unturned upon Exmoor, until he should be brought back again. Hereupon my mother grew very pale, and found fifty reasons against my going, each of them weightier than the true one, as Eliza (who was jealous of me) managed to whisper to Annie. On the other hand, I was quite resolved (directly the thing was mentioned) to see Uncle Reuben through with it; and it added much to my self-esteem to be the guard of so rich a man. Therefore I soon persuaded mother, with her head upon my breast, to let me go and trust in God; and after that I was greatly vexed to find that this dangerous enterprise was nothing more than a visit to the Baron de Whichehalse, to lay an information, and sue a warrant against the Doones, and a posse to execute it.

Stupid as I always have been, and must ever be no doubt, I could well have told Uncle Reuben that his journey was no wiser than that of the men of Gotham; that he never would get from Hugh de Whichehalse a warrant against the Doones; moreover, that if he did get one, his own wig would be singed with it. But for divers reasons I held my peace, partly from youth and modesty, partly from desire to see whatever please God I should see, and partly from other causes.

We rode by way of Brendon town, Illford Bridge, and Babbrook, to avoid the great hill above Lynmouth; and the day being fine and clear again, I laughed in my sleeve at Uncle Reuben for all his fine precautions. When we arrived at Ley Manor, we were shown very civilly into the hall, and refreshed with good ale and collared head, and the back of a Christmas pudding. I had never been under so fine a roof (unless it were of a church) before; and it pleased me greatly to be so kindly entreated by high-born folk. But Uncle Reuben was vexed a little at being set down side by side with a man in a very small way of trade, who was come upon some business there, and who made bold to drink his health after finishing their horns of ale.

"Sir," said Uncle Ben, looking at him, "my health would fare much better, if you would pay me three pounds and twelve shillings, which you have owed me these five years back; and now we are met at the Justice's, the opportunity is good, sir."

After that, we were called to the Justice-room, where the Baron himself was sitting with Colonel Harding, another Justiciary of the King's peace, to help him. I had seen the Baron de Whichehalse before, and was not at all afraid of him, having been at school with his son, as he knew, and it made him very kind to me. And indeed he was kind to everybody, and all our people spoke well of him; and so much the more because we knew that the house was in decadence. For the first De Whichehalse had come from Holland, where he had been a great nobleman, some hundred and fifty years agone. Being persecuted for his religion, when the Spanish power was everything, he fled to England with all he could save, and bought large estates in Devonshire. Since then his descendants had intermarried with ancient county families, Cottwells, and Marwoods, and Walronds, and Welses of Pylton, and Chichesters of Hall; and several of the ladies brought them large increase of property. And so about fifty years before the time of which I am writing, there were few names in the West of England thought more of than De Whichehalse.

But now they had lost a great deal of land, and therefore of that which goes with land, as surely as fame belongs to earth—I mean big reputation. How they had lost it, none could tell; except that as the first descendants had a manner of amassing, so the later ones were gifted with a power of scattering. Whether this came of good Devonshire blood opening the sluice of Low Country veins is beyond both my province and my power to inquire. Anyhow, all people loved this last strain of De Whichehalse far more than the name had been liked a hundred years agone.

Hugh de Whichehalse, a white-haired man, of very noble presence, with friendly blue eyes and a sweet smooth forehead, and aquiline nose quite beautiful (as you might expect in a lady of birth), and thin lips curving delicately, this gentleman rose as we entered the room; while Colonel Harding turned on his chair, and struck one spur against the other. I am sure that, without knowing aught of either, we must have reverenced more of the two the one who showed respect to us. And yet nine gentleman out of ten make this dull mistake when dealing with the class below them!

Uncle Reuben made his very best scrape, and then walked up to the table, trying to look as if he did not know himself to be wealthier than both the gentlemen put together. Of course he was no stranger to them, any more than I was; and, as it proved afterwards, Colonel Harding owed him a lump of money, upon very good security. Of him Uncle Reuben took no notice, but addressed himself to De Whichehalse.

The Baron smiled very gently, so soon as he learned the cause of this visit, and then he replied quite reasonably.

"A warrant against the Doones, Master Huckaback. Which of the Doones, so please you; and the Christian names, what be they?"

"My lord, I am not their godfather; and most like they never had any. But we all know old Sir Ensor's name, so that may be no obstacle."

"Sir Ensor Doone and his sons—so be it. How many sons, Master Huckaback, and what is the name of each one?"

"How can I tell you, my lord, even if I had known them all as well as my own shop-boys? Nevertheless there were seven of them, and that should be no obstacle."

"A warrant against Sir Ensor Doone, and seven sons of Sir Ensor Doone, Christian names unknown, and doubted if they have any. So far so good Master Huckaback. I have it all down in writing. Sir Ensor himself was there, of course, as you have given in evidence—"

"No, no, my lord, I never said that: I never said—"

"If he can prove that he was not there, you may be indicted for perjury. But as for those seven sons of his, of course you can swear that they were his sons and not his nephews, or grandchildren, or even no Doones at all?"

"My lord, I can swear that they were Doones. Moreover, I can pay for any mistake I make. Therein need be no obstacle."

"Oh, yes, he can pay; he can pay well enough," said Colonel Harding shortly.

"I am heartily glad to hear it," replied the Baron pleasantly; "for it proves after all that this robbery (if robbery there has been) was not so very ruinous. Sometimes people think they are robbed, and then it is very sweet afterwards to find that they have not been so; for it adds to their joy in their property. Now, are you quite convinced, good sir, that these people (if there were any) stole, or took, or even borrowed anything at all from you?"

"My lord, do you think that I was drunk?"

"Not for a moment, Master Huckaback. Although excuse might be made for you at this time of the year. But how did you know that your visitors were of this particular family?"

"Because it could be nobody else. Because, in spite of the fog—"

"Fog!" cried Colonel Harding sharply.

"Fog!" said the Baron, with emphasis. "Ah, that explains the whole affair. To be sure, now I remember, the weather has been too thick for a man to see the head of his own horse. The Doones (if still there be any Doones) could never have come abroad; that is as sure as simony. Master Huckaback, for your good sake, I am heartily glad that this charge has miscarried. I thoroughly understand it now. The fog explains the whole of it."

"Go back, my good fellow," said Colonel Harding; "and if the day is clear enough, you will find all your things where you left them. I know, from my own experience, what it is to be caught in an Exmoor fog."

Uncle Reuben, by this time, was so put out, that he hardly knew what he was saying.

"My lord, Sir Colonel, is this your justice! If I go to London myself for it, the King shall know how his commission—how a man may be robbed, and the justices prove that he ought to be hanged at back of it; that in his good shire of Somerset—"

"Your pardon a moment, good sir," De Whichehalse interrupted him; "but I was about (having heard your case) to mention what need be an obstacle, and, I fear, would prove a fatal one, even if satisfactory proof were afforded of a felony. The malfeasance (if any) was laid in Somerset; but we, two humble servants of His Majesty, are in commission of his peace for the county of Devon only, and therefore could never deal with it."

"And why, in the name of God," cried Uncle Reuben, now carried at last fairly beyond himself, "why could you not say as much at first, and save me all this waste of time and worry of my temper? Gentlemen, you are all in league; all of you stick together. You think it fair sport for an honest trader, who makes no shams as you do, to be robbed and well-nigh murdered, so long as they who did it won the high birthright of felony. If a poor sheep stealer, to save his children from dying of starvation, had dared to look at a two-month lamb, he would swing on the Manor gallows, and all of you cry 'Good riddance!' But now, because good birth and bad manners—" Here poor Uncle Ben, not being so strong as before the Doones had played with him, began to foam at the mouth a little, and his tongue went into the hollow where his short grey whiskers were.

I forget how we came out of it, only I was greatly shocked at bearding of the gentry so, and mother scarce could see her way, when I told her all about it. "Depend upon it you were wrong, John," was all I could get out of her; though what had I done but listen, and touch my forelock, when called upon. "John, you may take my word for it, you have not done as you should have done. Your father would have been shocked to think of going to Baron de Whichehalse, and in his own house insulting him! And yet it was very brave of you, John. Just like you, all over. And (as none of the men are here, dear John) I am proud of you for doing it."

All throughout the homeward road, Uncle Ben had been very silent, feeling much displeased with himself and still more so with other people. But before he went to bed that night, he just said to me, "Nephew Jack, you have not behaved so badly as the rest to me. And because you have no gift of talking, I think that I may trust you. Now, mark my words, this villain job shall not have ending here. I have another card to play."

"You mean, sir, I suppose, that you will go to the justices of this shire, Squire Maunder, or Sir Richard Blewitt, or—"

"Oaf, I mean nothing of the sort; they would only make a laughing-stock, as those Devonshire people did, of me. No, I will go to the King himself, or a man who is bigger than the King, and to whom I have ready access. I will not tell thee his name at present, only if thou art brought before him, never wilt thou forget it." That was true enough, by the bye, as I discovered afterwards, for the man he meant was Judge Jeffreys.

"And when are you likely to see him, sir?"

"Maybe in the spring, maybe not until summer, for I cannot go to London on purpose, but when my business takes me there. Only remember my words, Jack, and when you see the man I mean, look straight at him, and tell no lie. He will make some of your zany squires shake in their shoes, I reckon. Now, I have been in this lonely hole far longer than I intended, by reason of this outrage; yet I will stay here one day more upon a certain condition."

"Upon what condition, Uncle Ben? I grieve that you find it so lonely. We will have Farmer Nicholas up again, and the singers, and—"

"The fashionable milkmaids. I thank you, let me be. The wenches are too loud for me." (Methought this may have appertained to the antics of the night, though I said naught.) "Your Nanny is enough. Nanny is a good child, and she shall come and visit me." (This, I resolved, never should happen.) Uncle Reuben would always call her "Nanny"; he said that "Annie" was too fine and Frenchified for us. "But my condition is this, Jack—that you shall guide me to-morrow, without a word to any one, to a place where I may well descry the dwelling of these scoundrel Doones, and learn the best way to get at them, when the time shall come. Can you do this for me? I will pay you well."

I promised very readily to do my best to serve him, but, of course, would take no money for it, not being so poor as that came to. Accordingly, on the day following, I managed to set the men at work on the other side of the farm, especially that inquisitive and busybody John Fry, who would pry out almost anything for the pleasure of telling his wife; and then, with Uncle Reuben mounted on my ancient Peggy, I made foot for the westward, directly after breakfast. Uncle Ben refused to go unless I would take a loaded gun, and indeed it was always wise to do so in those days of turbulence; and none the less because of late more than usual of our sheep had left their skins behind them. This, as I need hardly say, was not to be charged to the appetite of the Doones, for they always said that they were not butchers (although upon that subject might well be two opinions); and their practice was to make the shepherds kill and skin, and quarter for them, and sometimes carry to the Doone-gate the prime among the fatlings, for fear of any bruising, which spoils the look at table. But the worst of it was that ignorant folk, unaware of their fastidiousness, scored to them the sheep they lost by lower-born marauders, and so were afraid to speak of it: and the issue of this error was that a farmer, with five or six hundred sheep, could never command, on his wedding-day, a prime saddle of mutton for dinner.

To return now to my Uncle Ben—and indeed he would not let me go more than three land-yards from him—there was very little said between us along the lane and across the hill, although the day was pleasant. I could see that he was half amiss with his mind about the business, and not so full of security as an elderly man should keep himself. Therefore, out I spake, and said,—

"Uncle Reuben, have no fear. I know every inch of the ground, sir; and there is no danger nigh us."

"Fear, boy! Who ever thought of fear? 'Tis the last thing would come across me. Pretty things those primroses."

At once I thought of Lorna Doone, and how my fancy went with her. Could Lorna ever think of me? Was I not a lout gone by, only fit for loach-sticking? Had I ever seen a face fit to think of near her? The sudden flash, the quickness, the bright desire to know one's heart, and not withhold her own from it, the soft withdrawal of rich eyes, the longing to love somebody, anybody, anything, not imbrued with wickedness—

My uncle interrupted me, misliking so much silence now, with the naked woods falling over us. For we were come to Bagworthy forest, the blackest and the loneliest place of all that keep the sun out. Even now, in winter-time, with most of the wood unriddled, and the rest of it pinched brown, it hung around us like a cloak containing little comfort. I kept quite close to Peggy's head, and Peggy kept quite close to me, and pricked her ears at everything. However, we saw nothing there, except a few old owls and hawks, and a magpie sitting all alone, until we came to the bank of the hill, where the pony could not climb it. Uncle Ben was very loath to get off, because the pony seemed company, and he thought he could gallop away on her, if the worst came to the worst, but I persuaded him that now he must go to the end of it. Therefore he made Peggy fast, in a place where we could find her, and speaking cheerfully as if there was nothing to be afraid of, he took his staff, and I my gun, to climb the thick ascent.

There was now no path of any kind; which added to our courage all it lessened of our comfort, because it proved that the robbers were not in the habit of passing there. And we knew that we could not go astray, so long as we breasted the hill before us; inasmuch as it formed the rampart, or side-fence of Glen Doone. But in truth I used the right word there for the manner of our ascent, for the ground came forth so steep against us, and withal so woody, that to make any way we must throw ourselves forward, and labour as at a breast-plough. Rough and loamy rungs of oak-root bulged here and there above our heads; briers needs must speak with us, using more of tooth than tongue; and sometimes bulks of rugged stone, like great sheep, stood across us. At last, though very loath to do it, I was forced to leave my gun behind, because I required one hand to drag myself up the difficulty, and one to help Uncle Reuben. And so at last we gained the top, and looked forth the edge of the forest, where the ground was very stony and like the crest of a quarry; and no more trees between us and the brink of cliff below, three hundred yards below it might be, all strong slope and gliddery. And now for the first time I was amazed at the appearance of the Doones' stronghold, and understood its nature.

The chine of highland, whereon we stood, curved to the right and left of us, keeping about the same elevation, and crowned with trees and brushwood. At about half a mile in front of us, but looking as if we could throw a stone to strike any man upon it, another crest just like our own bowed around to meet it; but failed by reason of two narrow clefts of which we could only see the brink. One of these clefts was the Doone-gate, with a portcullis of rock above it, and the other was the chasm by which I had once made entrance. Betwixt them, where the hills fell back, as in a perfect oval, traversed by the winding water, lay a bright green valley, rimmed with sheer black rock, and seeming to have sunken bodily from the bleak rough heights above. It looked as if no frost could enter, neither wind go ruffling; only spring, and hope, and comfort, breathe to one another. Even now the rays of sunshine dwelt and fell back on one another, whenever the clouds lifted; and the pale blue glimpse of the growing day seemed to find young encouragement.

But for all that, Uncle Reuben was none the worse nor better. He looked down into Glen Doone first, and sniffed as if he were smelling it, like a sample of goods from a wholesale house; and then he looked at the hills over yonder, and then he stared at me.

"See what a pack of fools they be?"

"Of course I do, Uncle Ben. 'All rogues are fools,' was my first copy, beginning of the alphabet."

"Pack of stuff lad. Though true enough, and very good for young people. But see you not how this great Doone valley may be taken in half an hour?"

"Yes, to be sure I do, uncle; if they like to give it up, I mean."

"Three culverins on yonder hill, and three on the top of this one, and we have them under a pestle. Ah, I have seen the wars, my lad, from Keinton up to Naseby; and I might have been a general now, if they had taken my advice—"

But I was not attending to him, being drawn away on a sudden by a sight which never struck the sharp eyes of our General. For I had long ago descried that little opening in the cliff through which

I made my exit, as before related, on the other side of the valley. No bigger than a rabbit-hole it seemed from where we stood; and yet of all the scene before me, that (from my remembrance perhaps) had the most attraction. Now gazing at it with full thought of all that it had cost me, I saw a figure come, and pause, and pass into it. Something very light and white, nimble, smooth, and elegant, gone almost before I knew that any one had been there. And yet my heart came to my ribs, and all my blood was in my face, and pride within me fought with shame, and vanity with self-contempt; at that moment, once for all, I felt that I was face to face with fate (however poor it might be), weal or woe, in Lorna Doone.

CHAPTER XVI

LORNA GROWING FORMIDABLE

Having reconnoitred thus the position of the enemy, Master Huckaback, on the homeward road, cross-examined me in a manner not at all desirable. For he had noted my confusion and eager gaze at something unseen by him in the valley, and thereupon he made up his mind to know everything about it. In this, however, he partly failed; for although I was no hand at fence, and would not tell him a falsehood, I managed so to hold my peace that he put himself upon the wrong track, and continued thereon with many vaunts of his shrewdness and experience, and some chuckles at my simplicity. Thus much, however, he learned aright, that I had been in the Doone valley several years before, and might be brought upon strong inducement to venture there again. But as to the mode of my getting in, the things I saw, and my thoughts upon them, he not only failed to learn the truth, but certified himself into an obstinacy of error, from which no after-knowledge was able to deliver him. And this he did, not only because I happened to say very little, but forasmuch as he disbelieved half of the truth I told him, through his own too great sagacity.

Upon one point, however, he succeeded more easily than he expected, viz. in making me promise to visit the place again, as soon as occasion offered, and to hold my own counsel about it. But I could not help smiling at one thing, that according to his point of view my own counsel meant my own and Master Reuben Huckaback's.

Now he being gone, as he went next day, to his favourite town of Dulverton, and leaving behind him shadowy promise of the mountains he would do for me, my spirit began to burn and pant for something to go on with; and nothing showed a braver hope of movement and adventure than a lonely visit to Glen Doone, by way of the perilous passage discovered long afore. Therefore I waited for nothing more than the slow arrival of new small-clothes made by a good tailor at Porlock, for I was wishful to look my best; and when they were come and approved, I started, regardless of the expense, and forgetting (like a fool) how badly they would take the water.

What with urging of the tailor, and my own misgivings, the time was now come round again to the high-day of St. Valentine, when all our maids were full of lovers, and all the lads looked foolish. And none of them more sheepish than I myself, albeit twenty-one years old. And what of all things scared me most was the thought of my own size, and knowledge of my strength, which came like knots upon me daily. In honest truth I tell this thing (which often since hath puzzled me, when I came to mix with men more), I was to that degree ashamed of my thickness and my stature, in the presence of a woman, that I would not put a trunk of wood on the fire in the kitchen, but let Annie scold me well, with a smile to follow, and with her own plump hands lift up a little log, and fuel it. Many a time I longed to be no bigger than John Fry was; whom now (when insolent) I took with my left hand by the waist-stuff, and set him on my hat, and gave him little chance to tread it; until he spoke of his family, and requested to come down again.

Now taking for good omen this, that I was a Valentine, though much too big for a Cupidon, I chose a seven-foot staff of ash, and fixed a loach-fork in it, to look as I had looked before; and leaving word upon matters of business, out of the back door I went, and so through the little orchard, and down the brawling Lynn-brook. Not being now so much afraid, I struck across the thicket land between the meeting waters, and came upon the Bagworthy stream near the great black whirlpool. Nothing amazed me so much as to find how shallow the stream now looked to me, although the pool was still as black and greedy as it used to be. And still the great rocky slide was dark and difficult to climb. After some labour, I reached the top; and halted to look about me well, before trusting to broad daylight.

The winter (as I said before) had been a very mild one; and now the spring was toward so that bank and bush were touched with it. The valley into which I gazed was fair with early promise, having shelter from the wind and taking all the sunshine. The willow-bushes over the stream hung as if they were angling with tasseled floats of gold and silver, bursting like a bean-pod. Between them came the water laughing, like a maid at her own dancing, and spread with that young blue which never lives beyond the April. And on either bank, the meadow ruffled as the breeze came by, opening (through new tufts of green) daisy-bud or celandine, or a shy glimpse now and then of the love-lorn primrose.

Though I am so blank of wit, or perhaps for that same reason, these little things come and dwell with me, and I am happy about them, and long for nothing better. I feel with every blade of grass, as if it had a history; and make a child of every bud as though it knew and loved me. And being so, they seem to tell me of my own delusions, how I am no more than they, except in self-importance.

While I was forgetting much of many things that harm one, and letting of my thoughts go wild to sounds and sights of nature, a sweeter note than thrush or ouzel ever wooed a mate in, floated on the valley breeze at the quiet turn of sundown. The words were of an ancient song, fit to laugh or cry at.

"Love, an if There Be One,
Come My Love to Be,
My Love is for the One
Loving Unto Me.

> Not for me the show, love,
>   Of a gilded bliss;
>   Only thou must know, love,
>   What my value is.
>
>   If in all the earth, love,
>   Thou hast none but me,
>   This shall be my worth, love:
>   To be cheap to thee.
>
>   But, if so thou ever
>   Strivest to be free,
>   'Twill be my endeavour
>   To be dear to thee.
>
>   So shall I have plea, love,
>   Is thy heart and breath
>   Clinging still to thee, love,
>   In the doom of death."

All this I took in with great eagerness, not for the sake of the meaning (which is no doubt an allegory), but for the power and richness, and softness of the singing, which seemed to me better than we ever had even in Oare church. But all the time I kept myself in a black niche of the rock, where the fall of the water began, lest the sweet singer (espying me) should be alarmed, and flee away. But presently I ventured to look forth where a bush was; and then I beheld the loveliest sight—one glimpse of which was enough to make me kneel in the coldest water.

By the side of the stream she was coming to me, even among the primroses, as if she loved them all; and every flower looked the brighter, as her eyes were on them. I could not see what her face was, my heart so awoke and trembled; only that her hair was flowing from a wreath of white violets, and the grace of her coming was like the appearance of the first wind-flower. The pale gleam over the western cliffs threw a shadow of light behind her, as if the sun were lingering. Never do I see that light from the closing of the west, even in these my aged days, without thinking of her. Ah me, if it comes to that, what do I see of earth or heaven, without thinking of her?

The tremulous thrill of her song was hanging on her open lips; and she glanced around, as if the birds were accustomed to make answer. To me it was a thing of terror to behold such beauty, and feel myself the while to be so very low and common. But scarcely knowing what I did, as if a rope were drawing me, I came from the dark mouth of the chasm; and stood, afraid to look at her.

She was turning to fly, not knowing me, and frightened, perhaps, at my stature, when I fell on the grass (as I fell before her that day), and I just said, "Lorna Doone!"

She knew me at once, from my manner and ways, and a smile broke through her trembling, as sunshine comes through aspen-leaves; and being so clever, she saw, of course, that she needed not to fear me.

"Oh, indeed," she cried, with a feint of anger (because she had shown her cowardice, and yet in her heart she was laughing); "oh, if you please, who are you, sir, and how do you know my name?"

"I am John Ridd," I answered; "the one who gave you those beautiful fish."

"Yes, the one who was frightened so, and obliged to hide here in the water."

"And do you remember how kind you were, and saved my life by your quickness, and went away riding upon a great man's shoulder, as if you had never seen me, and yet looked back through the willow-trees?"

"Oh, yes, I remember everything; because it was so rare to see any except—I mean because I happen to remember. But you seem not to remember, sir, how perilous this place is."

For she had kept her eyes upon me; large eyes of a softness, a brightness, and a dignity which made me feel as if I must for ever love and yet for ever know myself unworthy. Unless themselves should fill with love, which is the spring of all things. And so I could not answer her, but was overcome with thinking and feeling and confusion. Neither could I look again; only waited for the melody which made every word like a poem to me, the melody of her voice. But she had not the least idea of what was going on with me, any more than I myself had.

"I think, Master Ridd, you cannot know," she said, with her eyes taken from me, "what the dangers of this place are, and the nature of the people."

"Yes, I know enough of that; and I am frightened greatly, all the time, when I do not look at you."

She did not answer me in the style some maidens would have used; the manner, I mean, which now we call from a foreign word "coquettish." And more than that, she was trembling from real fear of violence, lest strong hands might be laid on me, and a miserable end of it. And to tell the truth, I grew afraid; perhaps from a kind of sympathy, and because I knew that evil comes more readily than good to us.

Therefore, without more ado, or taking any advantage— although I would have been glad at heart, if needs had been, to kiss her (without any thought of rudeness)—it struck me that I had better go, and have no more to say to her until next time of coming. So would she look the more for me and think the more about me, and not grow weary of my words and the want of change there is in me. For, of course, I knew what a churl I was compared to her birth and appearance; but meanwhile I might improve myself and learn a musical instrument. "The wind hath a draw after flying straw" is a saying we have in Devonshire, made, peradventure, by somebody who had seen the ways of women.

"Mistress Lorna, I will depart"—mark you, I thought that a powerful word—"in fear of causing disquiet. If any rogue shot me it would grieve you; I make bold to say it, and it would be the death of mother. Few mothers have such a son as me. Try to think of me now and then, and I will bring you some new-laid eggs, for our young blue hen is beginning."

"I thank you heartily," said Lorna; "but you need not come to see me. You can put them in my little bower, where I am almost always—I mean whither daily I repair to read and to be away from them."

"Only show me where it is. Thrice a day I will come and stop—"

"Nay, Master Ridd, I would never show thee—never, because of peril—only that so happens it thou hast found the way already."

And she smiled with a light that made me care to cry out for no other way, except to her dear heart. But only to myself I cried for anything at all, having enough of man in me to be bashful with some young maidens. So I touched her white hand softly when she gave it to me, and (fancying that she had sighed) was touched at heart about it, and resolved to yield her all my goods, although my mother was living; and then grew angry with myself (for a mile or more of walking) to think she would condescend so; and then, for the rest of the homeward road, was mad with every man in the world who would dare to think of having her.

CHAPTER XVII

JOHN IS BEWITCHED

To forget one's luck of life, to forget the cark of care and withering of young fingers; not to feel, or not be moved by, all the change of thought and heart, from large young heat to the sinewy lines and dry bones of old age—this is what I have to do ere ever I can make you know (even as a dream is known) how I loved my Lorna. I myself can never know; never can conceive, or treat it as a thing of reason, never can behold myself dwelling in the midst of it, and think that this was I; neither can I wander far from perpetual thought of it. Perhaps I have two farrows of pigs ready for the chapman; perhaps I have ten stones of wool waiting for the factor. It is all the same. I look at both, and what I say to myself is this: "Which would Lorna choose of them?" Of course, I am a fool for this; any man may call me so, and I will not quarrel with him, unless he guess my secret. Of course, I fetch my wit, if it be worth the fetching, back again to business. But there my heart is and must be; and all who like to try can cheat me, except upon parish matters.

That week I could do little more than dream and dream and rove about, seeking by perpetual change to find the way back to myself. I cared not for the people round me, neither took delight in victuals; but made believe to eat and drink and blushed at any questions. And being called the master now, head-farmer, and chief yeoman, it irked me much that any one should take advantage of me; yet everybody did so as soon as ever it was known that my wits were gone moon-raking. For that was the way they looked at it, not being able to comprehend the greatness and the loftiness. Neither do I blame them much; for the wisest thing is to laugh at people when we cannot understand them. I, for my part, took no notice; but in my heart despised them as beings of a lesser nature, who never had seen Lorna. Yet I was vexed, and drank a pail of water, when John Fry spread all over the farm, and even at the shoeing forge, that a mad dog had come and bitten me, from the other side of Mallond.

This seems little to me now; and so it might to any one; but, at the time, it worked me up to a fever of indignity. To make a mad dog of Lorna, to compare all my imaginings (which were strange, I do assure you—the faculty not being apt to work), to count the raising of my soul no more than hydrophobia! All this acted on me so, that I gave John Fry the soundest threshing that ever a sheaf of good corn deserved, or a bundle of tares was blessed with. Afterwards he went home, too tired to tell his wife the meaning of it; but it proved of service to both of them, and an example for their children.

Now the climate of this country is—so far as I can make of it—to throw no man into extremes; and if he throw himself so far, to pluck him back by change of weather and the need of looking after things. Lest we should be like the Southerns, for whom the sky does everything, and men sit under a wall and watch both food and fruit come beckoning. Their sky is a mother to them; but ours a good stepmother to us—fearing to hurt by indulgence, and knowing that severity and change of mood are wholesome.

The spring being now too forward, a check to it was needful; and in the early part of March there came a change of weather. All the young growth was arrested by a dry wind from the east, which made both face and fingers burn when a man was doing ditching. The lilacs and the woodbines, just crowding forth in little tufts, close kernelling their blossom, were ruffled back, like a sleeve turned up, and nicked with brown at the corners. In the hedges any man, unless his eyes were very dull, could see the mischief doing. The russet of the young elm-bloom was fain to be in its scale again; but having pushed forth, there must be, and turn to a tawny colour. The hangers of the hazel, too, having shed their dust to make the nuts, did not spread their little combs and dry them, as they ought to do; but shrivelled at the base and fell, as if a knife had cut them. And more than all to notice was (at least about the hedges) the shuddering of everything and the shivering sound among them toward the feeble sun; such as we make to a poor fireplace when several doors are open. Sometimes I put my face to warm against the soft, rough maple-stem, which feels like the foot of a red deer; but the pitiless east wind came through all, and took and shook the caved hedge aback till its knees were knocking together, and nothing could be shelter. Then would any one having blood, and trying to keep at home with it, run to a sturdy tree and hope to eat his food behind it, and look for a little sun to come and warm his feet in the shelter. And if it did he might strike his breast, and try to think he was warmer.

But when a man came home at night, after long day's labour, knowing that the days increased, and so his care should multiply; still he found enough of light to show him what the day had done against him in his garden. Every ridge of new-turned earth looked like an old man's muscles, honeycombed, and standing out, void of spring, and powdery. Every plant that had rejoiced in passing such a winter now was cowering, turned away, unfit to meet the consequence. Flowing sap had stopped its course; fluted lines showed want of food; and if you pinched the topmost spray, there was no rebound or firmness.

We think a good deal, in a quiet way, when people ask us about them—of some fine, upstanding pear-trees, grafted by my grandfather, who had been very greatly respected. And he got those grafts by sheltering a poor Italian soldier, in the time of James the First, a man who never could do enough to show his grateful memories. How he came to our place is a very difficult story, which I never understood rightly, having heard it from my mother. At any rate, there the pear-trees were, and there they are to this very day; and I wish every one could taste their fruit, old as they are, and rugged.

Now these fine trees had taken advantage of the west winds, and the moisture, and the promise of the spring time, so as to fill the tips of the spray-wood and the rowels all up the branches with a crowd of eager blossom. Not that they were yet in bloom, nor even showing whiteness, only that some of the cones were opening at the side of the cap which pinched them; and there you might count, perhaps, a dozen nobs, like very little buttons, but grooved, and lined, and huddling close, to make room for one another. And among these buds were gray-green blades, scarce bigger than a hair almost, yet curving so as if their purpose was to shield the blossom.

Other of the spur-points, standing on the older wood where the sap was not so eager, had not burst their tunic yet, but were flayed and flaked with light, casting off the husk of brown in three-cornered patches, as I have seen a Scotchman's plaid, or as his leg shows through it. These buds, at a distance, looked as if the sky had been raining cream upon them.

Now all this fair delight to the eyes, and good promise to the palate, was marred and baffled by the wind and cutting of the night-frosts. The opening cones were struck with brown, in between the button buds, and on the scapes that shielded them; while the foot part of the cover hung like rags, peeled back, and quivering. And there the little stalk of each, which might have been a pear, God willing, had a ring around its base, and sought a chance to drop and die. The others which had not opened comb, but only prepared to do it, were a little better off, but still very brown and unkid, and shrivelling in doubt of health, and neither peart nor lusty.

Now this I have not told because I know the way to do it, for that I do not, neither yet have seen a man who did know. It is wonderful how we look at things, and never think to notice them; and I am as bad as anybody, unless the thing to be observed is a dog, or a horse, or a maiden. And the last of those three I look at, somehow, without knowing that I take notice, and greatly afraid to do it, only I knew afterwards (when the time of life was in me), not indeed, what the maiden was like, but how she differed from others.

Yet I have spoken about the spring, and the failure of fair promise, because I took it to my heart as token of what would come to me in the budding of my years and hope. And even then, being much possessed, and full of a foolish melancholy, I felt a sad delight at being doomed to blight and loneliness; not but that I managed still (when mother was urgent upon me) to eat my share of victuals, and cuff a man for laziness, and see that a ploughshare made no leaps, and sleep of a night without dreaming. And my mother half-believing, in her fondness and affection, that what the parish said was true about a mad dog having bitten me, and yet arguing that it must be false (because God would have prevented him), my mother gave me little rest, when I was in the room with her. Not that she worried me with questions, nor openly regarded me with any unusual meaning, but that I knew she was watching slyly whenever I took a spoon up; and every hour or so she managed to place a pan of water by me, quite as if by accident, and sometimes even to spill a little upon my shoe or coat-sleeve. And oft times did I wonder if she realised that it was not mere thought of Lorna, but that she now knew that her son, the one she still called her boy, was now a man in every sense; for she must have known that long time now had I been old enough by dint of law and by nature to test my virility. But Betty Muxworthy was worst; for, having no fear about my health, she made a villainous joke of it, and used to rush into the kitchen, barking like a dog, and panting, exclaiming that I had bitten her, and justice she would have on me, if it cost her a twelvemonth's wages. And she always took care to do this thing just when I had crossed my legs in the corner after supper, and leaned my head against the oven, to begin to think of Lorna.

However, in all things there is comfort, if we do not look too hard for it; and now I had much satisfaction, in my uncouth state, from labouring, by the hour together, at the hedging and the ditching, meeting the bitter wind face to face, feeling my strength increase, and hoping that some one would be proud of it. In the rustling rush of every gust, in the graceful bend of every tree, even in the "lords and ladies," clumped in the scoops of the hedgerow, and most of all in the soft primrose, wrung by the wind, but stealing back, and smiling when the wrath was passed—in this, and many others there was aching ecstasy, delicious pang of Lorna. Lorna, a flower in every sense, her lips the roses about to bloom, soft and moist with dew, her nipples two rosebuds brought to fruition by a tender hand, their tips reaching up to meet the light, and her sex, the most prized flower of all, for only the most worthy of persons to pluck; and I, being of experience in dealings with the earth though not of high birth, could only pray to God that I would be the one always to tend her.

But however cold the weather was, and however hard the wind blew, one thing (more than all the rest) worried and perplexed me. This was, that I could not settle, turn and twist as I might, how soon I ought to go again upon a visit to Glen Doone. For I liked not at all the falseness of it (albeit against murderers), the creeping out of sight, and hiding, and feeling as a spy might. And even more than this, I feared how Lorna might regard it; whether I might seem to her a prone and blunt intruder, a country youth not skilled in manners, as among the quality, even when they rob us. For I was not sure myself, but that it might be very bad manners to go again too early without an invitation; and my hands and face were chapped so badly by the bitter wind, that Lorna might count them unsightly things, and wish to see no more of them.

However, I could not bring myself to consult any one upon this point, at least in our own neighbourhood, nor even to speak of it near home. But the east wind holding through the month, my hands and face growing worse and worse, and it having occurred to me by this time that possibly Lorna might have chaps, if she came abroad at all, and so might like to talk about them and show her little hands to me, I resolved to take another opinion, so far as might be upon this matter, without disclosing the circumstances.

Now the wisest person in all our parts was reckoned to be a certain wise woman, well known all over Exmoor by the name of Mother Melldrum. Her real name was Maple Durham, as I learned long afterwards; and she came of an ancient family, but neither of Devon nor Somerset. Nevertheless she was quite at home with our proper modes of divination; and knowing that we liked them best—as each man does his own religion—she would always practise them for the people of the country. And all the while, she would let us know that she kept a higher and nobler mode for those who looked down upon this one, not having been bred and born to it.

Mother Melldrum had two houses, or rather she had none at all, but two homes wherein to find her, according to the time of year. In summer she lived in a pleasant cave, facing the cool side of the hill, far inland near Hawkridge and close above Tarr-steps, a wonderful crossing of Barle river, made (as everybody knows) by Satan, for a wager. But throughout the winter, she found sea-air agreeable, and a place where things could be had on credit, and more occasion of talking. Not but what she could have credit (for every one was afraid of her) in the neighbourhood of Tarr-steps; only there was no one handy owning things worth taking.

Therefore, at the fall of the leaf, when the woods grew damp and irksome, the wise woman always set her face to the warmer cliffs of the Channel; where shelter was, and dry fern bedding, and folk to be seen in the distance, from a bank upon which the sun shone. And there, as I knew from our John Fry (who had been to her about rheumatism, and sheep possessed with an evil spirit, and warts on the hand of his son, young John), any one who chose might find her, towards the close of a winter day, gathering sticks and brown fern for fuel, and talking to herself the while, in a hollow stretch behind the cliffs; which foreigners, who come and go without seeing much of Exmoor, have called the Valley of Rocks.

This valley, or goyal, as we term it, being small for a valley, lies to the west of Linton, about a mile from the town perhaps, and away towards Ley Manor. Our homefolk always call it the Danes, or the Denes, which is no more, they tell me, than a hollow place, even as the word "den" is. However, let that pass, for I know very little about it; but the place itself is a pretty one, though nothing to frighten anybody, unless he hath lived in a gallipot. It is a green rough-sided hollow, bending at the middle, touched with stone at either crest, and dotted here and there with slabs in and out the brambles. On the right hand is an upward crag, called by some the Castle, easy enough to scale, and giving great view of the Channel. Facing this, from the inland side and the elbow of the valley, a queer old pile of rock arises, bold behind one another, and quite enough to affright a man, if it only were ten times larger. This is called the Devil's Cheese-ring, or the Devil's Cheese-knife, which mean the same thing, as our fathers were used to eat their cheese from a scoop; and perhaps in old time the upmost rock (which has fallen away since I knew it) was like to such an implement, if Satan eat cheese untoasted.

But all the middle of this valley was a place to rest in; to sit and think that troubles were not, if we would not make them. To know the sea outside the hills, but never to behold it; only by the sound of waves to pity sailors labouring. Then to watch the sheltered sun, coming warmly round the turn, like a guest expected, full of gentle glow and gladness, casting shadow far away as a thing to hug itself, and awakening life from dew, and hope from every spreading bud. And then to fall asleep and dream that the fern was all asparagus.

Alas, I was too young in those days much to care for creature comforts, or to let pure palate have things that would improve it. Anything went down with me, as it does with most of us. Too late we know the good from bad; the knowledge is no pleasure then; being memory's medicine rather than the wine of hope.

Now Mother Melldrum kept her winter in this vale of rocks, sheltering from the wind and rain within the Devil's Cheese-ring, which added greatly to her fame because all else, for miles around, were afraid to go near it after dark, or even on a gloomy day. Under eaves of lichened rock she had a winding passage, which none that ever I knew of durst enter but herself. And to this place I went to seek her, in spite of all misgivings, upon a Sunday in Lenten season, when the sheep were folded.

Our parson (as if he had known my intent) had preached a beautiful sermon about the Witch of Endor, and the perils of them that meddle wantonly with the unseen Powers; and therein he referred especially to the strange noise in the neighbourhood, and upbraided us for want of faith, and many other backslidings. We listened to him very earnestly, for we like to hear from our betters about things that are beyond us, and to be roused up now and then, like sheep with a good dog after them, who can pull some wool without biting. Nevertheless we could not see how our want of faith could have made that noise, especially at night time, notwithstanding which we believed it, and hoped to do a little better.

And so we all came home from church; and most of the people dined with us, as they always do on Sundays, because of the distance to go home, with only words inside them. The parson always sat next to mother, and was to be seen, when he thought no one else was taking notice, to place his hand gently on her knee in a most affectionate manner; and she, though the very model of propriety and loath to encourage gossip, did not remove his smooth hand unsullied by the field work of others around here; indeed Lizzie said she had seen his hand slip up to the top of mother's thighs and dig his stubby fingers into her, to which of course Annie and I gave no credence, for Lizzie was prone to exaggeration (though we had heard of such proclivities of the parson; and such thought may pervert Eliza's years), and we did not believe mother would entertain such attention from any man other than our dear father. The parson was afraid that he might have vexed us, and would not have the best piece of meat, according to his custom. But soon we put him at his ease, and showed him we were proud of him (saying not of Lizzie's imaginings, for such they were); and then he made no more to do, but accepted the best of the sirloin.

CHAPTER XVIII

WITCHERY LEADS TO WITCHCRAFT

Although well-nigh the end of March, the wind blew wild and piercing, as I went on foot that afternoon to Mother Melldrum's dwelling. It was safer not to take a horse, lest (if anything vexed her) she should put a spell upon him; as had been done to Farmer Snowe's stable by the wise woman of Simonsbath.

The sun was low on the edge of the hills by the time I entered the valley, for I could not leave home till the cattle were tended, and the distance was seven miles or more. The shadows of rocks fell far and deep, and the brown dead fern was fluttering, and brambles with their sere leaves hanging swayed their tatters to and fro, with a red look on them. In patches underneath the crags, a few wild goats were browsing; then they tossed their horns, and fled, and leaped on ledges, and stared at me. Moreover, the sound of the sea came up, and went the length of the valley, and there it lapped on a butt of rocks, and murmured like a shell.

Taking things one with another, and feeling all the lonesomeness, and having no stick with me, I was much inclined to go briskly back, and come at a better season. And when I beheld a tall grey shape, of something or another, moving at the lower end of the valley, where the shade was, it gave me such a stroke of fear, after many others, that my thumb which lay in mother's Bible (brought in my big pocket for the sake of safety) shook so much that it came out, and I could not get it in again. "This serves me right," I said to myself, "for tampering with Beelzebub. Oh that I had listened to parson!"

And thereupon I struck aside; not liking to run away quite, as some people might call it; but seeking to look like a wanderer who was come to see the valley, and had seen almost enough of it. Herein I should have succeeded, and gone home, and then been angry at my want of courage, but that on the very turn and bending of my footsteps, the woman in the distance lifted up her staff to me, so that I was bound to stop.

And now, being brought face to face, by the will of God (as one might say) with anything that might come of it, I kept myself quite straight and stiff, and thrust away all white feather, trusting in my Bible still, hoping that it would protect me, though I had disobeyed it. But upon that remembrance, my conscience took me by the leg, so that I could not go forward.

All this while, the fearful woman was coming near and more near to me; and I was glad to sit down on a rock because my knees were shaking so. I tried to think of many things, but none of them would come to me; and I could not take my eyes away, though I prayed God to be near me.

But when she was come so nigh to me that I could descry her features, there was something in her countenance that made me not dislike her. She looked as if she had been visited by many troubles, and had felt them one by one, yet held enough of kindly nature still to grieve for others. Long white hair, on either side, was falling down below her chin; and through her wrinkles clear bright eyes seemed to spread themselves upon me. Though I had plenty of time to think, I was taken by surprise no less, and unable to say anything; yet eager to hear the silence broken, and longing for a noise or two.

"Thou art not come to me," she said, looking through my simple face, as if it were but glass, "to be struck for bone-shave, nor to be blessed for barn-gun. Give me forth thy hand, John Ridd; and tell why thou art come to me."

But I was so much amazed at her knowing my name and all about me, that I feared to place my hand in her power, or even my tongue by speaking.

"Have no fear of me, my son; I have no gift to harm thee; and if I had, it should be idle. Now, if thou hast any wit, tell me why I love thee."

"I never had any wit, mother," I answered in our Devonshire way; "and never set eyes on thee before, to the furthest of my knowledge."

"And yet I know thee as well, John, as if thou wert my grandson. Remember you the old Oare oak, and the bog at the head of Exe, and the child who would have died there, but for thy strength and courage, and most of all thy kindness? That was my granddaughter, John; and all I have on earth to love."

Now that she came to speak of it, with the place and that, so clearly, I remembered all about it (a thing that happened last August), and thought how stupid I must have been not to learn more of the little girl who had fallen into the black pit, with a basketful of whortleberries, and who might have been gulfed if her little dog had not spied me in the distance. I carried her on my back to mother; and then we dressed her all anew, and took her where she ordered us; but she did not tell us who she was, nor anything more than her Christian name, and that she was eight years old, and fond of fried batatas. And we did not seek to ask her more; as our manner is with visitors.

But thinking of this little story, and seeing how she looked at me, I lost my fear of Mother Melldrum, and began to like her; partly because I had helped her grandchild, and partly that if she were so wise, no need would have been for me to save the little thing from drowning. Her grandchild was the offspring of the daughter Mother Melldrum had borne; with whom, though no one knew for sure, it were rumoured (and widely believed by those on both sides of the moors) that it had been a man of the cloth.

It is widely known—and this is not a mere gossiping—that these men, even Papist priests sworn to celibacy, might regard as a praxis to their work the taste of forbidden fruit, though they may well in their wisdom quicken their fancy without entering the woman. Whilst decrying witches and their ways from the pulpit, he had, it was said, oft visited her to exorcise any demons in her making.

Some told of how she had invited him unto her cave and practised her dark arts on him, unwilling and by now tied by the hands and feet; though how this might have taken place, even with such a man of puny strength (as are most of our sacerdotal gentlemen, often corpulent but not solidified by hard labours), against any woman, I know not.

John Fry had spoken of one of his acquaintance: a fellow labourer on the land making his way home from the inn, who had stumbled upon Mother Melldrum and the cleric (I shall, for the sake of propriety, though his own behaviour may not have been morally correct and proper given his calling, leave him unnamed). Methinks it be that this fellow had set out to cozen John Fry, or by dint of imagination well-entertained through ale warming his brain, he persuaded himself of the veracity of his story.

Though it were indeed true that the cleric be bound with rope better used to tether cattle, he was by no means an unwilling partner (or so sayeth this fellow). Standing naked, silhouetted by the moonlight (which had been serving well as a lanthorn for the labourer, and so his approach was neither seen nor sensed by the hag transcending the laws of nature), the outline of his body carved against the sky and his silvered semi-upstanding prick had caused this labourer to spur his sobriety and observe.

Urging her to do with him as she wished, he then lowered himself to the ground (for he was bound only unto himself though not, it may be argued, to God that night, and not to any fixed stake), lying himself prone, his bound hands behind him in the indentation of the small of his back. It was then that our prurient observer saw that the gentleman (if that be his epithet) in question was bound about the eyes with a strip of cloth.

Lighting a candle and not needing to shield it with her hand, so still and clear was the night, the crone (as he, the observer, called her) stood above him with a smile skimming her wild eyes, glistening in the flickering flame, and, placing the candle secure against some prop, knelt by his side to smear his body with an oil; his skin now so gliddery that her hands would continue without interruption over his back and up and down the length of his spine. His head turned to the side, he uttered a groan laced with a hissing exhalation as each time her hands would smooth over his buttocks and, but a few times (and there was to be no pattern or form to it), she drizzled more oil into her hands, palms rubbing over each other as though in relishment, and trailed her lengthy, bony fingers over his stones touching the ground between his legs. And with each of her ventures there, his breathing caught ragged and his body would writhe on the ground, the ample cheeks of his backside clenched in response to her touch.

Our observer's eyes sprang wider as, with no mention afore doing so, she raised her hand in the air so as to bring it down to smite his buttocks, delivering her blow with the palm of her hand and lifting it again as sharply as having touched a burning cinder. "Such exquisite pain," he moaned. "Again please of haste do it again," he begged. She raised her hand once more but stilled at the top of the arc whilst he begged further, his anticipation intensifying his excitement, not knowing exactly when or where she would deliver her next slap to him. Once again she rained a blow upon him, his whole body quivering in response. She rubbed at him gently as if to caress and soothe the ruddled buttocks, then with change of manner taking even the observer in surprise, she scolded him further with the weight of her hand and he shouted out, as though a cry (like that of a wild animal) were snared in his throat. With regular rhythm she then delivered a good baker's dozen or so strikes to him, so sharp that his body lifted from the ground with each one, as he (being a man of fancy words in the pulpit and so well able to describe) shouted out into the night (thinking no one around to hear him): "Such exquisite pain! It seeps its way into my very soul! 'Tis is no more than I deserve! 'Tis in your power to make me accept this! I am wretched—nay, I am fulfilled—consider your self and not me at all. I would fain die, that I might savour this esoteric delight! My blood flames at this arousal!"

And when she chose to desist, he lay groaning on the ground, still but for his cheeks twitching their wretched satisfaction. With her jaw set hard, lips in some tight smirk, and a deftness of hand, she (still on her knees by his side) turned him to lie on his back, his hands now secure below his body against the ground, and such was the mutual relish of this torture that his prick lay large over his belly, having entertained his arousal. As if in high dudgeon at being moved, he asked, some wariness in the tone: "Why have you turned me so, for I was indeed in some heavenly state afore? What pleasures will you dispense to me now?" Eliciting but a menacing quiet (and our observer related that a briar full of thorns seemed to prick the skin on his own head), he whimpered in a voice no more than a whisper carried in the still air, "I know not what darkness you have in store for me of this eve and I have indeed a greed for more, but be gentle of now, I beseech you, though your strikes be of such kind fault."

From its cradling place she took up the candle and held it over his body, silent, waiting, waiting, until allowing the wax from the mutton tallow to dribble, amongst other places, onto his nipples and balls of skin. Afore the first drop hit his body she incanted over him: "Know ye not, nor sight, nor hand; to place of my choosing it will land." With eyes bound shut he could not have known what was to befall, yet appeared not displeased: "Perform your superior devotions upon me." Each droplet of wax, hitting his skin and puddling slightly as it cooled, served to heat his ardour further; his breath quickening as he inhaled sharply through his nostrils and held the air for a second before blowing out through his mouth; his face creased as in pain, though "Yes, oh yes" was his panting plea to her. She took one of her fingers to his mouth and he sucked hard on it, afore she withdrew it and traced the moist finger gently around each circlet of wax now hardened. "Such glorious tickling," he moaned, his stomach rippling in pleasure.

"Save your breath on such bilge and prepare to consider seriously with yourself what I may do next," said she, a snarl in her voice, "and not seeing will bring you to the greatest of anticipation."

At this, his erection burst higher as a plant in spring, the blood having forsaken his cheeks for his prick, and his head tipped back, lips parted, teeth biting down on the bottom lip. She leaned over to straddle him, holding herself just at his tip so that he could feel her, and as he raised his hips to enter himself into her, she moved just far enough away to tantalise. "No, leave off your thrusting; it is I who will decide," she chid, prolonging his sweet agony until she lowered herself onto his awaiting fullness, steadying it with one hand to guide it swiftly within her. (Our prying observer had learned of a posturing previously not known to him, for she was not facing the man surrendered of his control, but away from him, her buttocks in his full view had not he been blindfolded.) She moved quickly and surely, sinking deep and leaning forward, holding at his knees, her breasts pendulous and sweeping over his legs, swaying from side to side as a ship riding the waves of pleasure afore sailing to port.

And at the time of his trembling spend she reached forward between his legs to rip off the wax (now hardened in the night air) from his bollocks. Crying out to God in reverence of the pain, his voice pierced the air, though naught but the owls and our observer may have had their ears so assaulted.

I could say a hundred things more to this assignation as I had been told, but suffice to say that each had been pleasured, though they knew not that all had been seen; which makes me surer that

Mother Melldrum is not of so great witchery, and this gentleman be of so little religion. The observer swore on his child's life that his tale was not taradiddle, and that as this couple parted, each traced the other's jaw tenderly with their fingertips and shared a kiss becoming of a coy couple with genuine affection, and he telling her that he would pray for the safety of her soul.

And little under a year later, Mother Melldrum gave birth to a child, said to be the result of her sin that night of a full moon (certain of mischief following such swiving). And with no husband to throw a cloak over the origins of the infant, she embraced an even more torpid life, shunning others and now decried by that most pediculous, pious man as one of whom others should be afraid.

But this tale being of that grandchild, therefore I stood up and said, though scarcely yet established in my power against hers,—

"Good mother, the shoe she lost was in the mire, and not with us. And we could not match it, although we gave her a pair of sister Lizzie's."

"My son, what care I for her shoe? How simple thou art, and foolish! according to the thoughts of some. Now tell me, for thou canst not lie, what has brought thee to me."

Being so ashamed and bashful, I was half-inclined to tell her a lie, until she said that I could not do it; and then I knew that I could not.

"I am come to know," I said, looking at a rock the while, to keep my voice from shaking, "when I may go to see Lorna Doone."

No more could I say, though my mind was charged to ask fifty other questions. But although I looked away, it was plain that I had asked enough. I felt that the wise woman gazed at me in wrath as well as sorrow; and then I grew angry that any one should seem to make light of Lorna.

"John Ridd," said the woman, observing this (for now I faced her bravely), "of whom art thou speaking? Is it a child of the men who slew your father?"

"I cannot tell, mother. How should I know? And what is that to thee?"

"It is something to thy mother, John, and something to thyself, I trow; and nothing worse could befall thee."

I waited for her to speak again, because she had spoken so sadly that it took my breath away.

"John Ridd, if thou hast any value for thy body or thy soul, thy mother, or thy father's name, have nought to do with any Doone."

She gazed at me in earnest so, and raised her voice in saying it, until the whole valley, curving like a great bell, echoed "Doone," that it seemed to me my heart was gone for every one and everything. If it were God's will for me to have no more of Lorna, let a sign come out of the rocks, and I would try to believe it. But no sign came, and I turned to the woman, and longed that she had been a man.

"You poor thing, with bones and blades, pails of water, and door-keys, what know you about the destiny of a maiden such as Lorna? Chilblains you may treat, and bone-shave, ringworm, and the scaldings; even scabby sheep may limp the better for your strikings. John the Baptist and his cousins, with the wool and hyssop, are for mares, and ailing dogs, and fowls that have the jaundice. Look at me now, Mother Melldrum, am I like a fool?"

"That thou art, my son. Alas that it were any other! Now behold the end of that; John Ridd, mark the end of it."

She pointed to the castle-rock, where upon a narrow shelf, betwixt us and the coming stars, a bitter fight was raging. A fine fat sheep, with an honest face, had clomb up very carefully to browse on a bit of juicy grass, now the dew of the land was upon it. To him, from an upper crag, a lean black goat came hurrying, with leaps, and skirmish of the horns, and an angry noise in his nostrils. The goat had grazed the place before, to the utmost of his liking, cropping in and out with jerks, as their manner is of feeding. Nevertheless he fell on the sheep with fury and great malice.

The simple wether was much inclined to retire from the contest, but looked around in vain for any way to peace and comfort. His enemy stood between him and the last leap he had taken; there was nothing left him but to fight, or be hurled into the sea, five hundred feet below.

"Lie down, lie down!" I shouted to him, as if he were a dog, for I had seen a battle like this before, and knew that the sheep had no chance of life except from his greater weight, and the difficulty of moving him.

"Lie down, lie down, John Ridd!" cried Mother Melldrum, mocking me, but without a sign of smiling.

The poor sheep turned, upon my voice, and looked at me so piteously that I could look no longer; but ran with all my speed to try and save him from the combat. He saw that I could not be in time, for the goat was bucking to leap at him, and so the good wether stooped his forehead, with the harmless horns curling aside of it; and the goat flung his heels up, and rushed at him, with quick sharp jumps and tricks of movement, and the points of his long horns always foremost, and his little scut cocked like a gun-hammer.

As I ran up the steep of the rock, I could not see what they were doing, but the sheep must have fought very bravely at last, and yielded his ground quite slowly, and I hoped almost to save him. But just as my head topped the platform of rock, I saw him flung from it backward, with a sad low moan and a gurgle. His body made quite a short noise in the air, like a bucket thrown down a well shaft, and I could not tell when it struck the water, except by the echo among the rocks. So wroth was I with the goat at the moment (being somewhat scant of breath and unable to consider), that I caught him by the right hind-leg, before he could turn from his victory, and hurled him after the sheep, to learn how he liked his own compulsion.

CHAPTER XIX

ANOTHER DANGEROUS INTERVIEW

Although I left the Denes at once, having little heart for further questions of the wise woman, and being afraid to visit her house under the Devil's Cheese-ring (to which she kindly invited me), and although I ran most part of the way, it was very late for farmhouse time upon a Sunday evening before I was back at Plover's Barrows. My mother had great desire to know all about the matter; but I could not reconcile it with my respect so to frighten her. Therefore I tried to sleep it off, keeping my own counsel; and when that proved of no avail, I strove to work it away, it might be, by heavy outdoor labour, and weariness, and good feeding. These indeed had some effect, and helped to pass a week or two, with more pain of hand than heart to me.

But when the weather changed in earnest, and the frost was gone, and the south-west wind blew softly, and the lambs were at play with the daisies, it was more than I could do to keep from thought of Lorna. For now the fields were spread with growth, and the waters clad with sunshine, and light and shadow, step by step, wandered over the furzy cleves. All the sides of the hilly wood were gathered in and out with green, silver-grey, or russet points, according to the several manner of the trees beginning. And if one stood beneath an elm, with any heart to look at it, lo! all the ground was strewn with flakes (too small to know their meaning), and all the sprays above were rasped and trembling with a redness. And so I stopped beneath the tree, and carved L.D. upon it, and wondered at the buds of thought that seemed to swell inside me.

The upshot of it all was this, that as no Lorna came to me, except in dreams or fancy, and as my life was not worth living without constant sign of her, forth I must again to find her, and say more than a man can tell. Therefore, without waiting longer for the moving of the spring, dressed I was in grand attire (so far as I had gotten it), and thinking my appearance good, although with doubts about it (being forced to dress in the hay-tallat), round the corner of the wood-stack went I very knowingly—for Lizzie's eyes were wondrous sharp—and then I was sure of meeting none who would care or dare to speak of me.

It lay upon my conscience often that I had not made dear Annie secret to this history; although in all things I could trust her, and she loved me like a lamb. Many and many a time I tried, and more than once began the thing; but there came a dryness in my throat, and a knocking under the roof of my mouth, and a longing to put it off again, as perhaps might be the wisest. And then I would remember too that I had no right to speak of Lorna as if she were common property.

This time I longed to take my gun, and was half resolved to do so; because it seemed so hard a thing to be shot at and have no chance of shooting; but when I came to remember the steepness and the slippery nature of the waterslide, there seemed but little likelihood of keeping dry the powder. Therefore I was armed with nothing but a good stout holly staff, seasoned well for many a winter in our back-kitchen chimney.

Although my heart was leaping high with the prospect of some adventure, and the fear of meeting Lorna, I could not but be gladdened by the softness of the weather, and the welcome way of everything. There was that power all round, that power and that goodness, which make us come, as it were, outside our bodily selves, to share them. Over and beside us breathes the joy of hope and promise; under foot are troubles past; in the distance bowering newness tempts us ever forward. We quicken with largesse of life, and spring with vivid mystery.

And, in good sooth, I had to spring, and no mystery about it, ere ever I got to the top of the rift leading into Doone-glade. For the stream was rushing down in strength, and raving at every corner; a mort of rain having fallen last night and no wind come to wipe it. However, I reached the head ere dark with more difficulty than danger, and sat in a place which comforted my back and legs desirably.

Hereupon I grew so happy at being on dry land again, and come to look for Lorna, with pretty trees around me, that what did I do but fall asleep with the holly-stick in front of me, and my best coat sunk in a bed of moss, with water and wood-sorrel. Mayhap I had not done so, nor yet enjoyed the spring so much, if so be I had not taken three parts of a gallon of cider at home, at Plover's Barrows, because of the lowness and sinking ever since I met Mother Melldrum.

There was a little runnel going softly down beside me, falling from the upper rock by the means of moss and grass, as if it feared to make a noise, and had a mother sleeping. Now and then it seemed to stop, in fear of its own dropping, and wait for some orders; and the blades of grass that straightened to it turned their points a little way, and offered their allegiance to wind instead of water. Yet before their carkled edges bent more than a driven saw, down the water came again with heavy drops and pats of running, and bright anger at neglect.

This was very pleasant to me, now and then, to gaze at, blinking as the water blinked, and falling back to sleep again. Suddenly my sleep was broken by a shade cast over me; between me and the low sunlight Lorna Doone was standing.

"Master Ridd, are you mad?" she said, and took my hand to move me.

"Not mad, but half asleep," I answered, feigning not to notice her, that so she might keep hold of me.

"Come away, come away, if you care for life. The patrol will be here directly. Be quick, Master Ridd, let me hide thee."

"I will not stir a step," said I, though being in the greatest fright that might be well imagined, "unless you call me 'John.'"

"Well, John, then—Master John Ridd, be quick, if you have any to care for you."

"I have many that care for me," I said, just to let her know; "and I will follow you, Mistress Lorna, albeit without any hurry, unless there be peril to more than me."

Without another word she led me, though with many timid glances towards the upper valley, to, and into, her little bower, where the inlet through the rock was. I am almost sure that I spoke before (though I cannot now go seek for it, and my memory is but a worn-out tub) of a certain deep and perilous pit, in which I was like to drown myself through hurry and fright. And even then I wondered greatly, and was vexed with Lorna for sending me in that heedless manner into such an entrance. But now it was clear that she had been right and the fault mine own entirely; for the entrance to the pit was only to be found by seeking it. Inside the niche of native stone, the plainest thing of all to see, at any rate by day light, was the stairway hewn from rock, and leading up the mountain, by means of which I had escaped, as before related. To the right side of this was the mouth of the pit, still looking very formidable; though Lorna laughed at my fear of it, for she drew her water thence. But on the left was a narrow crevice, very difficult to espy, and having a sweep of grey ivy laid, like a slouching beaver, over it. A man here coming from the brightness of the outer air, with eyes dazed by the twilight, would never think of seeing this and following it to its meaning.

Lorna raised the screen for me, but I had much ado to pass, on account of bulk and stature. Instead of being proud of my size (as it seemed to me she ought to be and indeed would be) Lorna laughed so quietly that I was ready to knock my head or elbows against anything, and say no more about it. However, I got through at last without a word of compliment, and broke into the pleasant room, the lone retreat of Lorna.

The chamber was of unhewn rock, round, as near as might be, eighteen or twenty feet across, and gay with rich variety of fern and moss and lichen. The fern was in its winter still, or coiling for the spring-tide; but moss was in abundant life, some feathering, and some gobleted, and some with fringe of red to it. Overhead there was no ceiling but the sky itself, flaked with little clouds of April whitely wandering over it. The floor was made of soft low grass, mixed with moss and primroses; and in a niche of shelter moved the delicate wood-sorrel. Here and there, around the sides, were "chairs of living stone," as some Latin writer says, whose name has quite escaped me; and in the midst a tiny spring arose, with crystal beads in it, and a soft voice as of a laughing dream, and dimples like a sleeping babe. Then, after going round a little, with surprise of daylight, the water overwelled the edge, and softly went through lines of light to shadows and an untold bourne.

While I was gazing at all these things with wonder and some sadness, Lorna turned upon me lightly (as her manner was) and said,—

"Where are the new-laid eggs, Master Ridd? Or hath blue hen ceased laying?"

I did not altogether like the way in which she said it, with a sort of dialect, as if my speech could be laughed at.

"Here be some," I answered, speaking as if in spite of her. "I would have brought thee twice as many, but that I feared to crush them in the narrow ways, Mistress Lorna."

And so I laid her out two dozen upon the moss of the rock-ledge, unwinding the wisp of hay from each as it came safe out of my pocket. Lorna looked with growing wonder, as I added one to one; and when I had placed them side by side, and bidden her now to tell them, to my amazement what did she do but burst into a flood of tears.

"What have I done?" I asked, with shame, scarce daring even to look at her, because her grief was not like Annie's—a thing that could be coaxed away, and left a joy in going—"oh, what have I done to vex you so?"

"It is nothing done by you, Master Ridd," she answered, very proudly, as if nought I did could matter; "it is only something that comes upon me with the scent of the pure true clover-hay. Moreover, you have been too kind; and I am not used to kindness."

Some sort of awkwardness was on me, at her words and weeping, as if I would like to say something, but feared to make things worse perhaps than they were already. Therefore I abstained from speech, as I would in my own pain. And as it happened, this was the way to make her tell me more about it. Not that I was curious, beyond what pity urged me and the strange affairs around her; and now I gazed upon the floor, lest I should seem to watch her; but none the less for that I knew all that she was doing.

Lorna went a little way, as if she would not think of me nor care for one so careless; and all my heart gave a sudden jump, to go like a mad thing after her; until she turned of her own accord, and with a little sigh came back to me. Her eyes were soft with trouble's shadow, and the proud lift of her neck was gone, and beauty's vanity borne down by woman's want of sustenance.

"Master Ridd," she said in the softest voice that ever flowed between two lips, "have I done aught to offend you?"

Hereupon an unbidden hardness sprang within me which I hoped that she could not see beneath my hosen, and it went hard with me, not to catch her up and kiss her, in the manner in which she was looking; only it smote me suddenly that this would be a low advantage of her trust and helplessness. She seemed to know what I would be at, and to doubt very greatly about it, whether she might permit the usage. All sorts of things went through my head, as I made myself look away from her, for fear of being tempted beyond what I could bear. And the upshot of it was that I said, within my heart and through it, "John Ridd, be on thy very best manners with this lonely maiden."

Lorna liked me all the better for my good forbearance; because she did not love me yet, and had not thought about it; at least so far as I knew. And though her eyes were so beauteous, so very soft and kindly, there was (to my apprehension) some great power in them, as if she would not have a thing, unless her judgment leaped with it.

But now her judgment leaped with me, because I had behaved so well; and being of quick urgent nature—such as I delight in, for the change from mine own slowness—she, without any let or hindrance, sitting over against me, now raising and now dropping fringe over those sweet eyes that were the road-lights of her tongue, Lorna told me all about everything I wished to know, every little thing she knew, except indeed that point of points, how Master Ridd stood with her.

Although it wearied me no whit, it might be wearisome for folk who cannot look at Lorna, to hear the story all in speech, exactly as she told it; therefore let me put it shortly, to the best of my remembrance.

Nay, pardon me, whosoever thou art, for seeming fickle and rude to thee; I have tried to do as first proposed, to tell the tale in my own words, as of another's fortune. But, lo! I was beset at once with many heavy obstacles, which grew as I went onward, until I knew not where I was, and mingled past and present. And two of these difficulties only were enough to stop me; the one that I must coldly speak without the force of pity, the other that I, off and on, confused myself with Lorna, as might be well expected.

Therefore let her tell the story, with her own sweet voice and manner; and if ye find it wearisome, seek in yourselves the weariness.

CHAPTER XX

LORNA BEGINS HER STORY

"I cannot go through all my thoughts so as to make them clear to you, nor have I ever dwelt on things, to shape a story of them. I know not where the beginning was, nor where the middle ought to be, nor even how at the present time I feel, or think, or ought to think. If I look for help to those around me, who should tell me right and wrong (being older and much wiser), I meet sometimes with laughter, and at other times with anger.

"There are but two in the world who ever listen and try to help me; one of them is my grandfather, and the other is a man of wisdom, whom we call the Counsellor. My grandfather, Sir Ensor Doone, is very old and harsh of manner (except indeed to me); he seems to know what is right and wrong, but not to want to think of it. The Counsellor, on the other hand, though full of life and subtleties, treats my questions as of play, and not gravely worth his while to answer, unless he can make wit of them.

"And among the women there are none with whom I can hold converse, since my Aunt Sabina died, who took such pains to teach me. She was a lady of high repute and lofty ways, and learning, but grieved and harassed more and more by the coarseness, and the violence, and the ignorance around her. In vain she strove, from year to year, to make the young men hearken, to teach them what became their birth, and give them sense of honour. It was her favourite word, poor thing! and they called her 'Old Aunt Honour.' Very often she used to say that I was her only comfort, and I am sure she was my only one; and when she died it was more to me than if I had lost a mother.

"For I have no remembrance now of father or of mother, although they say that my father was the eldest son of Sir Ensor Doone, and the bravest and the best of them. And so they call me heiress to this little realm of violence; and in sorry sport sometimes, I am their Princess or their Queen.

"Many people living here, as I am forced to do, would perhaps be very happy, and perhaps I ought to be so. We have a beauteous valley, sheltered from the cold of winter and power of the summer sun, untroubled also by the storms and mists that veil the mountains; although I must acknowledge that it is apt to rain too often. The grass moreover is so fresh, and the brook so bright and lively, and flowers of so many hues come after one another that no one need be dull, if only left alone with them.

"And so in the early days perhaps, when morning breathes around me, and the sun is going upward, and light is playing everywhere, I am not so far beside them all as to live in shadow. But when the evening gathers down, and the sky is spread with sadness, and the day has spent itself; then a cloud of lonely trouble falls, like night, upon me. I cannot see the things I quest for of a world beyond me; I cannot join the peace and quiet of the depth above me; neither have I any pleasure in the brightness of the stars.

"What I want to know is something none of them can tell me—what am I, and why set here, and when shall I be with them? I see that you are surprised a little at this my curiosity. Perhaps such questions never spring in any wholesome spirit. But they are in the depths of mine, and I cannot be quit of them.

"Meantime, all around me is violence and robbery, coarse delight and savage pain, reckless joke and hopeless death. Is it any wonder that I cannot sink with these, that I cannot so forget my soul, as to live the life of brutes, and die the death more horrible because it dreams of waking? There is none to lead me forward, there is none to teach me right; young as I am, I live beneath a curse that lasts for ever."

Here Lorna broke down for awhile, and cried so very piteously, that doubting of my knowledge, and of any power to comfort, I did my best to hold my peace, and tried to look very cheerful. Then thinking that might be bad manners, I went to wipe her eyes for her.

"Master Ridd," she began again, "I am both ashamed and vexed at my own folly. But you, who have a mother, who thinks (you say) so much of you, and sisters, and a quiet home; you cannot tell (it is not likely) what a lonely nature is. How it leaps in mirth sometimes, with only heaven touching it; and how it falls away desponding, when the dreary weight creeps on.

"It does not happen many times that I give way like this; more shame now to do so, when I ought to entertain you. Sometimes I am so full of anger, that I dare not trust to speech, at things they cannot hide from me; and perhaps you would be much surprised that reckless men would care so much to elude a girl's knowledge. They used to boast to Aunt Sabina of pillage and of cruelty, on purpose to enrage her; but they never boast to me. It even makes me smile sometimes to see how awkwardly they come and offer for temptation to me shining packets, half concealed, of ornaments and finery, of rings, or chains, or jewels, lately belonging to other people.

"But when I try to search the past, to get a sense of what befell me ere my own perception formed; to feel back for the lines of childhood, as a trace of gossamer, then I only know that nought lives longer than God wills it. So may after sin go by, for we are children always, as the Counsellor has told me: so may we, beyond the clouds, seek this infancy of life, and never find its memory.

"But I am talking now of things which never come across me when any work is toward. It might have been a good thing for me to have had a father to beat these rovings out of me; or a mother to make a home, and teach me how to manage it. For, being left with none—I think; and nothing ever comes of it. Nothing, I mean, which I can grasp and have with any surety; nothing but faint images, and wonderment, and wandering. But often, when I am neither searching back into remembrance, nor asking of my parents, but occupied by trifles, something like a sign, or message, or a token of some meaning, seems to glance upon me. Whether from the rustling wind, or sound of distant music, or the singing of a bird, like the sun on snow it strikes me with a pain of pleasure.

"And often when I wake at night, and listen to the silence, or wander far from people in the grayness of the evening, or stand and look at quiet water having shadows over it, some vague image seems to hover on the skirt of vision, ever changing place and outline, ever flitting as I follow. This so moves and hurries me, in the eagerness and longing, that straightway all my chance is lost; and memory, scared like a wild bird, flies. Or am I as a child perhaps, chasing a flown cageling, who among the branches free plays and peeps at the offered cage (as a home not to be urged on him), and means to take his time of coming, if he comes at all?

"Often too I wonder at the odds of fortune, which made me (helpless as I am, and fond of peace and reading) the heiress of this mad domain, the sanctuary of unholiness. It is not likely that I shall have much power of authority; and yet the Counsellor creeps up to be my Lord of the Treasury; and his son aspires to my hand, as of a Royal alliance. Well, 'honour among thieves,' they say; and mine is the first honour: although among decent folk perhaps, honesty is better.

"We should not be so quiet here, and safe from interruption; but that I have begged one privilege rather than commanded it. This was that the lower end, just this narrowing of the valley, where it is most hard to come at, might be looked upon as mine, except for purposes of guard. Therefore none beside the sentries ever trespass on me here, unless it be my grandfather, or the Counsellor or Carver.

"By your face, Master Ridd, I see that you have heard of Carver Doone. For strength and courage and resource he bears the first repute among us, as might well be expected from the son of the Counsellor. But he differs from his father, in being very hot and savage, and quite free from argument. The Counsellor, who is my uncle, gives his son the best advice; commending all the virtues, with eloquence and wisdom; yet himself abstaining from them accurately and impartially.

"You must be tired of this story, and the time I take to think, and the weakness of my telling; but my life from day to day shows so little variance. Among the riders there is none whose safe return I watch for—I mean none more than other—and indeed there seems no risk, all are now so feared of us. Neither of the old men is there whom I can revere or love (except alone my grandfather, whom I love with trembling); neither of the women any whom I like to deal with, unless it be a little maiden whom I saved from starving.

"A little Cornish girl she is, and shaped in western manner, not so very much less in width than if you take her lengthwise. Her father seems to have been a miner, a Cornishman (as she declares) of more than average excellence, and better than any two men to be found in Devonshire, or any four in Somerset. Very few things can have been beyond his power of performance, and yet he left his daughter to starve upon a peat-rick. She does not know how this was done, and looks upon it as a mystery, the meaning of which will some day be clear, and redound to her father's honour. His name was Simon Carfax, and he came as the captain of a gang from one of the Cornish stannaries. Gwenny Carfax, my young maid, well remembers how her father was brought up from Cornwall. Her mother had been buried, just a week or so before; and he was sad about it, and had been off his work, and was ready for another job. Then people came to him by night, and said that he must want a change, and everybody lost their wives, and work was the way to mend it. So what with grief, and over-thought, and the inside of a square bottle, Gwenny says they brought him off, to become a mighty captain, and choose the country round. The last she saw of him was this, that he went down a ladder somewhere on the wilds of Exmoor, leaving her with bread and cheese, and his travelling-hat to see to. And from that day to this he never came above the ground again; so far as we can hear of.

"But Gwenny, holding to his hat, and having eaten the bread and cheese (when he came no more to help her), dwelt three days near the mouth of the hole; and then it was closed over, the while that she was sleeping. With weakness and with want of food, she lost herself distressfully, and went away for miles or more, and lay upon a peat-rick, to die before the ravens.

"That very day I chanced to return from Aunt Sabina's dying-place; for she would not die in Glen Doone, she said, lest the angels feared to come for her; and so she was taken to a cottage in a lonely valley. I was allowed to visit her, for even we durst not refuse the wishes of the dying; and if a priest had been desired, we should have made bold with him. Returning very sorrowful, and caring now for nothing, I found this little stray thing lying, her arms upon her, and not a sign of life, except the way that she was biting. Black root-stuff was in her mouth, and a piece of dirty sheep's wool, and at her feet an old egg-shell of some bird of the moorland.

"I tried to raise her, but she was too square and heavy for me; and so I put food in her mouth, and left her to do right with it. And this she did in a little time; for the victuals were very choice and rare, being what I had taken over to tempt poor Aunt Sabina. Gwenny ate them without delay, and then was ready to eat the basket and the ware that contained them.

"Gwenny took me for an angel—though I am little like one, as you see, Master Ridd; and she followed me, expecting that I would open wings and fly when we came to any difficulty. I brought her home with me, so far as this can be a home, and she made herself my sole attendant, without so much as asking me. She has beaten two or three other girls, who used to wait upon me, until they are afraid to come near the house of my grandfather. She seems to have no kind of fear even of our roughest men; and yet she looks with reverence and awe upon the Counsellor. As for the wickedness, and theft, and revelry around her, she says it is no concern of hers, and they know their own business best. By this way of regarding men she has won upon our riders, so that she is almost free from all control of place and season, and is allowed to pass where none even of the youths may go. Being so wide, and short, and flat, she has none to pay her compliments; and, were there any, she would scorn them, as not being Cornishmen. Sometimes she wanders far, by moonlight, on the moors and up the rivers, to give her father (as she says) another chance of finding her, and she comes back not a wit defeated, or discouraged, or depressed, but confident that he is only waiting for the proper time.

"Herein she sets me good example of a patience and contentment, hard for me to imitate. Oftentimes, I am vexed by things I cannot meddle with, yet which cannot be kept from me, that I am at the point of flying from this dreadful valley, and risking all that can betide me in the unknown outer world. If it were not for my grandfather, I would have done so long ago; but I cannot bear that he should die with no gentle hand to comfort him; and I fear to think of the conflict that must ensue for the government, if there be a disputed succession.

"Ah me! We are to be pitied greatly, rather than condemned, by people whose things we have taken from them; for I have read, and seem almost to understand about it, that there are places on the earth where gentle peace, and love of home, and knowledge of one's neighbours prevail, and are, with reason, looked for as the usual state of things. There honest folk may go to work in the glory of the sunrise, with hope of coming home again quite safe in the quiet evening, and finding all their children; and even in the darkness they have no fear of lying down, and dropping off to slumber, and hearken to the wind of night, not as to an enemy trying to find entrance, but a friend who comes to tell the value of their comfort.

"Of all this golden ease I hear, but never saw the like of it; and, haply, I shall never do so, being born to turbulence. Once, indeed, I had the offer of escape, and kinsman's aid, and high place in the gay, bright world; and yet I was not tempted much, or, at least, dared not to trust it. And it ended very sadly, so dreadfully that I even shrink from telling you about it; for that one terror changed my life, in a moment, at a blow, from childhood and from thoughts of play and commune with the flowers and trees, to a sense of death and darkness, and a heavy weight of earth. Be content now, Master Ridd, ask me nothing more about it, so your sleep be sounder."

But I, John Ridd, being young and new, and very fond of hearing things to make my blood to tingle, had no more of manners than to urge poor Lorna onwards, hoping, perhaps, in depth of heart, that she might have to hold by me, when the worst came to the worst of it. Therefore she went on again.

About the Author

M. J. Porteus is the pen name of an author who writes in several other genres. She lives in *"Lorna Doone* country" in England with her husband. Learn more at *www.mjporteus.com*.

A Sneak Peek from Crimson Romance
(From *North and South: The Wild and Wanton Edition, Vol. 1* by Brenna Chase and Elizabeth Gaskell)

"Wooed and married and a'."

"Edith!" said Margaret, gently, "Edith!"

But, as Margaret half suspected, Edith had fallen asleep. She lay curled up on the sofa in the back drawing-room in Harley Street, looking very lovely in her white muslin and blue ribbons. If Titania had ever been dressed in white muslin and blue ribbons, and had fallen asleep on a crimson damask sofa in a back drawing-room, Edith might have been taken for her. Margaret was struck afresh by her cousin's beauty. They had grown up together from childhood, and all along Edith had been remarked upon by every one, except Margaret, for her prettiness; but Margaret had never thought about it until the last few days, when the prospect of soon losing her companion seemed to give force to every sweet quality and charm which Edith possessed. They had been talking about wedding dresses, and wedding ceremonies; and Captain Lennox, and what he had told Edith about her future life at Corfu, where his regiment was stationed; and the difficulty of keeping a piano in good tune (a difficulty which Edith seemed to consider as one of the most formidable that could befall her in her married life), and what gowns she should want in the visits to Scotland, which would immediately succeed her marriage; but the whispered tone had latterly become more drowsy; and Margaret, after a pause of a few minutes, found, as she fancied, that in spite of the buzz in the next room, Edith had rolled herself up into a soft ball of muslin and ribbon, and silken curls, and gone off into a peaceful little after-dinner nap.

Margaret had been on the point of telling her cousin of some of the plans and visions which she entertained as to her future life in the country parsonage, where her father and mother lived; and where her bright holidays had always been passed, though for the last ten years her Aunt Shaw's house had been considered as her home. But in default of a listener, she had to brood over the change in her life silently as heretofore. It was a happy brooding, although tinged with regret at being separated for an indefinite time from her gentle aunt and dear cousin. As she thought of the delight of filling the important post of only daughter in Helstone parsonage, pieces of the conversation out of the next room came upon her ears. Her Aunt Shaw was talking to the five or six ladies who had been dining there, and whose husbands were still in the dining-room. They were the familiar acquaintances of the house; neighbours whom Mrs. Shaw called friends, because she happened to dine with them more frequently than with any other people, and because if she or Edith wanted anything from them, or they from her, they did not scruple to make a call at each other's houses before luncheon. These ladies and their husbands were invited, in their capacity of friends, to eat a farewell dinner in honour of Edith's approaching marriage. Edith had rather objected to this arrangement, for Captain Lennox was expected to arrive by a late train this very evening; but, although she was a spoiled child, she was too careless and idle to have a very strong will of her own, and gave way when she found that her mother had absolutely ordered those extra delicacies of the season which are always supposed to be efficacious against immoderate grief at farewell dinners. She contented herself by leaning back in her chair, merely playing with the food on her plate, and looking grave and absent; while all around her were enjoying the mots of Mr. Grey, the gentleman who always took the bottom of the table at Mrs. Shaw's dinner parties, and asked Edith to give them some music in the drawing-room. Mr. Grey was particularly agreeable over this farewell dinner, and the gentlemen staid down stairs longer than usual. It was very well they did—to judge from the fragments of conversation, which Margaret overheard.

"I suffered too much myself; not that I was not extremely happy with the poor dear General, but still disparity of age is a drawback; one that I was resolved Edith should not have to encounter. Of course, without any maternal partiality, I foresaw that the dear child was likely to marry early; indeed, I had often said that I was sure she would be married before she was nineteen. I had quite a prophetic feeling when Captain Lennox"—and here the voice dropped into a whisper, but Margaret could easily supply the blank. The course of true love in Edith's case had run remarkably smooth. Mrs. Shaw had given way to the presentiment, as she expressed it; and had rather urged on the marriage, although it was below the expectations, which many of Edith's acquaintances had formed for her, a young and pretty heiress. But Mrs. Shaw said that her only child should marry for love,—and sighed emphatically, as if love had not been her motive for marrying the General. She had encouraged Margaret to do the same: to marry for love. Margaret remembered the conversation well:

"Marry a man you can love as well as respect and admire. Money alone cannot fill the cold places in your heart." Then to both Margaret and Edith's surprise, she had added, "And when you do find someone, do not wait for your wedding nights. Remember: one does not purchase a pair of gloves without trying it on."

And as if that had not been enough to make both girls blush, she had described in a matter-of-fact way what went on in the bedroom between husband and wife, so that they should not be surprised, as she had been on her own wedding night. Edith had recently confessed to Margaret that she had taken her mother's advice. In fact, what Margaret did not know was that Edith was not actually sleeping, but enjoying the rather delightful memory of that event.

They had gone to the Blanchard's one evening for a ball, and Edith had danced several times, mostly with Captain Lennox, to whom she was newly affianced. She whirled round in his arms during one of the waltzes played, thankful that she knew the steps by heart, for his nearness had its usual unsettling effect upon her. The touch of his hands, even through gloves, made her pulse race. This led her to imagine how his hands would feel on her skin, and caused her to miss a beat. Then she wondered how his body looked out of his clothes, and how it would feel to run her hands over his tall, lean form. It did not help matters much that she had been thinking of doing as her mamma had suggested. She wondered what he would think of that if she told him.

"I'm going out for a bit of fresh air," Captain Lennox murmured, his mouth close to her ear, causing little goose bumps to work their way down Edith's spine. "Would you care to join me?"

Edith glanced around. The dance had ended. "I'd love to."

He led her out onto one of the balconies on the back of the house. The moon drifted behind a cloud, casting them in shadow. Edith breathed in the cool air and slowly regained her composure. She looked at Captain Lennox, who stood beside her, his hand on the rail next to hers.

"Thank you. It's lovely out here."

"I had an ulterior motive," he admitted, as the strains of another waltz drifted out to them. He held out his hand. "Dance with me."

"Delighted, Captain Lennox," Edith said, taking on the coquettish voice of several of her contemporaries inside.

He took her hand and drew her flush against his body and all thoughts of light flirtation fled. Edith stiffened in shock at first, but relaxed into him as if he had held her thusly many times before. He was lean and hard, and her pulse began to race faster than before as they moved in time to the music. If she had been unable to concentrate earlier, this was worse. And better. How good he felt! But she could barely breathe, and she trembled and tingled from head to foot. Her breasts ached and between her thighs she felt dampness form. Edith looked up at Captain Lennox as she felt something rigid between them. He smiled, but it was strained, and she wondered what was wrong.

Before she could ask, Captain Lennox danced them over next to the side of the house. He bent his head, his mouth claiming hers with soft, gentle brushes of lips. Edith's hands moved over his shoulders, at last touching him as she had longed to do. Her hands slipped up next to the back of his neck, where she caressed the taut muscles. Captain Lennox groaned and increased the pressure of his mouth on hers, his tongue darting against the seam of her lips. Edith parted them on a gasp and it swept in to stroke her palate, slide over her teeth, twine with and suckle her own.

He jerked away from her at the sound of her mother calling her name. She watched his throat work up and down and his hands tighten into fists.

"I'm not angry, Edith," he assured her. "I nearly lost control. If it weren't for your mother I don't know what I'd have done."

"Lost control?"

Captain Lennox stepped closer. "I want to make love with you, dearest."

"So do I. I mean I want to make love with you, as well," she whispered. Edith's mind raced. She wanted to be with him, now, this instant. "Come to my house later on. I'll let you inside."

They had parted reluctantly, but a few hours later, Captain Lennox followed Edith as she let him in the house, a finger over her lips, unnecessarily warning him to be as quiet as possible, and led him up to her room. She locked the door and moved back around to face him. With shaky fingers, she unfastened and let her nightgown slide to the floor. Captain Lennox let his gaze travel over her body as he removed his own clothing.

"You're beautiful, Edith."

"I was going to say the same of you," she whispered.

He reached for her, and Edith eagerly pulled him close. His kiss was more insistent than before, hot and ravaging, his tongue plunging in and out of her mouth while his hands roamed over her bare skin, setting trails of fire across her skin. One squeezed in between them and found a breast. He palmed it, brushed the tight bud of her nipple until she whimpered. Each thrust of his tongue, each caress, made Edith's core ache, and soon she was drenched with need, longing to feel his rigid length inside her.

Captain Lennox manoeuvred her back to the bed and soon she was sprawled upon it, her legs hanging off the side. He knelt between them, his hands and fingers tickling her as he spread her nether lips apart. But her soft laughter died as she felt his tongue slowly swipe over her flesh again and again until she could do little more than mewl in pleasure. And just when she thought she could not feel anything more wonderful, heat exploded inside her.

Limp and replete, she moved further onto the bed, Captain Lennox following. He settled between her thighs and she felt the press of him against her wet and still sensitive opening before he pushed into her. Edith stiffened in pain and clutched at him, gasping as she tried not to cry out. But when he kissed her and began to move, Edith wound her arms around him as the wonderful friction wiped away all traces of discomfort. Her body followed his lead, and soon she raised her hips and wrapped her legs around him, drawing him farther inside.

Captain Lennox leaned back on his heels and his fingers caressed the spot his tongue had moments before, the one that had driven her wild. Edith tumbled over the edge, moaning, her hands fisting her bed sheets, her hips rising frantically to meet him. Abruptly he withdrew and spilled his seed on her belly, only to collapse over her. He smiled and kissed her tenderly, whispering words of love. At last when he raised his head, Edith said, "That was wonderful! Can we do it again soon?"

He brushed her lips with another kiss. "As often as you like."

He had stayed a while after that, but dressed and let Edith lead him from her room and out the door before the servants stirred.

She had told Margaret all of that, as much as she dared, at least. Her cousin had not seemed scandalised, which Edith was glad of, for she hoped one day Margaret would know such rapture in a man's arms. And with that happy thought, Edith did indeed fall asleep.

But Margaret had no plans to "try on" any man. She had never met anyone to whom she could give her heart, let alone her body. Still, she was happy for her cousin, for her coming marriage. Her aunt was even more ecstatic. Mrs. Shaw enjoyed the romance of the present engagement rather more than her daughter. Not but that Edith was very thoroughly and properly in love; still she would certainly have preferred a good house in Belgravia, to all the picturesqueness of the life, which Captain Lennox described at Corfu. The very parts which made Margaret glow as she listened, Edith pretended to shiver and shudder at; partly for the pleasure she had in being coaxed out of her dislike by her fond lover, and partly because anything of a gipsy or make-shift life was really distasteful to her. Yet had any one come with a fine house, and a fine estate, and a fine title to boot, Edith would still have clung to Captain Lennox while the temptation lasted; when it was over, it is possible she might have had little qualms of ill-concealed regret that Captain Lennox could not have united in his person everything that was desirable. In this she was but her mother's child; who, after deliberately marrying General Shaw with no warmer feeling than respect for his character and establishment, was constantly, though quietly, bemoaning her hard lot in being united to one whom she could not love.

"I have spared no expense in her trousseau," were the next words Margaret heard.

"She has all the beautiful Indian shawls and scarfs the General gave to me, but which I shall never wear again."

"She is a lucky girl," replied another voice, which Margaret knew to be that of Mrs. Gibson, a lady who was taking a double interest in the conversation, from the fact of one of her daughters having been married within the last few weeks.

"Helen had set her heart upon an Indian shawl, but really when I found what an extravagant price was asked, I was obliged to refuse her. She will be quite envious when she hears of Edith having Indian shawls. What kind are they? Delhi? With the lovely little borders?"

Margaret heard her aunt's voice again, but this time it was as if she had raised herself up from her half-recumbent position, and were looking into the more dimly lighted back drawing-room. "Edith! Edith!" cried she; and then she sank as if wearied by the exertion. Margaret stepped forward.

"Edith is asleep, Aunt Shaw. Is it anything I can do?"

All the ladies said "Poor child!" on receiving this distressing intelligence about Edith; and the minute lap-dog in Mrs. Shaw's arms began to bark, as if excited by the burst of pity.

"Hush, Tiny! You naughty little girl! You will waken your mistress. It was only to ask Edith if she would tell Newton to bring down her shawls: perhaps you would go, Margaret dear?"

Margaret went up into the old nursery at the very top of the house, where Newton was busy getting up some laces, which were required for the wedding. While Newton went (not without a muttered grumbling) to undo the shawls, which had already been exhibited four or five times that day, Margaret looked round upon the nursery; the first room in that house with which she had become familiar nine years ago, when she was brought, all untamed from the forest, to share the home, the play, and the lessons of her cousin Edith. She remembered the dark, dim look of the London nursery, presided over by an austere and ceremonious nurse, who was terribly particular about clean hands and torn frocks. She recollected the first tea up there—separate from her father and aunt, who were dining somewhere down below an infinite depth of stairs; for unless she were up in the sky (the child thought), they must be deep down in the bowels of the earth. At home—before she came to live in Harley Street—her mother's dressing-room had been her nursery; and, as they kept early hours in the country parsonage, Margaret had always had her meals with her father and mother. Oh! Well did the tall stately girl of eighteen remember the tears shed with such wild passion of grief by the little girl of nine, as she hid her face under the bed-clothes, in that first night; and how she was bidden not to cry by the nurse, because it would disturb Miss Edith; and how she had cried as bitterly, but more quietly, till her newly-seen, grand, pretty aunt had come softly upstairs with Mr. Hale to show him his little sleeping daughter. Then the little Margaret had hushed her sobs, and tried to lie quiet as if asleep, for fear of making her father unhappy by her grief, which she dared not express before her aunt, and which she rather thought it was wrong to feel at all after the long hoping, and planning, and contriving they had gone through at home, before her wardrobe could be arranged so as to suit her grander circumstances, and before papa could leave his parish to come up to London, even for a few days.

Now she had got to love the old nursery, though it was but a dismantled place; and she looked all round, with a kind of cat-like regret, at the idea of leaving it for ever in three days.

"Ah Newton!" said she, "I think we shall all be sorry to leave this dear old room."

"Indeed, miss, I shan't for one. My eyes are not so good as they were, and the light here is so bad that I can't see to mend laces except just at the window, where there's always a shocking draught—enough to give one one's death of cold."

"Well, I dare say you will have both good light and plenty of warmth at Naples. You must keep as much of your darning as you can till then. Thank you, Newton, I can take them down—you're busy."

So Margaret went down laden with shawls, and snuffing up their spicy Eastern smell. Her aunt asked her to stand as a sort of lay figure on which to display them, as Edith was still asleep. No one thought about it; but Margaret's tall, finely made figure, in the black silk dress which she was wearing as mourning for some distant relative of her father's, set off the long beautiful folds of the gorgeous shawls that would have half-smothered Edith. Margaret stood right under the chandelier, quite silent and passive, while her aunt adjusted the draperies. Occasionally, as she was turned round, she caught a glimpse of herself in the mirror over the chimney-piece, and smiled at her own appearance there—the familiar features in the usual garb of a princess. She touched the shawls gently as they hung around her, and took a pleasure in their soft feel and their brilliant colours, and rather liked to be dressed in such splendour—enjoying it much as a child would do, with a quiet pleased smile on her lips. Just then the door opened, and Mr. Henry Lennox was suddenly announced. Some of the ladies started back, as if half-ashamed of their feminine interest in dress. Mrs. Shaw held out her hand to the new-comer; Margaret stood perfectly still, thinking she might be yet wanted as a sort of block for the shawls; but looking at Mr. Lennox with a bright, amused face, as if sure of his sympathy in her sense of the ludicrousness at being thus surprised.

Her aunt was so much absorbed in asking Mr. Henry Lennox— who had not been able to come to dinner—all sorts of questions about his brother the bridegroom, his sister the bridesmaid (coming with the Captain from Scotland for the occasion), and various other members of the Lennox family, that Margaret saw she was no more wanted as shawl-bearer, and devoted herself to the amusement of the other visitors, whom her aunt had for the moment forgotten. Almost immediately, Edith came in from the back drawing-room, winking and blinking her eyes at the stronger light, shaking back her slightly-ruffled curls, and altogether looking like the Sleeping Beauty just startled from her dreams. Even in her slumber she had instinctively felt that a Lennox was worth rousing herself for; and she had a multitude of questions to ask about dear Janet, the future, unseen sister-in-law, for whom she professed so much affection, that if Margaret had not been very proud she might have almost felt jealous of the mushroom rival. As Margaret sank rather more into the background on her aunt's joining the conversation, she saw Henry Lennox directing his look towards a vacant seat near her; and she knew perfectly well that as soon as Edith released him from her questioning, he would take possession of that chair. She had not been quite sure, from her aunt's rather confused account of his engagements, whether he would come that night; it was almost a surprise to see him; and now she was sure of a pleasant evening. He liked and disliked pretty nearly the same things that she did. Margaret's face was lightened up into an honest, open brightness. By-and-by he came. She received him with a smile that had not a tinge of shyness or self-consciousness in it.

"Well, I suppose you are all in the depths of business—ladies' business, I mean. Very different to my business, which is the real true law business. Playing with shawls is very different work to drawing up settlements."

"Ah, I knew how you would be amused to find us all so occupied in admiring finery. But really Indian shawls are very perfect things of their kind."

"I have no doubt they are. Their prices are very perfect, too. Nothing wanting." The gentlemen came dropping in one by one, and the buzz and noise deepened in tone.

"This is your last dinner-party, is it not? There are no more before Thursday?"

"No. I think after this evening we shall feel at rest, which I am sure I have not done for many weeks; at least, that kind of rest when the hands have nothing more to do, and all the arrangements are complete for an event which must occupy one's head and heart. I shall be glad to have time to think, and I am sure Edith will."

"I am not so sure about her; but I can fancy that you will. Whenever I have seen you lately, you have been carried away by a whirlwind of some other person's making."

"Yes," said Margaret, rather sadly, remembering the never-ending commotion about trifles that had been going on for more than a month past: "I wonder if a marriage must always be preceded by what you call a whirlwind, or whether in some cases there might not rather be a calm and peaceful time just before it."

"Cinderella's godmother ordering the trousseau, the wedding-breakfast, writing the notes of invitation, for instance," said Mr. Lennox, laughing.

"But are all these quite necessary troubles?" asked Margaret, looking up straight at him for an answer. A sense of indescribable weariness of all the arrangements for a pretty effect, in which Edith had been busied as supreme authority for the last six weeks, oppressed her just now; and she really wanted some one to help her to a few pleasant, quiet ideas connected with a marriage.

"Oh, of course," he replied with a change to gravity in his tone. "There are forms and ceremonies to be gone through, not so much to satisfy oneself, as to stop the world's mouth, without which stoppage there would be very little satisfaction in life. But how would you have a wedding arranged?"

"Oh, I have never thought much about it; only I should like it to be a very fine summer morning; and I should like to walk to church through the shade of trees; and not to have so many bridesmaids, and to have no wedding-breakfast. I dare say I am resolving against the very things that have given me the most trouble just now."

"No, I don't think you are. The idea of stately simplicity accords well with your character."

Margaret did not quite like this speech; she winced away from it more, from remembering former occasions on which he had tried to lead her into a discussion (in which he took the complimentary part) about her own character and ways of going on. She cut his speech rather short by saying:

"It is natural for me to think of Helstone church, and the walk to it, rather than of driving up to a London church in the middle of a paved street."

"Tell me about Helstone. You have never described it to me. I should like to have some idea of the place you will be living in, when ninety-six Harley Street will be looking dingy and dirty, and dull, and shut up. Is Helstone a village, or a town, in the first place?"

"Oh, only a hamlet; I don't think I could call it a village at all. There is the church and a few houses near it on the green—cottages, rather—with roses growing all over them."

"And flowering all the year round, especially at Christmas—make your picture complete," said he.

"No," replied Margaret, somewhat annoyed, "I am not making a picture. I am trying to describe Helstone as it really is. You should not have said that."

"I am penitent," he answered. "Only it really sounded like a village in a tale rather than in real life."

"And so it is," replied Margaret, eagerly. "All the other places in England that I have seen seem so hard and prosaic-looking, after the New Forest. Helstone is like a village in a poem—in one of Tennyson's poems. But I won't try and describe it any more. You would only laugh at me if I told you what I think of it—what it really is."

"Indeed, I would not. But I see you are going to be very resolved. Well, then, tell me that which I should like still better to know what the parsonage is like."

"Oh, I can't describe my home. It is home, and I can't put its charm into words."

"I submit. You are rather severe to-night, Margaret."

"How?" said she, turning her large soft eyes round full upon him. "I did not know I was."

"Why, because I made an unlucky remark, you will neither tell me what Helstone is like, nor will you say anything about your home, though I have told you how much I want to hear about both, the latter especially."

"But indeed I cannot tell you about my own home. I don't quite think it is a thing to be talked about, unless you knew it."

"Well, then"—pausing for a moment—"tell me what you do there. Here you read, or have lessons, or otherwise improve your mind, till the middle of the day; take a walk before lunch, go a drive with your aunt after, and have some kind of engagement in the evening. There, now fill up your day at Helstone. Shall you ride, drive, or walk?"

"Walk, decidedly. We have no horse, not even for papa. He walks to the very extremity of his parish. The walks are so beautiful, it would be a shame to drive—almost a shame to ride."

"Shall you garden much? That, I believe, is a proper employment for young ladies in the country."

"I don't know. I am afraid I shan't like such hard work."

"Archery parties—pic-nics—race-balls—hunt-balls?"

"Oh no!" said she, laughing. "Papa's living is very small; and even if we were near such things, I doubt if I should go to them."

"I see, you won't tell me anything. You will only tell me that you are not going to do this and that. Before the vacation ends, I think I shall pay you a call, and see what you really do employ yourself in."

"I hope you will. Then you will see for yourself how beautiful Helstone is. Now I must go. Edith is sitting down to play, and I just know enough of music to turn over the leaves for her; and besides, Aunt Shaw won't like us to talk." Edith played brilliantly. In the middle of the piece the door half-opened, and Edith saw Captain Lennox hesitating whether to come in. She threw down her music, and rushed out of the room, leaving Margaret standing confused and blushing to explain to the astonished guests what vision had shown itself to cause Edith's sudden flight. Captain Lennox had come earlier than was expected; or was it really so late? They looked at their watches, were duly shocked, and took their leave.

Edith drew Captain Lennox away from the foyer and into a nearby corridor. Once away from the view of everyone she threw her arms around his neck.

"You're here!" She studied his face by the light from a nearby sconce as if she had forgotten his warm brown eyes, straight nose, and perfect teeth. He was the handsomest, most gallant man she had ever seen, not to mention an attentive lover. And he was hers, she thought, with no small amount of pride.

"I couldn't stay away. I know I'm early. I hope that's all right?" he said, his voice and eyes teasing.

His arms went round her waist, and he pulled her close. Edith sighed at the feel of his hard muscles against her own soft frame. She trembled, and her nipples pearled as desire began to simmer in her veins. "I've been longing to see you." She peeked around, but no one was nearby. "Quick, let's go in here."

Edith reached behind her for the handle of the door that led into a rarely used room where there was no chance of being disturbed. She pulled Captain Lennox in behind her and shut the door. Moonlight spilled in from the window on the far wall, revealing coverings draped over sofas and chairs. Edith paid it all little heed, turning her attention instead to her fiancé. She had surprised him, she could tell, by her bold action, but he seemed to have recovered sufficiently, for once again he pulled her into his arms.

"Did you miss me, then?" Captain Lennox asked, leaning down toward her.

Head tilted back, she said, "You know I did."

His mouth covered hers, a warm sweep of lips that sent a burst of pleasure through her. He had recently shaved, but his moustache tickled slightly, heightening the sensation. Edith moaned and pressed closer still. Her hands moved once more to caress the back of his neck and tug on his close-cropped hair. Captain Lennox drew back slightly and nipped at her lower lip before sucking it into his mouth. She felt that light caress between her thighs and knew a simple kiss would not be enough. When he released her, she opened her eyes in protest.

His gaze seared her, thrilling her as she beheld the tempered lust in its depths. A kiss would not be enough for him, either.

"I missed you as well," he murmured.

And he bent his head, capturing her mouth again, this time his tongue sweeping inside to mate with hers. Edith's breasts tingled and her nipples hardened further. She ached to have his rough palms cupping them, his thumbs brushing over the tight buds before he took them into his mouth. Just the thought of it sent another answering flare of heat to her nether regions.

"Yes," she sighed as his lips left hers once again.

His mouth travelling down to the base of her throat before moving to nibble at the sensitive flesh beneath her ear, Captain Lennox caught Edith by her buttocks and lifted her up against him. His arousal pressed against the juncture of her thighs while Edith trembled with desire as she imagined him sliding into her, filling her. Heat pooled in her belly and moisture dampened her core.

"I want to feel you inside me again."

His lips stilled near her ear, hot breath ghosting over her skin. "We can't. There's not enough time."

But Edith felt the slide of muslin over her silk stockings, then his hand brushing over them as he pushed her skirts up. She caught the material, bunching her skirts up in her fist. Captain Lennox's fingers eased into her drawers, brushing her thigh, and a tremor swept through her as she realized his target.

His fingers teased her flesh, parting her lips, circling her slick opening. At her whispered plea he pushed a digit up inside her. Her walls tightened and her thighs clenched together to hold him there as Captain Lennox began to slide it out again. But no! She wanted him to move, to feel that glorious friction that brought her such ecstasy. Edith relaxed and stepped further apart, and he pushed another finger inside her. He set a languid rhythm at first, gradually moving faster.

His mouth hovered near her ear again, his voice husky. "I love the way your cunny feels. So hot and tight. I can't wait to be inside you again."

Edith's pulse jolted at the naughty words. Her body moved with him as his touch commanded, thrumming with pleasure. His thumb found the bud of flesh at the apex of her cleft, softly stroking it and driving her mad. She caught at Captain Lennox's arm for support.

"Oh yes!" Edith gasped, just before Captain Lennox's mouth closed over hers again, swallowing the scream that followed with a scorching kiss.

Weak-kneed and breathless, she collapsed against Captain Lennox, but not before she saw him lick his fingers clean. She moaned and closed her eyes as another thrill rushed through her. When she had recovered somewhat she glanced at him. His expression was strained, and his smile tight. "You still need relief."

"I'll be fine," Captain Lennox murmured, bending down to kiss her yet again.

But he did not object when Edith undid his trousers and took his cock into her hand. With faltering strokes, then more sure ones, she moved her barely closed fist up and down his shaft. With a groan, he shoved himself into her hand until they were both panting. It was not long before Captain Lennox gasped her name, jerked, and Edith moaned again as his hot seed spilled over her hand.

She smiled, quite pleased and proud of herself that he had found release at her touch. He grinned back before fumbling for his handkerchief to clean her hand before wiping and tucking himself back into his trousers. Her skirts down and smooth, Edith quickly helped him right his clothing, and a moment later Captain Lennox drew her into a gentle embrace.

"I love you, Edith."

"I love you, too," she whispered. And though they wanted to linger, and make love without rushing, they hurried from the room hand in hand to return to the others.

Margaret, meanwhile, remembering the long absence of Edith and the Captain at another function, as well as Edith's confession, sought to keep her aunt and the remaining guests occupied with wedding talk. Henry added to the conversation, quite enthusiastically for a single man, but Margaret put it down to his happiness for his brother's coming marriage and thought no more of it. She kept up a steady stream of questions and responses, and wished that Edith and Captain Lennox would join them soon. She was just about to give up and go in search of them when she caught movement out of the corner of her eye.

Then Edith came back, glowing with pleasure, half-shyly, half-proudly leading in her tall handsome Captain. His brother shook hands with him, and Mrs. Shaw welcomed him in her gentle kindly way, which had always something plaintive in it, arising from the long habit of considering herself a victim to an uncongenial marriage. Now that, the General being gone, she had every good of life, with as few drawbacks as possible, she had been rather perplexed to find an anxiety, if not a sorrow. She had, however, of late settled upon her own health as a source of apprehension; she had a nervous little cough whenever she thought about it; and some complaisant doctor ordered her just what she desired,—a winter in Italy. Mrs. Shaw had as strong wishes as most people, but she never liked to do anything from the open and acknowledged motive of her own good will and pleasure; she preferred being compelled to gratify herself by some other person's command or desire. She really did persuade herself that she was submitting to some hard external necessity; and thus she was able to moan and complain in her soft manner, all the time she was in reality doing just what she liked.

It was in this way she began to speak of her own journey to Captain Lennox, who assented, as in duty bound, to all his future mother-in-law said, while his eyes sought Edith, who was busying herself in rearranging the tea-table, and ordering up all sorts of good things, in spite of his assurances that he had dined within the last two hours.

Mr. Henry Lennox stood leaning against the chimney-piece, amused with the family scene. He was close by his handsome brother; he was the plain one in a singularly good-looking family; but his face was intelligent, keen, and mobile; and now and then Margaret wondered what it was that he could be thinking about, while he kept silence, but was evidently observing, with an interest that was slightly sarcastic, all that Edith and she were doing. The sarcastic feeling was called out by Mrs. Shaw's conversation with his brother; it was separate from the interest which was excited by what he saw. He thought it a pretty sight to see the two cousins so busy in their little arrangements about the table. Edith chose to do most herself. She was in a humour to enjoy showing her lover how well she could behave as a soldier's wife. She found out that the water in the urn was cold, and ordered up the great kitchen tea-kettle; the only consequence of which was that when she met it at the door, and tried to carry it in, it was too heavy for her, and she came in pouting, with a black mark on her muslin gown, and a little round white hand indented by the handle, which she took to show to Captain Lennox, just like a hurt child, and, of course, the remedy was the same in both cases. Margaret's quickly-adjusted spirit-lamp was the most efficacious contrivance, though not so like the gypsy-encampment which Edith, in some of her moods, chose to consider the nearest resemblance to a barrack-life. After this evening all was bustle till the wedding was over.

In the mood for more Crimson Romance?
Check out *A Treasure Worth Keeping* by Marie Patrick at
CrimsonRomance.com.

www.ingramcontent.com/pod-product-compliance
Lightning Source LLC
Chambersburg PA
CBHW010636100726
47900CB00011B/2853